UNDERSTORIES

UNDERSTORIES

TIM HORVATH

BELLEVUE LITERARY PRESS

NEW YORK

First Published in the United States in 2012 by
Bellevue Literary Press, New York

FOR INFORMATION ADDRESS:
Bellevue Literary Press
NYU School of Medicine
350 First Avenue
OBV A612
New York, NY 10016

Bellevue Literary Press would like to thank all its generous
donors—individuals and foundations—for their support.

 This publication is made possible by the New York State Council on
the Arts with the support of Governor Andrew Cuomo and the New
NYSCA York State Legislature.

Cataloging-in-Publication Data is available
from the Library of Congress.

The following stories were previously published, sometimes in slightly
different forms or with different titles: "The Lobby" in *JMWW*, "Urban
Planning: Case Studies Numbers One, Two, and Three" in *Sein und
Werden*, Circulation by sunnyoutside press, "The Understory" in *Carve*,
"The Discipline of Shadows," "Urban Planning: Case Study Numbers
Four and Seven: The City in the Light of Moths," and "Altered Native"
in *Conjunctions*, "Planetarium" in *Puerto del Sol*, "A Box of One's Own"
in *Mad Hatters' Review*, "Internodium" in *Everyday Genius*, "Pocket" in
DIAGRAM, "Urban Planning: Case Study Number Five" in *Alimentum*,
"Urban Planning: Case Study Number Six" in *Wigleaf*, "The Conversations"
in *The Collagist*, "Tilkez" in *The Normal School*, and "Urban Planning: Case
Study Number Eight" in *Fiction*.

Book design and composition by Mulberry Tree Press, Inc.
Manufactured in the United States of America.
FIRST EDITION
1 3 5 7 9 8 6 4 2
ISBN 978-1-934137-44-4

For Mary Ann and Ella

Contents

The Lobby   9

Urban Planning: Case Study Number One   12

Circulation   15

Urban Planning: Case Study Number Two   48

The Understory   51

Urban Planning: Case Study Number Three   76

The Discipline of Shadows   79

Urban Planning: Case Study Number Four   103

Planetarium   107

The Gendarmes   129

A Box of One's Own   133

Internodium   137

Urban Planning: Case Study Number Five   139

Runaroundandscreamalot!   149

Urban Planning: Case Study Number Six   185

Pocket   188

Altered Native   190

Urban Planning: Case Study Number Seven
     The City in the Light of Moths   195

The Conversations   220

Tilkez   239

Urban Planning: Case Study Number Eight   250

The Lobby

Welcome! Please stop at the desk for a moment to sign this waiver. Though we wish you to enjoy the architectural apotheosis that surrounds you, since you are a mere pedestrian onlooker (henceforth "voyeur") rather than a lessee (henceforth "resident"), you are subject thereby to certain restrictions and provisions. Continued presence in this lobby constitutes tacit acceptance of the following terms and conditions:

Management cannot be held responsible for any physical or psychological damage pursuant to the perceptual intake of this lobby, including but not limited to hyperventilation, fainting, seizures (epileptic or non), hives, acid reflux, anomie, ennui, generalized anxiety, mania, lethargy, manic lethargy, chromosomal ambivalence, rugburn (psychosomatic or otherwise), stiffarm, etc.

Note that any form of recording, photographic, videographic, sketch pad doodling, or representation in any traditional or untraditional mode of painting, whether in vogue or otherwise (this includes Impressionist, Postimpressionist, Rococo, pre-Raphaelite, prelapsarian, Expressionist, neo-Expressionist, neo-Lascauxian, agitprop, Dadaist and Surrealist, Mamaist and hyperrealist, Futurist, installation, uninstallation, Pointillist, smudgist, etc.) is strictly prohibited. Failure on the part of this document to anticipate new developments and/or movements in the arts not covered by the aforementioned does not exonerate voyeur from attempted portrayal.

Note that remembering is strictly prohibited, current

research being staunchly ambivalent on the representationality of memory.

At the request of residents, no description of their habitation shall be given in ink, sound waves transmitted from vocal launching apparatus to aural landing pad, sign/gesture, semaphore, biophysical reenactment, encoded encapsulation, or telekinetic approximation. Failure on the part of this document to anticipate unprecedented forms of signification not covered by the aforementioned (else they'd hardly be "unprecedented") does not exonerate voyeur from attempted description. Additionally, metaphorical and literal depictions of lobby are interchangeable, and from a legal standpoint, any such distinction is entirely moot. Blood-ethanol level exceeding threshold of diminished inhibitory mechanisms in voyeur also does not excuse voyeur from blabbing about the astonishing visual properties of the lobby of this building.

(If you want a bar, incidentally, I'd recommend Errol's around the corner.)

Note that voyeur is not even capable of fully appreciating the lobby, since architect's express mission was "to create a transitional venue to be absorbed molecularly in daily passage, subordinating ocular experience to a dopaminergic rush and overcoming the perils of habit(u)ation." Note that even we have only a partial clue of what the fuck the architect was talking about; hence, to pretend that you, a mere pedestrian onlooker (henceforth "voyeur"), will "get it" in some fell swoop like some mathematical savant bypassing all the dirty little scratch pad pencil and eraser work is just plain ludicrous.

Dos?

Do wallow in silent appreciation. Bask, even. Marvel at how the lintels, by way of fractal tilework, suggest the expansion and eventual contraction of the universe. Ooh and aah at the way the right angles ooze and the curves flatten. Twitter at the use of barklike textures. Gape at the juxtaposition of so-called choosy mirrors that resolve age-old paradoxes of regress through their tasteful editing of visual ephemera. Revel in the inimitable touches—the portrait of the yeti hung mischievously aslant, the coquettish positioning of the mailboxes.

Then, at some point, exit, returning to your (henceforth "your") existence as pedestrian, free to merge into the anonymous tumult of human transit, speaking nil of what you've seen today, abiding no scar of it in the retention orifices of your mind, for to recall it thusly will entail your having become part of the lobby; hence, according to the provisions set forth above, prohibited from speaking of oneself, crippled, I tell you, as one who must fall silent and expressionless each time I walk through those heart-rendingly simple doors.

Those, there.

Urban Planning:

Case Study Number One

The mayor of Morrisania decreed that no longer would its citizens be plagued by rain. Over the airwaves, the voice that the pundits had dubbed "fascist . . . in a good way" rang out as though outrage were a stringed instrument; he plucked, bowed, implied nonintuitive fingerings. "What century are we living in," he thundered, "that I still even need to *think* before I set forth from my door about what I will wear, for fear of getting drenched to the bone? Do not our heads have roofs over them? Do awnings not jut out from our doorways to curbs? Must we constantly adjust to the whims of outmoded gods and goddesses?"

Immediately, building began citywide with fanfare and all-hands-on-deck resolve. Grandmothers simmered marvelous soups, salvaging bones from the near oblivion of trash mounds. Construction teams lent out their brawniest, resplendent in colorful T-shirts sporting memorable slogans. Street performers busked with renewed vigor, sending sweat and falcons skyward and forging their own signatures in luminous contrails. Philosophers set up tables at which they contemplated in lively and vigorous fashion the premises and consequences of the whole endeavor, debating, for instance, whether the open or closed form of the umbrella was more authentic and fundamental. Closed was originary, yet its very existence had meaning only in the context of the open; never had these pallid intellectuals come so close to blows. School was canceled—what teacher, no matter how inventive, could hope to minister about roots of square in the midst of such fervor? The streets were closed to traffic and attics swiftly divested of twine, canvas, and wire—in sum, anything remotely resembling a tarpaulin or a zip line that would bear a covering.

Pulling aside those canvases that were least water-resistant upon which to work, artists rendered their visions of Morrisania. The futurists depicted pulleys and levers controlling a many-tiered canopy that would emerge from apartments and rooftops, and would come into existence as though instantaneously, each covering sloped and hemmed with gutters that, in labyrinthine fashion, would bear each drop on its cascade downward. Via these it would be shunted out to the Longinard River, coursing toward the sea after passing through a series of turbines that would keep the city energized for days. The surrealists' visions were no less inspired, though their canopies were made of earlobes and genitals and their raindrops were engulfed by the sky.

Then, it began to rain. More, it began to pour, no ordinary rain, not even that which cats and dogs have long been associated with—through no fault of their own, I might add. No, this rain began as butter and moss and chinchilla pelts, gradually picked up until it was repo men and tenterhooks and foyers, and finally coalesced into an onslaught of grand piano lids and conveyer belts and marketing departments. Everyone ducked, tried to shield themselves, ran for cover. Cover was indoors, of course. Unfazed, the mayor planted himself firm in the crosshairs of an intersection and got on a megaphone. His voice was toxic violet putty. He called them cowards—no one knew whether he meant the citizens of Morrisania or the gods themselves. He pointed the megaphone skyward, wielding it as a makeshift umbrella, but the water funneled through it and it hit him like bottled riptide. He'd always been a bachelor, and his genes tried to jump ship at the last minute, but their life rafts were old and uninspected and had been devoured by the moths and rats and other vermin that had had the word *plague* hurled at them countless times before and now found only serenity in the fricative rub of its consonants.

Circulation

When we were awash with youth, we were all led to believe that our father was assembling a book called *The Atlas of the Voyages of Things*, or, as we shortened it, *The Atlas*. That it was eventually destined to enter the world was incontestable—one day, assuredly, we would march into the bookshop behind his gallant stride, and there, on the shelf, would sit the book, sprawling, coffee table–ready, his name beaming from the front as on a theater marquee. "You see, boys?" he'd say, and we would solemnly nod.

But before you get overly swept away in such childhood reverie, I owe you a snapshot of him from years later, nearer the present: in a hospital bed, riggered to a set of machines that monitored many of his bodily functions. My memories of the strapping man I once knew—almost fiendish in his independence, wearing his learning like his plaid flannel at barbecues and on vacations, splitting hairs with the tour guide in an underground cave about this or that obscure fact—vied with the presence of the helpless man before me. His body itself had been extended through tubes into clear hanging bags—transparent, clearly labeled external organs. His body was being perpetually translated into the language of quantification, via feedback machines through which rates and levels looped again and again.

His body; his body. In such mantras, electronic and otherwise, I could achieve a semblance of peace. Amid the faint hum of fluorescent lights and machines, an image would sometimes materialize for me of a brown-haired girl with a Hula-hoop. She was so adept and satisfied with its steady motion that she could gyrate it indefinitely. At some point in each of my visits, I arrived at some version of that peace, which came to stand, however fleetingly, for infinity. Those visits were frequent. I was trying to make up for the fact that Aidan, my brother, was far away, and that when these rhythms reverted to silence, it would register barely a blip, I think, in my mother's day.

Seeing him so reduced, though, it was impossible not to think of *The Atlas* and the fervid energy it had once commanded. Behind the door of his office, which jutted proudly at the stern of our first house, overlooking the yard and taking in maddening sunsets, he was supposedly huddled amid his papers in the evening hours, piecing together a masterwork, a lifelong enterprise. There was a certain comfort in glancing up on summer evenings while we built a fort at the edge of our yard where the woods began, with the volley of dogs barking back and forth nearby. It was the comfort of your tongue tripping on your own sweat, a friendly reminder that of the world's salt, a share is yours. His presence hovered over us.

For a long time, my brother, Aidan, and I had a rather comical misunderstanding of what an ordinary atlas actually was, our definition warped by what we were told about this book. We revealed this to each other years later, our own laughter backed by that of Aidan's family. His wife, son, and daughter could not get over how "weird" we both were, Daddy and "silly Uncle Jay."

It was not our only failure of understanding. Until I was older—I couldn't pinpoint exactly when—I held intuitions about the nature of paper that would be considered by most profoundly strange. My father worked as an editor by day, and one of the perks of his job was the paper he would bring home for us to color or scrawl on, piles consisting of scrap versions of manuscripts. One side of each page was still blank;

on the "reverse" of each page was a smattering of text. Without even considering that it might be otherwise, I assumed that *paper itself* was one-sided. All things that could be said or drawn were thus built upon the backs of words already written: dancing constellations of musings on metaphysics, the mineral composition of scarabs, the origins of the treble clef. I am, of course, projecting backward with an adult's grasp of the world. At the time, they were simply the "wrong" side of the page, bearing no more meaning than the dull gray backing of aluminum foil or the mineral deposits on the underbelly of a rock.

But atlases. Our misunderstanding was exacerbated by the constant references made to *The Atlas*. No occasion or gathering could take place without it being invoked. If my Uncle Gerry was in from Detroit, it would only be a matter of time before he would growl, "How's that book of yours coming?" his voice bearing its precarious mix of support and doubt like an overly full soup bowl.

"It's coming along great, Gerry," my father would say emphatically. "I tell you, though, I'm gonna need your help on the part about cars, you being up there in Detroit and all."

"Yes, but I'm a chemist, Gus," Gerry would shoot back.

"I *know* that, Gerry, but you're up there in Detroit and, well, by God, you're my man on assignment for those particular pages," my dad would insist.

Always, when asked about the status of the book, even as a form of small talk, my father would plead for the personal assistance of the person asking, making him or her feel, at least for a few moments, indispensable to the project. That included the guy at the corner store, our dentist, the fellow who checked out our water meter. And through my child's eyes, they all seemed both flattered and willing.

The premise, for all of the book's unwieldy history, was disarmingly straightforward. My father was eternally fascinated by how things came to be where they currently were. In the case of the automobile entry that he'd repeatedly vowed to coauthor with Gerry, he wanted to know where the metal had come from, where the leather or vinyl for the seats had been manufactured, where the paint had come from, the glass, et cetera. The page would then be cross-referenced so that you could look up a page on paint itself and determine where the chemical components of paint had originated, where the particles that formed glass had once been granules of sand, how that sand had been deposited and swept around by ocean currents, based on the best understanding then available. Maps would untuck from each of its opposing pages on whatever cartographic scale was merited, and, spread like wings, would chart the voyages of things, as heroic in my father's mind as the boldest venture in the Age of Exploration.

He'd gone so far as to write up a book jacket for the book itself, although leaving enough gaps in it so that he could, as he phrased it, "put forth his best stuff when it's all done." The jacket, which he shared with us as proudly, as though it was draped around an actual book, read thusly:

> The *Atlas of the Voyages of Things* is a lavishly illustrated book that documents the marvelous, intricate, globe-trotting chain of events by which things come to be *what* and *where* they are. It is a book that is somewhat scholarly in tone, yet addressed to the general reader. One finds oneself learning that _____ originates in _____, that in fact, to one's amazement, _____ comes from _____, and that the _____ in _____ is actually derived from _____. Anyone, almost anyone—anyone with the slightest degree of susceptibility to the specific as it impinges on the universal, or vice versa, in short anyone with an iota of curiosity—will find something to mull over in it. It is *eminently*

mullworthy. It is decidedly not a book that one reads straight through—who could bear to do so? For to do so would mean that, rather than catching one's breath after learning that _____ is of _____-ian origin, and allowing the ramifications, however great or small, of this discovery to sink in, one would go on in the next breath to learn that _____ is of _____. And like some defiance of the principle of *res extensa*, two bodies (facts) occupying the same space (logical) at once, this would flout all that is harmonious and tolerable. How narrowly or broadly are "things" to be defined? There is the section on the circulation of fluids in the body, that of the winds known as the trade winds, maps of various epidemics, as they are believed to have been transmitted, a map of the spread of languages as they are believed to have emanated out of Africa, or simultaneously in many regions, depending on whether one subscribes to the monogenetic or polygenetic theory of origins. There are maps of the drug trade whose degree of detail might send tremors through the most Kevlar-entrenched drug dealer. There are maps of genetic modification of foods, delineating how they have sprawled all over the American landscape, picked up and buffeted by winds lacking policy agendas. [*He updated some of these over the years, as you have surely noted.*]

In short, it is a tome to marvel at, and to pick up and browse at will. And it has just arrived on the shelves of the Mid-Manhattan Library right at Fortieth Street and Fifth Avenue, shelved logically under Dewey classification _____.____P, ready to be checked out, gaped at, ogled, handled, caressed, ignored, flung, tiger-charged, and any of the other innumerable postures available within the *Kama Sutra* of the readerly imagination that books might be seduced into trying in the middle of the year AD 19____.

We, too, were part of that collective effort, and felt our responsibility as burden and badge. I can recall a garage sale: neighbors, the Larsens. My mother was picturing their furniture, mentally rearranging it in our house, while my father walked around as if he were at a hands-on museum. He seemed to be particularly drawn by the most impractical items—a battery hold-down for cars that had not been manufactured in decades, a set of binoculars that were unwieldy even for that time. I remember him calling us over, turning the knob of the eyepiece while panning around as he said, "These once belonged to the Margolises, and now I'm going to buy them for a song from the Larsens. And we'll probably hold a garage sale of our own in a few months, at which point, hopefully, I will dump them off to someone else." He looked sagely at Aidan and me. "You see," he said in a hushed tone, "the way things make their way even around our little neighborhood." I don't recall ever having a garage sale.

Do all families have such unifying themes? And if not, what replaces them? How, otherwise, do they make sense of it all, bring together the noblest and the basest in their histories within a single binding? We were driving to Detroit, once, to see Uncle Gerry. It was the excitement of anticipation—the big city and greasy roadside fare along the way. As we pulled back on the highway after a stop at a diner, my body betrayed me with a riptide of a fart. Aidan immediately began writhing and pinching his nose. He cranked down his window, air rushing into the car. It smelled worse outside, at that moment in eastern Michigan. My hair whipping up, I reached over and, his own hand grabbing my arm midway up, wrestled him. I was bigger, stronger—that was before Aidan shot up and overtook me in every physical sense—but he was next to the handle. My mother's "Boys, stop that!" could barely be heard in the melee, when my father's voice roared over the wind: "Now listen here. We're going to track that fart for *The Atlas*, by God, Jay. I'm putting you and Aidan in charge of those pages. And if anyone's going to open up the window, you'd better make note of *exactly* where we are!" Yes, we were reduced to howling laughter, and the fighting was subdued, but more, that fart became the stuff of legend. Years later, we'd mime unsuspecting readers whistling with exaggerated innocence as they flipped through the pages, and then overacted scratching of heads, and eventually wide-eyed horror.

Only later, once my mother had divorced my father and removed herself several states from his lingering charms, did I learn that she'd been skeptical of the book's ever seeing the light of day. And, indeed, her doubt was justified—when my father eventually went into the hospital, the complications ensuing from a laryngectomy gouging his ability to take care of himself even more acutely than his ability to speak, I was given the charge of cleaning out his apartment. By this point, he was headed for assisted living if he made it out of the hospital. As I rummaged through his stuff, mostly books and papers, but also a remarkable collection of rocks, I came upon only bits and traces of anything like a work in progress. There were pages and pages of research notes, written out on legal pads and on the blank sides of manuscript pages, and copies of maps with incomprehensible annotations and arrows plunging and swooping about, but nothing that even approximated a coherent text. I tried to keep together anything that I thought might have belonged in *The Atlas*. It turned out that his apartment abounded with as much pornography as geography, and the former made more sense, at least, to one sifting through the detritus of a life lived largely alone. As I worked, I noted the relative heights of the two piles, rooting for *The Atlas* pile but knowing it would likely be a dead heat.

At various points in what felt like an excavation, I would phone Aidan to discuss what to do with certain items that looked like they might have value—this sterling silver unpromisingly packed in a crushed cardboard carton, a broach that depicted a woman—our grandmother?—in solemn sepias. During these conversations, I felt as though Aidan was making a concerted effort to avoid sounding impatient, and I was made starkly aware of how different we were, how successfully he'd managed to extricate himself from the radius of our father's magnetism. He was a stockbroker in New York, trading in oil futures, and, if his standard of living was any gauge, damned good at it. I was somewhat fascinated by what he did. Sometimes I'd come across a book about Wall Street while contemplating library purchases, and I'd seize the opportunity to consult with him.

"Sure," he'd say. "If someone in Michigan wants to read about the New York financial markets, that sounds as good as anything else."

Sometimes I was more direct. "What is it that you *do* all day?"

He'd shrug aside the question. "It's not really interesting. Then again, it's not supposed to be. Only type *interest* that matters to my company is percent on the dollar." He had an accent that I otherwise heard only on television and in movies.

It was the same when it came to asking Aidan about being a parent. His answers were terse; there was the occasional extended anecdote, usually about something "cute," like his daughter's "One of Everything" collection, but other than that, minimal info. I liked being able to look things up—that's just my way. As a source, Aidan seemed rich, substantive, and reputable but was frustratingly lacking in an index.

Like Aidan, my mother had bolted when she saw daylight, I think. The way I'd construed it, after staying in the Midwest to marry him upon graduating from college, she must have undergone a sort of Copernican revolution at some point, realizing she wasn't anywhere near the center of my father's self-contained cosmos. Her own family came from outside Philadelphia, and they welcomed her back until she could re-locate with the childhood sweetheart who was conveniently just the other side of a divorce himself. It might have been mere coincidence, just as it might have been coincidence that her geographical proximity to Aidan seemed to correspond to a greater emotional closeness, as was the case, I suppose, with my father and me. Then again, her closeness with Aidan may have stemmed from the fact that as a grandmother, as it turned out, she was a natural, a singer of strictly arias. Her disappointment that I wasn't seeing anyone, or anyone worth really talking about for more than a few awkward moments, was ever pal-pable; my emphatic recommendations of the latest mysteries that she would love, no matter how right I was, fell ever short.

At some point in the process of sorting through my father's things, I realized that caves and cave-related items were de-manding the formation of a third pile. Indeed, this would keep me on my toes—pictures of the interiors of caves bear a striking resemblance to certain close-up treatments of the human body. You see, my father wouldn't go to the hereafter without leaving behind something cataloged in the Library of Congress—after all that, he was an author. GB603.P46, to be exact, or Dewey 551.4P. I haven't memorized these systems, no, though they are our periodic tables. When I was getting my library science degree, there was a period in which if you handed me a book, I could have turned it over a couple of times, scanning its exterior only, and spit out a pretty reason-able guess as to where exactly it would be shelved. Nowadays, I've only retained those that stir specific passions.

The book, *Spelos: An Ode to Caves*, had been available at the local store for a while, propped above the handwritten sign proudly proclaiming "Local Author Gus Pardo!!!!!!!" but the copy there never budged more than an inch or two. It got slightly dog-eared over the years, its pages turning creamy and mottled—when he self-published, my father did not know to use paper that would withstand time and other elements. The real moment it hit me with desolation was when I held it aloft, once, and noted a fresh smudge. That fingerprint looked, at a certain angle, like slime creeping its way out of the cave entrance that graced the cover. When I saw the smeared copy, I thought about buying it at the local store, but somehow it seemed like it would cause too much commotion in the small town where we lived—Sam, the guy who ran the bookstore, knew my dad well, and would surely ask him, "Hey, why's your *son* buying your book, Gus?"

But the copy of *Spelos* that was housed in our nation's capital was another story. I remember visiting Washington, D.C. with the family, when Aidan was thirteen and I sixteen, and making our way to the glorious library amid the other palatial buildings, as they seemed to my decidedly midwestern sensibility. I remember spending much of the three days we were there bedazzled, in awe of dimensions, buildings that appeared to have been stretched out like the limousines we saw on the streets, and brightness that seemed to dance off every surface. My mother had to yell out my name a couple of times in intersections, and Aidan premiered the "jaywalking" jokes that immediately entered the permanent database of obnoxious family references.

Our stop at the Library of Congress was surely one of the highlights of that trip. Our father kept announcing that there were "thousands of miles of books" there, adding, "That's more than the distance that we traveled to get here." I remember my mother shaking her head—she really wanted more face time with the seats of power: the Capitol, the White House, the Washington Monument; for her, the LC was a glorious architectural specimen, but, at the end of the day, just a library. My father's insistence that it really was "the library *of* Congress" seemed to carry some appeal for her—she thought she might spot a congressperson. Once there, we got the needed special permission to go back into the stacks, as Aidan and I were technically too young. My dad even half-joked with the guard that they had better reserve a slot, "yea wide and yea high," for the atlas he was eventually to finish; he actually, as I recall, apologized for making them wait.

Finally, after various delays, we located the book. Unlike the much-handled version in the bookstore back home, this copy had had its cover stripped, and the black spine declaring the title in gold lettering seemed more hardened, as though it had gone off to join the military and been forced to toughen up, gather an austere dignity. And the very cataloging itself was revelatory for me. The transition between Dewey and LC is a conversion accomplished in seconds with a computer program nowadays, but I can still remember marveling at the unfamiliar codes on the books as we strode through, which seemed like intimations of an adult world I could barely glimpse, tantalizingly and dauntingly complicated.

Of course, we had always had copies sitting around in the house—since it was self-published, he got more than the customary ten copies or whatever it is that an author receives. Oddly enough, while over the years I'd opened it many times, and read many pages, I'd never read the book straight through from start to finish. I knew it was about caves, of course, and that it was about more than caves, too. That in its 137 pages, my father had captured a passion for going into caves that had flourished in the years before I'd been born. That he'd mused on their natural history, their flora and fauna, their dankness and darkness, their labyrinthine souls. He'd touched on sleep cycles, prehistoric aesthetics, philosophy, oracles, blindness. (His eclecticism and the solipsism of self-published work, less common then, threw the catalogers, Deweyan and LC alike, for a loop; I knew, based on my dips in, that they'd probably gotten it wrong.) He'd gotten a cult following among spelunkers, a cult if ever there was one, judging by the occasional fan mail that he received, sometimes bearing the name of a cave as its return address ("Funny guy, this one!"), which he would share with us boomingly over the dinner table. "This guy, I've got to get him to do a section of *The Atlas*," he'd say on occasion if he got a particularly eccentric letter—let's say one featuring a handwritten map of a set of caverns.

It was written when I was an infant, and so from the time I was young it was sort of always around. But quickly I'd passed well beyond the point where it had been assumed that we had all read it—I know Aidan lapped me in this regard—and so as often as I urged myself to do so, it seemed that the other, more urgent reading material kept piling up. First there was high school, then college, where I studied literature, which certainly didn't leave me a whole lot of time to catch up on such back reading. And then, on to a library science degree, where the reading was much more technical and technologically oriented than anything I'd encountered before, demanding a whole new way of reading. It was the beginning of the heyday of the Internet; suddenly, bibliophilia was just another trait among many that qualified one to be a top-notch librarian, and even those of us who put books first had to embrace "information management."

I was familiar enough with the book that I could carry on the small talk that usually circulated around the book— it wasn't as though spelunkers were making pilgrimages to Esoch, Michigan, where I got my first library job, or anything of that nature. Mostly, friends and relatives would make reference to it, and occasionally a woman whom I was seeing. Somehow, none of them ever got past the first question, "What's it about?" My stock answer—"It's all about caves . . . it's hard to describe, though, because it's not *just* about the actual physical caves"—was more than sufficient for them. Part of me, perhaps the part that had always yearned to be a fiction writer instead of a librarian who nonetheless trafficked so often in fictions, would itch to say more, to make it up, to conjure a version of what I thought the book was about, based on my skimmings and perusals over the years. Another part of me, though, was relieved that I didn't have to lie about something so fundamental to how I thought about my family. Not even the biggest wiseass I dated, Erica—six months—would press me: "Well, what's the first *sentence*, at least?" No, come to think of it, Erica would have been more ruthless still, would have asked about the *last* sentence. Glad she never got around to it.

At the Esoch Library, I put in an order for a copy right away. The head librarian was more than glad to oblige. "Well, of course, it's your father's book," she said, positively tickled to have the son of a bona fide local author join the staff. Later, I moved to Biltchrist and ordered a copy there, too. There, Lucy, the reference librarian, ruled the nonfiction orders with an iron fist. She was less than enthusiastic about ordering a copy, less game to do so on a whim, suspicious that I was trying to slip something past her. A bulldog of a woman, she'd intimidated me from day one.

"Are there any reviews of it I could read?" she inquired.

I thought about the reviews I knew of. One in the local paper in Esoch, where I'd grown up, written by a guy who was posed in several fishing photos on my dad's walls. I knew him as the shorter guy, in height somewhere between my father and the dangling fish. A couple of write-ups in spelunking magazines, which were, believe it or not, obscure. Not a whimper in *Publishers Weekly* or *Library Journal* or *Book Trade*, the sources that Lucy relied upon with an almost religious fervor, and that we were expected to swear by also. Not even a blurb in *Outside* or anywhere with journalistic cachet or popular standing.

"I think I can get ahold of some fan mail from some read-ers," I tried. She thought I was kidding. "Yes, well, bring in whatever *reviews* you have." In that moment, I made a men-tal vow not to be so slavishly bound to the serendipities and stratagems of the marketplace when I had the opportunity, to seek out the obscure and the overlooked.

The copy I brought in wound up on the shelf. That was okay—at that time, my dad didn't need the $14.95, plus ship-ping and handling, that he was charging for it, but years later, sitting in his hospital room, I thought, Medicare and health insurance notwithstanding, we could both use it now.

In that very hospital room, I was caught red-handed for never having read *Spelos*. One day I was confronted by, of all people, a nurse named Désirée, to whom my father had appar-ently talked about the book. She was making small talk with me, a better diversion than the paper, while he was asleep one day, and she was tending to him, cleaning, et cetera.

"So, is it true he's written a book?" She was wise to confirm, as the greatest, most jarring postoperative complication had been a form of delirium. His connection with reality came and went unpredictably, and of course there was no mechanism yet sensitive enough to detect it, unlike the more autonomic functions.

"Indeed it is," I said. "He's not making that up."

"So how does it feel to be the son of a writer?"

"Oh," I said. "It's an honor, I suppose."

She smiled. "Tell me about the book he's written again?"

I led with the standard line, but she wasn't going anywhere. She scrubbed his arm.

"Well, what about caves, then, if not the actual physical caves?"

I stumbled. I think I stammered something about the deeper meaning in caves. Something about going deeper, the way you could venture into caves. I felt as though among the machines in the room there was a bullshit detector whose needle was flailing in the red zone.

"Hmmm, sounds interesting," she murmured, cocking an eyebrow. It was unmistakable—she *knew* that I was a cheat. That night, I yanked it almost angrily off the shelf where it had been gathering dust; people always expect a librarian's home shelves will somehow be immune to residue, and speech immune to clichés, but neither is the case. Thus I began to plow through it. One hundred and thirty-seven pages in a matter of hours, and the sense that my father's soul had once been, perhaps still was, magma, lit and surging.

The next time I was there, another nurse was on call, but about a week later I overlapped with Désirée again. "Hello," I said.

My father was conscious now. He did not speak much, for he couldn't, but his whisper still had a robustness to it.

"Hey," I said. "About my father's book, you know, that we were talking about last time?"

"Mmmmm."

"Since you expressed curiosity," I said, "I brought a copy. In case you were interested in reading it." It was checked out under my own name from the Biltchrist Public Library.

My father spotted as much immediately. He said, "You check out library? *Your*?" He left out words that he felt he didn't need.

"I did, I did," I said.

"What if someone needs?" he said.

I couldn't quite gauge where he was vis-à-vis reality. I said, "That's true, but it will be due back in three weeks." I gestured to Désirée. "And I'm sure Désirée won't hang on to it longer than that." She nodded in affirmation. I didn't have the heart to tell him that as far as I knew, the book had never left the library. Perhaps it had, but I certainly had never checked it out to anyone.

A few minutes went by. Then he squinted at me. "What is it you do . . . library?"

"I'm the Director of Circulation," I said.

He paused for a moment, stared out at the wall across from the bed, from where sometimes the Hula-Hoop girl emerged. She was nowhere near now. Then he asked a question I was not quite expecting, yet somehow dreading. "Who else checked it out? When?"

It was indeed one of the older books, old enough that it still had the pocket in the back where a card had once designated the due dates of the book. Any book up until a certain point wore its history on its sleeve, its record of encounters, its promiscuity or chasteness. Only in high school libraries was there an actual signature; for public libraries, a date stamp did the trick. I peered in the pocket, just to be sure. Those cards had been discarded with the advent of the computerized system. For a period of time, those records had been recorded and archived electronically, but after the Patriot Act, many librarians, myself included, were wary about this government—I am tempted to use the word *regime*—meddling in the privacy of our patrons. We've felt tested by this possibility: we've become versed in the Privacy Act to an unprecedented degree, and I know many of us who have responded by destroying checkout records with a newfound urgency. There is no way to tell who has checked out many of our books and when, and there was no way to know for sure that this book had never left the library.

More likely, it had sat on the shelf next to its companions, growing old, peering out at the movements of patrons, sizing them up perhaps just as readily as they were sized up. Yes, I know it sounds strange—you might conclude that I, and not my father, was the one suffering from delirium, but I have occasionally tried to take the perspective of the books on my shelves, imagining that they choose their recipients as much as they are chosen. Like animals in the wild, they can, I suppose, camouflage themselves such that at times they blend in with their surroundings as readily as tree frogs, hugging the walls of the shelves around them, appearing less palatable than the plump bestsellers they lean against. Or like abandoned puppies in pet stores—I was going to say prostitutes, but fear it could single-handedly shatter your impression of me, and perhaps I, like these books, can only hope to make an impression—they can poke themselves out just a bit farther than the nearest competitor, jutting forth an irresistible moist black nose between pouting eyes.

These are fanciful notions, of course, and who is to say which is the stranger phenomenon in the grand view—Man Seeking Book, or Book Seeking Man? And why not a mutual wooing?

I glanced down into the pocket anyway, indeed empty. My father was a man who would have cared deeply about the Patriot Act and its implications for American citizens, privacy, and freedom. But instead of going into that, I told a half-truth, a truth that five years earlier would have been intact. I said, "We have that information on the computer now, Dad."

He nodded. Désirée took the book, thanked me. Said the last book she read was months ago. These hospital shifts are killing her.

—◇◇◇—

One of the most striking stories I read when I was in college was Borges's "Library of Babel," and on occasion I have thought myself the proprietor of that very library. Borges envisions a metaphysical marvel, a library that essentially comprises the whole of the universe—the universe *as* library. Its volumes are random and contain every possible permutation of text, from gibberish to the complete works of Shakespeare. Within the library that Borges conjures, not only is every book ever written shelved somewhere but every *possible* book, every conceivable configuration of the alphabet. The conceit is too dizzying to think about for very long, but it serves as a good antidote to certain fundamental realities: funds are limited, books go unread, tumble out of print, serve as door-stops—all too effectively, I might add; the greatest libraries of civilizations burn down, suns collapse, abandon planets without child support. And each life is limited—there is only so much reading that one can consume in the course of a life-time, and the guests are waiting for the ham. No, that's my brother Aidan's life, and his line, too—once we were speak-ing in his bedroom, and he was expressing concern for me, my solitude, the dearth of female companionship in my life. I had just broken off an apparently blossoming relationship shortly before coming for Thanksgiving. At some point, de-spite my brother's better intentions, it became apparent that there was nothing more to be said—we could both hear the mirth below, the hubbub of Aidan's kids and those of the neighbors who were over, the clatter of dishes being hoisted from the kitchen to prime spots on the table, sloshing sauce. And Aidan, at last, smiling at the futility of his words: "Well, the guests are waiting for the ham."

⬥

Désirée had called me and warned me my dad wasn't doing well, that he seemed less cognizant of his surroundings. He was talking about Lake Superior and hunting lodges and a mother bear. She said that, by the way, she had read the book, and while she wasn't sure she had understood most of it, and it was unlike any other book that she had ever read, she'd found it to be "powerful and very, very emotional." I thanked her without quite knowing why, and added, "I bet he'd be glad to know that."

She said, "Oh, I told him. I told him I particularly liked the part about bats."

"Oh, yes," I shot right back, perhaps a bit too eagerly. "Where he goes into the whole thing about insideness and outsideness, and how we are becoming more batlike as we spend more and more of our lives indoors."

"Yes." I could hear her smiling over the phone as she noted that I had read it, perhaps concurrently with her. "I could identify with that. I *never* seem to get outside these days." She paused for a moment. "Some of that stuff was strange, though."

"About the proportions of the bat's head to its body?"

"That's it," she said, and I could sense her nodding and even laughing.

"My dad's a strange guy," I said. "He has some strange notions about the world."

Later, when I arrived at the hospital, and Désirée had left the book behind with a note, he came awake. He couldn't really gesture, lacking the facial control to do so, but I could sense that inwardly he was motioning to it as he said, "She liked it."

"So I hear."

Then, a few minutes later: "Who'll have it next?"

I said, "I'll bring it back to the library."

"Hmm. Then?"

"It will go back on the shelf."

"Then?"

At what point does one recognize that the truth is precisely the wrong instrument for a task? I was in charge of circulation. A slowness, a quasi-geological time governs the circulation of books: the punctuation of frantic movements as a book takes on a buzz, gets reviewed, followed by years of stillness, silence, neglect. Perhaps a motion picture is commissioned, produced, released; the book stirs, reenters the commerce of the world, mingles and becomes inebriated in the gala of its success, and eventually tapers off, only somewhat reluctantly, into a second retirement. Envision a remake thirty years later—it happens. There is always hope, you see.

But imagine if one could speed up time, fast-forward and rewind over longer intervals, see at once all the permutations of a book's lifetime. From this vantage point, the Director of Circulation might appear the ringleader of a circus—co-ordinating acrobats, elephants, fire-breathing ladies, third-rate clowns, contract renegotiations. Books would fly off the shelves in a blur, leaving gaps like children's debut teeth, making their forays out into the world, and swooping back to their perches eventually like osprey. Indeed, sideways and spines up, with their covers spread out, would they look like anything other than birds? I paused, though, as I realized that what was missing from this vision were the temporary habitations of the book outside, its journeys through the neighborhood. Or, as I knew all too well from the day-to-day job, throughout the *world*. How laughably common is it to hear "I returned that— I'm absolutely positive!" only to receive a sheepish note from a return address far away—New Mexico?—that reads, "*This* turned up while unpacking. Sorry!" One would have hoped for a jar of salsa, at least.

I thought, inevitably, of that Other Book. *The Atlas*. Un-written, perhaps unwritable. I pictured the ideal version of that book; once one has admitted the impossible, one might as well usher in its unruly companions. Picture a tracer placed in the book that would record its travels to and fro. No, too much of a concession to the regime. Rather, render a version of the book itself that includes a sheaf of blank pages and empty maps. These would be pages reserved for the recording of the book's own journey, not merely where it went but what went on in the lives of those around it while it was in their abodes. I foresee, and you do, too, that gradually the journal grows and grows, till it subsumes the book, essentially *becomes* the book. Worry about that then.

I was the Director of Circulation. I said, "It is checked out by a boy."

He seemed pleased with this answer. But not satisfied. Perhaps he, too, at that moment was thinking of *The Atlas*; perhaps he never ceased thinking of it; perhaps it was error to think that it *was* a book at all, that it was anything other than the very medium of thought itself. "And then?" The machines pulsed and bleeped; the room waited for more. The Hula-hoop froze, though it did not tumble; it hovered around the waist of the girl—did I neglect to mention that she was there?

I continued: "He needs it for school." It was all I could think of. The hoop was still poised. "For earth science class."

He laughed. "Required text?" he said.

My father didn't mind imaginative leaps, but he was no Panglossian. "Nope," I said. "For extra credit." The story pushed on. With these minimal legs, it somehow staggered to its feet, however awkwardly. "They're . . . not covered in the regular curriculum. The teacher . . . gave them a list. 'Topics Not Covered,' it read. Passed it around the room." Somehow with the contrivance of that list, the story started to plod forward in my mind, then to lumber forth with increased momentum as the sheet worked its way around the room. I didn't know where any of these images, which had the materiality and authority of memories, were coming from, except in the vaguest sense. I could see my father was transfixed. "The kid, he signed up first . . . for avalanches. He wanted avalanches, desperately. Who wouldn't? He was overjoyed when the list came around . . . and the four people ahead of him hadn't signed up for avalanches. What were the odds?

"So he signs his name. But when the list comes around and the teacher wants to double-check . . . she reads off Billy Fletcher's name for avalanches. He wants to protest; he can see from where he's sitting that Billy has crossed off his name— it's Heath, and he—gets mocked for it sometimes, especially next year when they're doing *Macbeth*. Anyway, it's crossed, blatantly, off, but Billy's bigger, more developed, works out, football player. So Heath keeps his mouth shut. Caves is left, still. Anybody want caves? He shoots up his hand. He *needs* the extra credit way more than he needs avalanches. He's fallen behind, barely passing the class. He doesn't mind earth science, rather enjoys it, actually, but it's . . . a *lot* of memorization. Doesn't have time. Most of his free time is spent over in . . . the hunting store where he works, helps out his dad, exhausting.

"So he gets one day off, the start of actual hunting season. Everything's closed, but . . . for some reason the library's open. Let's say . . . the librarian there is antihunting. Heath heads for the library and finds your book on caves. Takes it out. Takes out a couple of other books. But he knows the project has to be good. He doesn't have a lot of time, though—next day it's back to the store. He's strapped in math class, too, where Mrs. Clayman is going over the Cartesian graphs. He doesn't get functions. So . . . he copies a bit, more than a bit, in truth, three pages."

As I related this, a part of me was observing myself, and that part wanted to discern where the details were coming from. They seemed conjured from anywhere and nowhere at once, at first trickling, then gushing forth as though from some reservoir of necessity. A thought that I had vaguely had before crystal-lized in my mind: nonfiction could be pinned down, assigned its plot of shelf real estate, where it could reliably be located in the continuum of knowledge, in any library in any country in the world. But fictions were like transient, shifty renters—all we could do with them was alphabetize them by the arbitrary condition of the authors' last names and hope they stayed put.

"So," my father murmured. "He get away with it?"

The tip of my tongue rooted around between my lip and the top of my gums as I pondered, as though the answer were wedged there like food caught in teeth. It was a good question, and it felt like any answer was irrevocable; somehow, too, it needed to be dictated by the book. "He gets caught . . . when his teacher asks him about the part about 'uterine walls.' The class snickers . . . so she knows it is her professional duty to do something, and when she confronts him, Heath is stymied, tongue-tied." I paused for a moment here. My dad was not Pollyannaish, but why I had been lured into such a cynical cavern of possibility, a seeming dead end? Somehow, glancing over at his sallow cheeks, I felt I needed to push around this.

It came to me all at once, and I said it as quickly as though I was on a fading phone connection. "But he will read the book later for a literature class and understand it much more and look back in disgust and pathos on his younger ways. And he will write his college essay on the book and the whole experience, and it will get him into his second choice."

I looked over at my father; he appeared to be in something akin to a trance. As for me, I'd gotten so caught up in the story that I hadn't even seen Désirée come into the room.

"This is what happens next to the book," I explained, as if this explanation would make sense to her. But if it didn't— I shrugged—so be it; I'd realized something that my father, perhaps, had already known: that delirium is a form of understanding.

As Désirée crouched over him to give him his medication, he said, "We are cave people," perhaps by way of his own explanation. Somehow, the words were comedic and weighty at once. Neither of us responded, except by smiling, which seemed about right.

Afterward, as I drove home, I retraced my story as though I had just surfaced from a particularly vivid dream, trying to figure out from whence its ingredients had grown, by what recipe it had been put together. I had dated a woman once who was a high school teacher, and she had told me a couple of stories about plagiarists she had caught; I hadn't thought about her recently. The other details—avalanches, buff football players—seemed like miracles.

The next evening, I told him about the couple who had checked the book out next. Somehow, a fragment set me off—something I heard about once on NPR? "They're a couple who are getting married in a cave. She's an archaeologist; he's a dean at the school where she works. She has a vision of a splendid wedding that actually will be set in a cave—hundreds of candles illuminating the lush walls, dripping sounds in the background, chains of flowers lining the mantel that happens to run along the cave's contours, a photographer who must crane his neck around stalactites.

"The groom, the dean, he's a little stiff, but he decides to go along with it. She's brought out so many wonderful aspects of him—spontaneity, adventure—that he can't complain. They get out books about caves, look for 'Cave Readings.' *Spelos* looks promising, looks like it was written for that target audience of brides and grooms looking for pithy cave quotes. Doing his part, dutifully, he reads the passage on bats, somehow panics. It's not about the bats; it's about something deeper that she represents, someplace she's leading him. Too much. Soon, for consecutive nights, he's having dreams, nightmares, bats swarming.

"They split up. She marries a local chef, who is delighted to get married in a cave. They have a cave-aged cheese spread at the wedding that rivals anything anyone's ever seen.

"He neglects to return the book. Pining for her, he clings to it, a remnant of that relationship, what once was, even though it is too painful to actually read it.

"Then one day, he meets a new girl. Everything's great—she loves the symphony and the opera. It's what he's always imagined. A couple of years go by. They are moving . . . to New Mexico, of all places. He's a little bit wary but hears the Santa Fe Symphony is fantastic. As they are packing up, she turns up the book, which is absurdly overdue at this point. She can't believe he hasn't returned it. Not only that, but she knows that he was previously all but married in a cave, and she's savvy—she actually puts two and two together; she interprets the reasons for the book's continued presence there and continued absence from the library all too accurately. They fight—about other last-minute scrambles, the need to return the cable box, et cetera—she never lets on that she sees the significance of it, besides its being long overdue. He doesn't quite understand why she wants him to return it *immediately*—they are in the middle of rolling lamps in bubble wrap—but he does. Dutiful. At first, they want to charge him at the library, but the librarian is in a lighthearted mood and clears the fine when he explains the situation. The librarian sleeps well that night, thinking of him as she is drifting off.

"The book is back but it's not there for long. There is a woman who has been taking a class in the evening." I looked up; I had been so immersed in the story that I had forgotten the presence of my audience. I glanced over at him. He was fast asleep, his snoring steady and serene.

The next night, I told the story of the woman. The stories continued to unfold over the next several nights. Sometimes Désirée was present, and sometimes not. I had never told stories before—it felt exhilarating. I would leave and pick up my car and pay the ticket at the gate, imagining SCHEHERAZADE on a vanity plate—how could you pare it down to six characters and still make it recognizable? Immediately, I reprimanded myself for being so flippant—my father was on his deathbed, and I was hardly saving my own life. Or was I?

I thought about Aidan reading his children stories, and I wondered if I would be any good at it. My father had seen and experienced enough of the world that that there was very little I would bite my tongue about with him; almost anything that popped into my head would be fair game. But if you were telling stories to children, you would have to limit what you could say. Did you just make exotic dishes with minimal ingredients, or were the expectations lower for items ordered off the children's menu? When I'd visited Aidan in New York, I'd always been anxious about bedtime—it seemed like a nightly trial, a forum in which all of your shortcomings and neuroses as a parent and as a person would be showcased. Were you a pushover, or were you "just not the creative type," or, perhaps worse, too preoccupied with budgets and deadlines to suspend disbelief even fleetingly—your own and another's—in outspoken mice and yawning moons?

I would wait downstairs, nervously thumbing the remote through cable channels, gnawed at by the sense that I should be doing something to help, something to make the night special because I was there. Meanwhile, I'd let Aidan and Jen tend to those duties, like any other night. Eventually, they would rejoin me, shaking their heads, swapping a detail or two about their ordeals, and every so often glancing at the head of the stairs, looking for the pajama-clad figure they hoped would not appear. Next time I was out at Aidan's, I vowed, I would volunteer for bedtime services.

For now, though, I was in the thicker woods of the adult story world. "It's a continuing ed class. She's getting her life back on track after a series of abusive or nondescript relationships. Doing something good for the soul.

"Needless to say, she develops a crush on her handsome thirtysomething teacher, who has been ushering her into the realm of philosophy—the class is called 'The Moderns on the Ancients,' or maybe it's 'The Ancients on the Moderns,' whatever. She shoots him glances; he might or might not be responding, but she confirms her initial impression that he isn't wearing a ring.

"After she *finally* gets her grade in the mail—she did just fine—she musters up the courage to call him and ask him out. He is surprisingly appreciative and charmingly awkward all at once, and says it would be great to go out for dinner sometime.

He tells her that her paper on Nietzsche on Plato was great, and that he was just surprised that she made no mention of Plato's Allegory of the Cave—apologizes that they never had time for it on the syllabus, but surely she's read it. She hasn't? Oh, he tells her, oh, she must.

"She goes to the library immediately, and locates the Platonic dialogues. There's nothing there that even looks cave-related, just a bunch of Greek names: *Meno, Crito*, no *Cavo*. Disheartened, she heads for the computer and looks up caves—maybe it's nestled next to other cave books, maybe there's an *Anthology of Cave Literature*; she'll try *allegory* last. She goes to the cave shelf—the 551s—and there, lo and behold, is something called *Spelos: An Ode to Caves*. The book seems to be beckoning to her—it all but has Plato's autograph on it.

"She reads a hundred and thirty-seven pages in one fell swoop. There are references throughout the volume to Plato's myth, but they're oblique, scattered like clues. Over dinner, she says something about bats and the sizes of their heads relative to their bodies—he hears 'hats,' though, and finds the comment crass and trivial. She senses his boredom and the disparity of their intellects.

"After he drops her off, she takes the book, which was in her purse, and flings it off a bridge, where it flips over three times and hurtles into the back of a flatbed filled with gravel and dust. It rains a bit; the book is partly sheltered. The next morning, the driver picks it up and brings it back to the library. It's the last day of the library book sale, and he gets three children's books about construction and trucks dirt cheap, and takes them home to his kids and is proud because it is his profession and they will be readers.

"But he's taken it to the wrong library—the name got slightly obscured by the rain, and he took it to the library one town over. As they attempt to check it in, of course, they recognize that. And they do what they always do *in these cases*.

"They send it to the Greenvale in the next state over, because there are two Greenvales within thirty miles of each other and this happens *all the time*.

"Well, at this point the book is a little bit tattered, a little bit scruffy. When it arrives at the Greenvale, Indiana Public Library, they roll their eyes a bit, relabel it, figuring that at some fundamental level all the libraries of the world are united—head librarian there fancies herself a bit of a socialist, anyhow. So they treat it like a new book; it spends a week at the bindery.

"When it hits the shelves again, they put it on display as a new book—really an understandable error, because it is shimmering in its new packaging. It happens that a man who has recently been diagnosed with obsessive-compulsive disorder has recently had a major breakthrough after years of therapy and failed remedies. His therapist has recommended that rather than attempting to beat his obsessions by avoiding them, he needs to find an outward focus *for* his obsessive energy, an object worthy of affection. He cites Freud; the patient is game.

"He heads to the library immediately and hits the 'New Nonfiction' shelves, then plunges into the older books. He pulls down four or five, each of which seems to promise a lifetime, or at least many months, of promising obsessional material. He clutches a stack and heaves it on the circulation desk up front: a book on kites and kite making, one on mutual funds, one on the Civil War, one on stargazing, and all of them balancing on the slenderest of the bunch, the afterthought he has grabbed on spelunking."

At this point, I'd taken to actually plotting and writing up the scenarios the night before. Having never composed fiction before, I'd grown restless in the evening hours, thinking about where the book would go next. At first, I wrote simply in order to sleep, but it also seemed as though the stories would be more meaningful for him, since he'd been such a reader himself throughout his life but didn't have the fine motor control needed to operate a book at this point. As for the oral tradition, I could always embellish in the moment of performance, too. I could not quite discern pride in his minimal responses; his gestural repertoire was confined to the eyes and the muscles around the orbits at this point, but I felt that he couldn't be disappointed at my stabs at writing. I wrote about my OCD patient:

"When he reads it, though, he reads with fervor. He's a Dostoyevskian reader, and though that could mean many things, in his case, it means that he reads in the manner in which he imagines that Dostoyevsky wrote—ravenous, staggering through his dimly lit apartment clutching the book, luminous with something teetering between ecstasy and epilepsy, ingesting swathes of prose in desperate gulps, like an infant born undersized, suckling harder. When once he misplaces the book and locates it at last, after a forty-minute search, concealed under an errant cushion, he collars it like a treacherous friend; he is at once too furious and too attached to reprimand for long. It goes without saying that he takes it into the bathroom, and sometimes loses himself on the porcelain seat, as though this was the most natural reading position, as if reading was only one part of *that*. His bathroom, anyway, overlooks an alley fraught with the stink and presence of people, and when he is reading the book, it is summer; thus windows are wide open and the whole building seems to be singing, a chorus of vague suggestions and clashing soloists. He devours it like a novel, fastening on the dramas of the explorers, their obsessions with going farther and with firsts—the first to conquer a particular cave or to prove, slithering on their stomachs, that two caves were ultimately connected in some remote channel inaccessible to all but those willing to die for an idea, the idea that all things must be connected.

"At some point in the bathroom, a slight but terrible thing happens; he drops the book onto the toilet seat. He grabs as though it is his only pair of glasses tumbling over the railing of an ocean liner, and manages to prevent the book from falling in, but for a brief moment it lands unmistakably on the toilet seat. Disgusting, to him. More than that, it sends him spiraling into thoughts, thoughts that only an obsessive would have—how many other times might this book have landed near toilets, been handled by germ-laden people, people with no regard for hygiene whatsoever, and no regard for the fact that this book will be read by the purer and more innocent, oblivious to its former depravities? Reason returns momentarily—he recalls that it is a New Book, glistening, can only have been checked out once or twice, but then *what to think of these other books*? Now the thought has taken up lodging—it is too late to unthink it, and he can't shake it. He cannot even bring himself to handle the other books, not even to take them back. He tells his friend, who knows about his condition. His friend, ever loyal, aware and sympathetic, will return them— he makes a joke: put the kite book on a string and read it at arm's length. As his friend departs with the books, the obsessive actually considers this as a possibility for future library excursions.

"The friend returns most of the books. But the cave book seems special, somehow. He decides to recheck it out under his own name. Is so provoked by its magnificent descriptions and reflections that he decides to try spelunking. He takes it along—pocket-sized, it isn't exactly going to do any lasting damage to his back."

Have you forgotten, for even an instant, as I must admit I had, that these stories were meant for my father, that he was listening all along? Indeed, he had passed away at some point during my reading of this last story, which thus never was told. Little in his features distinguished this latest placidity from that sleep that had become our ritual, our agreement. I found it hard to believe that there wouldn't be another story tomorrow.

With some trepidation, that evening I phoned my mother to inform her of the news. I was almost relieved when her voice betrayed sorrow, perhaps a mourning for some ineradicable part of herself, though her words were no more than "Well, I'm deeply glad you could be there for him."

The funeral was later that week. Aidan and his wife and the kids flew in, Gerry, and even Désirée made an appearance with her son—it was oddest to see her in black instead of her nurse's attire. A chilly, rainy day, flood warnings. The flash storms were made more dramatic by the flatness all around; Aidan's children would remember the Midwest as strung up by lightning throughout their lives. Afterward, everyone came over to my place, the profusion of voices and bodies like armor against the cataclysm without.

But afterward, left alone in my apartment, I felt as though something was still unresolved. It was selfish, I knew; my story had been prematurely cut off. I knew, at least by reputation, of a set of caves, nearly a day's drive away, but I was the Director of Circulation, after all, and my father had just passed away, and so I could take some time off. Into the mouth of one of the caves I plunged, the copy of the book borne in one hand, flashlight in the other illuminating the walls. I was mindful of my father's own words in *Spelos*—at the spot you needed light most in a cave, you could never quite get it: right where your head would eventually, no matter how careful and experienced you were, smack into an expected lintel of rock. I didn't have a helmet, but the book made a good temporary stand-in.

The immediate sensation was coldness, a roaming cold that shook free of the walls and crept around, the kind you get standing shoulder-deep in a lake under passing clouds. There was a cave smell, too, like wet pavement, only slightly metallic. Once I had my bearings, I could understand "mouth" more viscerally; the interior was like the ominous pictures of periodontal disease that hang on dentists' walls. Rock spears oozed like fleshy icicles, and the glazed walls glittered with what looked like sugar residue in a downed mug of coffee—what an onslaught of detail in those walls, and what a staggering thought that without illumination, they would remain forever invisible, inaccessible.

After several false leads, I found a crevice in an overhang. It seemed as though the likelihood of its being disturbed back here was slim. I wedged myself upward and thrust my body in the direction that my light revealed this slight opening. My shoulders found themselves between two walls, as though I were being held by the cave. This was mildly comforting, and I paused to savor it, but at once felt a twinge of danger—a few feet away, these same walls, angled slightly closer, could crush. I reached out and with a flick of the wrist sent the book off into the darkness, then retreated.

Checking it back into the library system in a few days would require little other than a passworded function override, and the records would, of course, be swept clean in a couple of weeks. If anyone ever sought it, it would be tagged MISSING and the usual searches would ensue; I'd go through the motions, use it as an opportunity to look for fresh mouse droppings. I had no idea what fate would befall the book itself. Would the temperature of the cave preserve its molecular structure like fine cheese, or would dampness eat away at it, inviting microorganisms to feast upon its pages, cannibalize descriptions of their own likenesses? Would an intrepid spelunker eventually stumble across it and send it back, or see it as a sign and take it to the next cave on his itinerary?

As I decided to depart, then, pitch-darkness at my back, I felt that whatever future lay before his book, it would be safer here, more permanent even than in the Library of Congress itself, more faithful to my father's ultimate ambition. And surely it was self-delusion, but I'd driven all that day fueled by coffee and a vision: the words and the *Ding an sich* of the cave reaching out, embracing each other. In the embrace, whether eternal embalming or disintegration into cave sludge, I'd felt sure I would sense both what had created me and what would ultimately end me. En route, I'd pictured it cinematically, as sculpture, as jewelry; the reality was less dramatic, and now even that was gone.

For a moment, though, I risked flicking off the lamp. It was the sheerest darkness I could recall, and I instantly lost track of my limbs. I knew I needed to steer myself with arms extended; I knew the fingers of my left hand were still poking through the handle of the flashlight and my right palm was fully splayed. It was a directionless dark in which I could still distinguish degrees of cold but not myself. I kept expecting to smack into something, almost willing it to happen, because I'd lost all recollection of pain, of sensation. Not wishing to push my luck, I flicked the light back on, to exit—I'd gone only a yard or so.

I took in the cave one last time. Its shadows were restless, already arranging themselves into the stories I'd carry to Aidan's kids, much like the ones I might one day tell my own. As I neared the mouth, children's voices were audible just outside. Abruptly, I reentered at once light, warmth, clamor. At first, it was too much—I threw the hand with the lamp straight up to shield my eyes, but the other remained stubbornly outstretched as I pointed myself in the direction where I recalled the parking lot to be. I could feel my skin awakening to the moist air. With each step blinking my way back, I gradually lowered the lamp. It was tougher in daylight, but I wanted to see how long I could maintain that feeling of open, open arms.

Urban Planning:
Case Study Number Two

All that about apples not falling far from the tree—shit, that. I know; I tumbled ass-first earthward and fell where I fell, and where I fell, I rolled, only then recognizing how rounded parts of me must have been. I wound up whole deserts from Morrisania, deserts that gleamed and those dull as obverse mirrors, deserts lush with indifference and misinformation. If sand can turn to glass without human ordination, surely that was what had happened here time and time again. I passed shards that had never been part of anything larger than themselves, whose only shot at survival was to stow away in passing flesh, lodging in soles and ankles that no longer could tell agony apart from ordinary touch.

But when at last I arrived in Delagotha, how I longed for those distances, their quaint assimilations of glass. Immediately past her gates, I was accosted by stacks of marketplaces where smaller marketplaces were for sale, themselves selling nothing other than still-smaller marketplaces. This regress wasn't infinite—sure, it took many purchases, but eventually you'd arrive at the "atoms"—the goods—and you'd tremble at the prospect of dropping one and losing it forever.

All the while, getters, the closest thing the city had to beggars, moved hither and thither with the compulsive synchronicity of zebra finches or a crew team at break of day. They bounded off one another's shoulders in a choreography of beguiling signals. Finally, I just asked one what it all meant. It was not *what* was said, he insisted, turning his stubble-ridden face aside as if speaking to someone beyond me. No, it was what was on their breath when they spoke that delineated meaning. *That* depended largely on what they'd eaten most recently, which hinged, in turn, on what had tumbled their way—thrice-scorched crescent breads, globules of the sweet balm gondoliers slather on their cankers, the cankers themselves, and, for the luckiest only, the city's famed tomatoes, in which succulent pulp and ceramic likeness lie spooning like lovers.

Like a kid with a new decoder ring, I boarded one of Delagotha's octens of rails, which plunge, capillarylike, improvising their routes as they go, bearing passengers to destinations that they'll be convinced in retrospect they've chosen. So it was breath and odors I should attend to. I sniffed, hoping for caramel but bracing for something fetid. Nothing—smell reduced to a nullity. Instead, socketed into a sheer mesh of interlocking elbows, I felt the skin of my fellow commuters, a blind man's brothel of textures that mocked endings and beginnings like objects of a misplaced nostalgia.

It was then that I first noticed the assembly of musicians who'd begun to jostle the crowd at its fringes. I tried to observe them. Their musical extrusions acted like they were sentient, jostling for attention and dominance. Some performers spewed their notes into the fray, as if trying to edge out those emanating from their fellow musicians. Others stacked chords and arpeggios, forging walls and stairways for other notes to climb on. Still others dispatched castanet shoes that tripped notes but somehow left passengers standing. I wanted to plug my ears. I worked my hand upward through the thicket of limbs, but a G7 chord slapped it away, taking down my glasses, too. I groped, but I couldn't even get near the floor, where, unless a getter had snagged them in midair, they must have tumbled.

I was mystified, as I would be those early weeks. How was it that no one in Delagotha complained about these suffocating crowds, this steady bombardment, this all-at-onceness? How could a place persist under such conditions? Why didn't its citizens unite their voices and demand respites—parks, plazas, sound-swallowing walls? And yet I was stunned at how easily and smoothly I was able to get along without the glasses, girded by the flesh of those around me. Slowly, eventually, it started to dawn on me: five senses was madness, four mild insanity, three delusion, two wrongheadedness, and one, quite simply, ideal. In Delagotha, they'd learned to burrow into a single sense at a time, dwelling utterly there, and thus treading calmly and rationally amidst pandemonium.

The Understory

*A**nyone but Lear*, Schöner thinks. He hobbles across the pebbled path, toward the periphery of the woods, where he can still plant the walker almost flat. On he goes, "Let not . . . to true mind's marriages . . . admit . . . impediments." Even as he pitches himself forward on hard end consonants, he senses the quote is off: the right author but the wrong words, the right words, the wrong play, maybe not even a play. Not only wrong but ironically wrong. Anyone but Lear, he has vowed for a long time, and he is none other.

As he pauses to survey the woods, he feels them staring back, judging, rejecting his desire for entrance. Like he is some illegal, trying to cross a border without the proper papers. The sun catches him as he curses the wood that he wants to be in. This is the most devastating part of age, he thinks. He can laugh at slipshod memory along with the others, the misplaced glasses and pills. The hearing aid is no picnic, but he does not miss the birds nearly as much as the trees they sit in. Aches and pains are jarring, but there are medication and sleep for such things.

He can even deal with the way objects double and then vanish like sea lions bobbing at the ocean's surface—all of these are compromises he can come to terms with and has. But to be repudiated by the woods, *his* woods—this is intolerable. Of course, he must recognize that the walker (an overly optimistic name, he thinks) cannot possibly commandeer the undergrowth, the splay of fallen wood overgrown with moss and fungus, the tip-up mounds with sideways roots that permeate the plot. From here, he can almost enter in memory. Every inch of the plot is stored somewhere in his brain. Even now, he can taste rampant leaf litter, inhale the ground's rank riches. Mosquitoes left him alone. Maybe he scrambled their signals. Whatever the reason for their aloofness, their indifference to him afforded him many hours in the woods alone.

But he won't be alone for long now. In a matter of hours, he will see the blue Subaru hatchback pull up, carrying his daughter and Alan. That assortment alone makes it radically different from Lear's situation—not three sisters vying for land, and affection in the form of land, but merely one daughter and her husband. He breathes relief at the divergence. They will try to convince him, again, as they used to do every few years, as they now do more insistently, less obliquely, to clear out the fallen debris, to clean up that forest. They love the woods, they insist, but the plot is a mess. "A rain forest," his daughter, Sabine, calls it, "in the middle of Peterborough, New Hampshire."

He jokes that if they can find an anaconda there, they can have the woods, do with them what they will. Raise cattle. Put in a roller coaster. Sell the land to the "developers" who wait like pitcher plants for their prey to stumble in.

Sabine insists that developing the land is not what they want. "We want to be able to walk to the lake on the property. Imagine if we could do that. We could hire someone to carve a trail through there. I've already gotten an estimate—a local guy who loves this area, not some tree-hating jerk. And then we could walk to sit by the lake. Our kids could, and your great-grandkids, whenever they arrive. And we won't have to exploit the McElroys from Rhode Island and wait for invitations to go out on their boat."

He is familiar with the arguments. And not necessarily opposed, at least not to the principle behind them. He has nothing against boats and lakes to cool down in in midsummer heat, and trails to access those lakes.

But he will wait it out until they drag out that anaconda. Will not submit to the desire to clean up the woods, to haul away the degenerating matter that trips one up at every turn. It is not purity that he is after; on the contrary, it is precisely the lack of purity on which he insists.

⸺◈◈◈⸺

In the spring of 1930, he is honored with the *venia legendi*, followed swiftly by an appointment as *Privatdozent* on the faculty of Botanical Sciences at the university in Freiburg im Breisgau. He is twenty-four. He is euphoric upon learning of his position. Suddenly he is a peer of his own teachers. But more importantly, Freiburg abuts the Black Forest, the Schwarzwald, and yet it is a big city, too, so much more colorful and stately than the small village in which he was raised. He is further honored with an office in a building dating from the 1700s. Then again, in this university, which goes back to medieval times, this does not even qualify as the *Alte Universität*.

But it would be more accurate to call the woods both his office and his classroom. Though he is expected to do research, and it is clear that he had better be seen hunched over his library carrel from time to time, the head of his department supports his idea to take the students out into the woods, their notebooks poised to sketch out the leaves, trunks. He makes them draw, damnit, makes them see. Some drop out, and that is precisely the way he wants it. For soon he makes them learn a good deal of Latin, insistent that they not only know everyday German terms. "That's *Fagus sylvatica*. Over there, *Picas abies*," he says. "You must be able to speak of the trees in a way that your mother will not always understand." As he teases them, he prods them gently with the knotted end of the gnarled stick that he otherwise carries to point to signs of incipient disease, or lightning scars in the bark.

The students want to carry him down the streets on their shoulders, chanting "Schöner! Schöner!" with steins in their free hands. He teases them about carving their initials in the trees. "If I ever see yours, I will carve the tree's own initials in you," he says, aiming the stick at Gunther, a promising student who everyone knows is lovesick. Gunther asks for a repetition and then he calls out, with moderate confidence, "AB." The professor nods; a balsam fir. The students know that he adores them and the trees. They know that his family is days away, that he has no car, no wife, and that his life consists of them and arboreal species.

Their ventures into the woods afford them more time to talk than they would have in an ordinary class or in a laboratory. When they are not bending down to examine an unusual fungus or char marks on the trunk of a tree, they fall into step with one another, and conversation unfurls. Over the semester, he learns whose fathers fought and died in the Great War, whose families' businesses went belly-up, who studied their plant biology by candlelight after sweeping up the floor in the store beneath their parents' cramped apartment. And so he gains an intimacy that only the rarest professors achieve so quickly and most never do. Meanwhile, they ask him why he doesn't have a *Fräulein* of his own. At first he dodges the question, but they drop hints that some suspect he is a bit of a *Fräulein* himself, and so he feels perhaps it would be in his best interest to respond.

"Hans, where can I find a woman who will put up with my long walks? She will wonder where I've been all day, whom I've been frolicking with. I smell like a peasant. And what will I bring her, a spruce cone for a ring?"

But what really gets him famous is the way he makes them clamber up trees. It is what he did as a boy, whenever he could. He remembers his arms extending desperately toward the lowermost branches of a beech behind the cottage in which he was born, and then the day he woke up and could reach them, and then the sense years later that the branch he was perched on was about to snap under his own weight. "If you are not willing to climb, how else will you see what is truly in the canopy?" he asks them. Then he turns their stratagem against them. "If you want to be *Fräulein*, stay down here on the ground. If you want to be scientists, then up and away."

They call him 'Schimmler' because he has taught them the English word "shimmy," which he learned at an international conference held in Paris. Paris! He is the first member of his family to travel out of the country, as far as he knows. It is just a play on words and a generic German name. No one has heard of Himmler yet.

And so he teaches them about forest succession, not out of a textbook, but in the woods themselves, standing in a *Lichtung*, a clearing, calling upward to Rudolf, asking, "What do you see?" If Rudy fell out, would he lose his position and be forced to take up a broom of his own? Worse, would he be jailed? Possibly, but he doesn't worry about such contingencies. He chooses trees that are sturdy and broad-branched, oaks of hundreds of years, and he has his dream job and he has hundreds of years himself, he thinks.

When he says the word *succession*, he thinks of the royal families of England and France, the border of which is only a few kilometers away. He envisions trees vying for the throne of the canopy, Tudor Firs and Stuart Oaks, and the revolutions of fires and winds that could upend the existing lineages, bringing forth new pretenders and contenders alike. The top of a tree is called a crown. This cannot be coincidence. It signifies, rather, that no matter how rigorous the science, no matter how precisely calibrated one's instruments, trees are, in the end, regal beings to whom we are obligated to bow.

<><><>

It is late September of 1931, and the class is heading back from an eight-hour hike that took them into a favorite stand of oak and yellow beech, a quiet spot a way's off the notched trail, overlooking a hidden waterfall. He will take them there again in winter to mark the differences. By then they will be different, the students. He will ask them to note the changes, some obvious, others more subtle, in the grove, and then to note the changes in themselves. In the silent vacancy left by the dormant falls, they will seem much more than a couple of months older, and will feel it, too. As for himself, the mustache he has cultivated in order to distinguish himself from his students will have thickened. He will have allowed it to do so in spite of knowing full well that appearance can belie age—a thin tree can be deceptively old, and a thick one, even peeling with shaggy bark, rather young. It's a favorite lesson, the sort of intuition-defying phenomenon that astonishes them in September, though it might leave them unmoved in December.

As they are returning from the stand, a mood of mirth permeating the group after a swim at the falls, Max, one of his quieter students, gets his attention.

"Herr Dr. Schöner?"

"Yes, Max."

"I'm afraid I may have to . . . switch from the class."

It is late for a student to leave class except for medical reasons. He is accustomed to students dropping from the roster—many find themselves unprepared for the onslaught of information and the discipline of Latin nomenclature. Others, though they might like the idea of the class, find their tendons and knees aren't up to the challenge. Still others find that a day of strenuous hiking is no way to nurse a hangover. Of course, those who are cowed by climbing trees have not even signed up for the course, as Schöner's reputation is already well established by now.

He has watched Max carefully for the past couple of weeks. He is a superb student, and through quizzes and the first exam, he can see that Max has a knack for it, and he'll be sad to lose him. He'll be sadder by far, though, if it has to do with Schöner's being a Jew. So far, he hasn't lost any students that he knows of to this fact, but Freiburg has no shortage of anti-Semitism; odds are, he's lost some he doesn't even know about.

So he's relieved when Max says, "It's not that I want to cut out this class. It's just that with the hour earlier, I miss out on Herr Heidegger's lectures."

Now it makes sense. He has asked them to gather at eight rather than nine, so that they can make the most of daylight hours and cover more ground. There has never been a conflict before. But he knows that Heidegger is the university's true superstar. Winning him from Marburg was a great coup. Students come not only from all over Germany but from throughout the Continent to hear the author of *Being and Time* hold forth at the podium. Some swear to his greatness and brilliance, while others consider him the biggest sham in the university, a propounder of mystical terms, a spider weaving webs in midair. He's heard the mockeries, as students parody his jargon—"*Dasein* yawns in its being-toward-bed"—and scoff at his rustic appearance. He thinks about it for a few minutes.

Then he turns to Max and says, "How badly do you want to be there for Herr Heidegger?"

Max curls his lip. "I want to do both. It's not an insult to your class."

"Well, suppose we leave at the original time from now on?"

"I'd still need to leave his lectures early."

"Perhaps I can write a note to Herr Heidegger for you."

"That might work," says Max. "I'm always there for his seminar, and I enter into discussion a lot. I mean, he forces us to. But I feel like he notices that I'm not at all the lectures."

Hunched over a magnifying glass the next morning,

examining a diseased bit of bark, Schöner receives a knock on his office door. When he says "Come in," he is surprised by the presence of the striking figure he recognizes immediately as Martin Heidegger. He knows him from faculty meetings, but up close, certain features are accented: the high, barren forehead, hair arching back, the mustache tightly clipped on the upper bank of the lips, and, most of all, the penetrating eyes. His outer garb is that of a peasant, though a tie lurks beneath.

"Herr Professor Heidegger," he greets him. "Herr Schöner. What brings you to this part of campus?"

From what he has heard of Heidegger's lectures, he expects a booming, larger-than-life figure, but the man is soft-spoken, almost shrinking his way into the tiny office. "Call me Martin," he says. Heidegger looks him over. "So, here he is," he goes on, the slightest trace of a smile visible. "The teacher who climbs trees."

"Yes," Schöner laughs. "It's a necessary part of my job."

"Hmmm, yes," Heidegger says. "Well, it's as Hölderlin says, 'Others climb higher/To ethereal Light who've been faithful/To the love inside themselves, and to the spirit/Of the gods.'"

"Well," says Schöner. "I just do it to get the best view of the canopy."

Heidegger looks mildly embarrassed, or perhaps disappointed. He clears his throat. "In any case, it seems that we have a student in common."

"Ah, yes, Max."

"Indeed. He is a talented thinker."

"He's a talented young man, then, because he shows signs of doing well in my class, too."

"So he'll be leaving my lectures a few minutes early."

"If that's all right. You see, I asked the students at the beginning of the term if they could leave a bit earlier for some of our walks, if they had any conflict. But if it imposes on you, I would certainly discourage him from—"

"Nonsense." Heidegger waves him off. "It's all right. To be frank, he'll learn more in the open air than sitting in a hard chair daydreaming about pine trees."

"Well, I'm sure that's hardly the case," says Schöner, somehow embarrassed himself now.

There is a protracted silence. Then Heidegger says, "That piece of bark . . ."

Schöner looks back at his specimen. "Yes?"

The philosopher looks puzzled. "What can you learn from it? I mean, by examining it thusly?"

"Well, I'm trying to figure out what got to it first, animal, fungus, or pathogen."

Heidegger nods, and Schöner can't tell whether this is genuine interest or mere politeness. He hears Heidegger's intense breath, then hears him ask, "How well do you know these woods?"

"Fairly well," Schöner replies. Probably an understatement—he knows them, by now, better than any professor at Freiburg, surely as well as some of the woodsmen who earn a living there.

"Perhaps you can show me, sometime, some of your favored routes."

"It would be an honor, Herr Professor Heidegger," says Schöner.

"Please. Martin," he says, scratching above his mustache right into his nostrils.

—◆◆◆—

Schöner and Heidegger go on lengthy walks through the Schwarzwald. "How is your work?" is always the first thing Heidegger asks him the moment they've gone beyond the garden and through the gate at the edge of the foothills. Schöner points out the various kinds of trees, explains the dynamics of the cycles of growth, decay, and regeneration, while Heidegger holds forth on poetry, art, music. Schöner knows some scattered lines of poetry from secondary school, his Goethe and some Trakl.

On one of their earliest walks, Heidegger recoils in horror as he rattles off names with which Schöner has only the faintest familiarity. "Schlegel? Heine? Hölderlin?"

It is only when Schöner realizes he's being, at least in part, had that he retaliates with equally exaggerated dismay: "Not know a black spruce from a red spruce? Norway from white?" This prompts a lengthy excursus from Heidegger on Goethe's theory of colors. Schöner, accusing him of trying to change the subject, insists on bringing him back to the trees, offering up the same mnemonics he does to his students. After several misidentifications, Heidegger throws his arms up in despair, and Schöner drops it.

After they've gone for several of these jaunts, Heidegger gets him a copy of Schlegel's Shakespeare. He explains that Schlegel was influenced by Herder in his translation, recognizing the playwright not merely as a great dramatist, tragedian, and shaper of characters but as a splendid wordsmith, whose puns and poetry and musicality are inextricable from the works' greatness.

"In Schlegel's rendering," Heidegger says, "Shakespeare is almost German."

Looking through it in the evening, Schöner sees that he has inscribed the volume: "To my tree climber, who lends me his forest spectacles."

Schöner, in turn, gets him a tree-identification guide, which he inscribes: "May this be soon as dog-eared as *Viburnum plicatum*." Though it is a plant he's pointed out to the philosopher, Schöner worries that his inscription is too impersonal. Nevertheless, he cannot risk a joke such as "Great being-in-the-woods with you," since Heidegger is highly sensitive about the accusations that he coins terms and phrases with flagrant disregard for clarity and logic.

As for Schöner, he feels certain that there is clarity in Heidegger's thought. As they are walking, sometimes, he loses himself in Heidegger's voice, as soothing as though they've been following the banks of a stream. There is always a sense of connectedness, of going somewhere, even if Schöner is lost mostly in the sounds of the words. He can distinguish the grammatical distinctions between *Sosein* ("Being-as-it-is"), *Sein-bei* ("Being-alongside"), and his namesake, *Schon-sein-in* ("Being-already-alongside") but he cannot follow the conceptual distinctions that the philosopher is attempting. At times, Heidegger makes him feel a little like he doesn't speak German at all. It is something that the scientists will often poke fun at the philosophers for, this lofty propensity for abstraction, which sometimes seems to be a peculiarly German affliction. But in Heidegger's voice the words are infused with something that makes them as palpable as the furrows in bark.

Though the pair return continually to the joke of their respective intellectual blind spots, they also find themselves returning again and again to science. Heidegger vehemently maintains that philosophy is a science, and Schöner remains skeptical. Further, Heidegger says, science has become too fragmented—he rattles off the various divisions and disciplines in the university as if he is a judge pronouncing a lengthy sentence. "But," he says, "it is not too late. All science needs to do, really, is to recover its essence." He praises the Greeks, how in the true spirit of discovery they had no separate designations for chemistry, astronomy, philosophy, physics, and so were better able to apprehend nature as a whole. At first, Schöner is thrilled to learn of Heidegger's enthusiasm for such work, for he has secretly lamented such divisions, the petty snobberies and snubbings that they invite. The mathematicians look down on the physicists, who can't quite do the pure math. In turn, the chemists couldn't cut it in physics, and the biologists, like himself, are at the bottom of the pecking order, dealing with spotted haunches and big leafy greens, even while the physicists are plying away at the atomic limit of matter. Schöner feels that he is viewed by many, in spite of Freiburg's prestige, as a taxonomist, or, worse, a glorified gardener.

He is also delighted by Heidegger's reverence for classical civilizations. At last he's found an ally who will sympathize with his own insistence on instilling Latin terms in his students' minds. Heidegger, though, never simply agrees or disagrees, and in this case he frowns.

"The Romans translated everything, but the essences were destroyed in the act. Unlike the Greeks, remember, the Romans were a brutal, materialistic people right down to the morpheme."

Schöner is no match for him as a philologist, so he tries to swing the conversation back to the need for interdisciplinarity, where they will surely agree. "Anything else is sheer stupidity," says Schöner. The trees grow in the soil. For that, we need to understand nitrogen compounds. To understand these, we must understand nitrogen atoms, right down to physics. Labels impede scientific work. Worse, they impede progress." He practically sings the last word.

Heidegger seems more amenable as he speaks, but in the end he continues to hem and haw. "*Progress.* A word to be infinitely suspicious of," he says. "Science needs to get back to its roots, its origins. In its essence, science has no divisions. But the essence of science has little to do with its practical forms."

"I'm afraid," admits Schöner, "that maybe I don't understand what you mean by the 'essence.'"

"You're not alone, then," says Heidegger.

On many occasions, they loop around to a spot they've been that morning, and Heidegger will ask, "Were we here earlier?"

"We were."

In these cases, Schöner is so sure that the other is thinking,

"As with our conversations," he doesn't bother remarking it himself.

In late November, crunching through fresh-fallen snow, they come upon a veritable army of towering pines. Heidegger asks, "How old are these?"

Schöner looks over them, tightly bound with crisscrossing bands of branches at chest height and upward, a stand of the type that gives the Black Forest its name. "Probably a couple of hundred years." Together, they search for a downed tree that will reveal its rings.

After they confirm that the trees are at least 250 years old, Heidegger gazes up, marveling at their lattice formation. "They live so much longer than us. For that, and lacking consciousness of their mortality, they call our attention to our own."

As winter comes through, they ski, and Heidegger is a daredevil, even though he claims he did not start skiing until he was an adult. The philosopher teases him for taking turns too wide, especially on precipitous slopes, and Schöner wonders if this is how his students feel when he antagonizes them for being reluctant to climb. At some point, several minutes behind, he hears Heidegger's scalding laughter from below, echoing off the walls of a canyon. As he skis downhill toward the sound, for a moment he feels a sudden urge to run Heidegger down. Instead, as he pulls into a stop, he tears off his skis and leaps into the lower branches of a beech tree and begins ascending, panting and calling down, "If I'm such a coward, you won't start to look like a little mouse as I get higher and higher above you." Heidegger stays on the ground, and his voice sounds faint as he calls up, "Schöner, you're braver than I thought."

<><><>

By 1932, the university is beginning to feel the effects of political ferment, which are still just a ripple, not quite a shudder, throughout Germany. Freiburg may be far from Berlin and Munich, but the National Socialists have struck the universities, like the bark disease striking beeches, youngest first. Of course, soon nothing will be intact; for now, the Nazis are overrepresented in the schools but still a minority elsewhere.

Over time, Schöner has taken on greater responsibilities, sitting on various committees and administrative bodies, which all take away from time he'd rather be spending in the forest. Still, he teaches his class, and gets outside as much as possible. Heidegger, too, has increased his commitments, and while they see each other less regularly, their relationship is still cordial.

The students seem different, though, more brazen, more disaffected, less drawn in by his enthusiasm and his humor. The enthusiasm feels more forced, too. He is reluctant to prod students, even gently, with his walking stick. He doesn't climb trees anymore, after a couple of students filed an anonymous complaint and he was reprimanded. That felt like a gut punch, and while he always suspected who it was, and that it was resentment and laziness that had motivated the complaint rather than genuine concern for the well-being of their fellow students, he could never pin it down with certainty. During classes, he has begun to feel as though he's being watched.

Moreover, the students are more inclined to challenge him directly. "What exactly is the point of all this?" one asks.

He's heard the question before, in a less acidic tone. Nevertheless, he holds his ground and answers patiently. "Germany's forests are a source of her history, her greatness. If we do not understand what is around us, we will never understand who we are or where we are going."

But the students are not as quickly appeased by this sort of answer as they once had been. "Where we are going has nothing to do with the woods and these Hansel and Gretel fairy tales," one says. "Germany's greatness is in its blood, its resolve. Our science ought to be about the *Volk*, not the trees."

On a desk in his classroom, someone has written "Who gives a flying damn what's in the canopy?" Because he holds class inside more often now, he is forced to look at it day after day. And in different handwriting, frighteningly neat and compact, someone has written, "Is a Jew hanging in a tree shade-tolerant?" beside a drawing of a hanged man dangling from a noose. No longer does he admonish them about carving in the trees. Recently, he has sighted a couple of swastikas etched into them, and he shook his head and said nothing. It occurred to him then that the swastika, with its many straight lines, might very well have been invented by a veteran carver of trees.

⋘⊗⋙

But there is one consolation for Schöner in Hitler's rise to power: a mere five months after his ascension on January 30, 1933, none other than Heidegger is elected unanimously to the position of rector of Freiburg University. The news echoes through the hallways and from building to building, filling Schöner with some combination of euphoria and relief. It is not merely that by now he considers Heidegger a dear personal friend, although they have not spoken much in the past few months, and not been on one of their outings since they last skied during the winter holidays of the year before. Rather, it is that his colleagues have selected Heidegger, wise, sensitive, and keenly nuanced, to lead them. This can only mean that there is greater balance in the National Socialist party than meets the eye. It means that the bullies and the thugs who protest outside the Jewish Union are but one faction, albeit the one Hitler has exploited in his rise. It means that although Jewish teachers and those who have spoken out against the Nazi cause have been dismissed from their posts at universities throughout Germany, here in Freiberg there will be a beacon of reason and conscience to carry them through these dark times. Heidegger, who has never breathed an anti-Semitic word, for whom policies and notions of biological racialism would surely be as reprehensible as a proposal to clear-cut the Black Forest and supplant it with a city the size of Berlin. Heidegger, who rails against the "common sense of the they," and thus who would turn a deaf ear to the student outcries that have turned many classrooms into courtrooms and put professors on trial.

So it is with an eagerness verging on rapture that he looks forward to Heidegger's rectoral address. The program has been printed, and its title, "The Self-Assertion of the German University," is already creating a buzz. Heidegger will, it is thought, speak out against tyranny. He will speak up for the intellectual life, Hitler's impatience for such things be damned. Schöner arrives in his purple robes with Kindler, a geophysicist in whom Schöner can confide these hopes. The stage is laid out with Nazi regalia, flags, and insignia. Behind the podium, gathered around Heidegger, are men who look no older than students, many in military garb. The crowd is filled with restless students, many in the nondescript brown shirts that make his own outfit feel ostentatious, even decadent. He thinks he sees a former student of his several feet away in brown, but in his studied expressionlessness he might be anyone. The ceremony opens with a few preliminary spurts of bureaucratese, flags twirling, the deafening stomp of boot heels, which rattle the stage. Next there is an oompah-pah band, and at last Heidegger takes the podium, diminutive even on his decisive day.

A pause, maybe for effect, then the voice Schöner knows so well, strange through the microphone. Schöner closes his eyes, and as he does, he can almost imagine they are ambling through the woods. Branches dip down upon his retina, so real-looking that he feels an involuntary urge to duck. He forces his eyes open. The words sound familiar, too, ordered just slightly differently from many of their conversations. He half-expects Heidegger's xeric laugh, which barely leaves his jaw, and he begins to drift into the usual reverie. But he's jarred awake. Phrases like "German destiny" and "the historical spiritual mission of the German people." He hears "'Knowing, however, is far weaker than necessity.'" Again and again—it is unmistakable. "German." "Destiny." "Historical mission." "Spiritual." "German." "German." The new rector repeats them like mantras. Wide awake now, Schöner shivers at the thunderous applause that greets each one. He looks around, expecting monsters, and sees worse: aught but the ruddy enthusiasm of a pep rally. Then he hears something about a proposal for labor service. Worse, military service. What is this doing in his speech? "Teachers . . . students . . . primary responsibility to the state." "The will of the people . . . asserted itself." "This . . . destiny." Where is the assertion of the university that was promised? Where is Heidegger? Schöner turns to Kindler, who will not return his gaze. Finally, with the flourish Schöner imagines he must bring to his great lectures, Heidegger quotes Plato: "'All that is great stands in the storm.'" And he is done.

More applause erupts. For some reason, he thinks suddenly of Max, the one who slipped out of Heidegger's lectures early, years ago.

❧

His final conversation with Heidegger is a blur to him now—how much more clearly he recalls the aftermath, the implication that he is on the short list of those to be considered for termination. Only because his discipline is out of alignment with the immediate goals and needs of the National movement. Heidegger never utters the words "It's not because you are a Jew," but the two men know each other well enough to understand that whether true or not, this is the unsaid thing. There is a certain coldness in Heidegger's demeanor, as though by granting Schöner the ten minutes he did, he was shortchanging someone else.

But even the months afterward, before he can secure a visa to look elsewhere for teaching positions, are hazy. There are conversations with Kindler and others about options. It is still early enough to get out of the country without too much hassle if you have been dismissed from a first-rate teaching job. No one, Heidegger least of all, wants to invoke the outrage of the international scholarly community. Given the events to follow, this will soon seem like a laughable reason to have granted him a visa, but there you have it.

There are conversations with his parents, who urge him to go. He will send for them once he is established somewhere, they decide.

There are conversations with other scientists who have been cut or who know they are next to feel the ax's swing, whether because Jewish or labeled pacifists or Communists or simply strapped with the designation "un-German." The consensus, particularly of the physicists, is that America is where they'll be most welcome, where they can wait out this passing era and keep pace with the relentless curve of scientific knowledge until they can return to German institutions.

Years later, when it has become apparent how narrow the window he's slipped through is, that already two concentration camps for those deemed political enemies are operating in Baden, where Freiburg is located, he conjures a fantasy. That fantasy looks something like this: He, Schöner, Schimmler, shimmying his way up a tree and slipping effortlessly from branch to branch in the uppermost canopy, right across the border into France or Switzerland.

Even the first years in America, when he has to reckon with the fact that his lack of English means he is essentially denuded of academic laurels and qualifications, unlike the physicists, who speak a subatomic language that transcends words and who are, in fact, being courted by the American government—even these are somewhat hazy now. Like most

German refugees of the time, he goes first to New York, to Washington Heights and Inwood, where other German Jews have established a veritable diaspora. Unlike most, though, he feels almost immediately confined by the city, a rat familiarizing itself with its cage. He has no Berlin in his past to become sentimental about, and while Fort Tryon and Inwood Park offer him enclaves of lushness, the city's traffic and smells and grime threaten to smother him. For the moment, he is reborn under the sign of the ailanthus, the plant that manages to grow out of cracks in the pavement in the unlikeliest places. This sustains him long enough for it to dawn on him that he can offer himself up for a pittance as a landscaper for a family of wealthy German New Yorkers, whose handsome brownstone holds a courtyard that quickly becomes putty in his hands, transformed into a veritable slice of the Homeland. A family with whom he can communicate. With a daughter self-assured enough to choose love over social status, and who loves the sounds of the Latin names of trees and the German ones as they waltz together up the path that rims the edge of the Hudson. A family that purchases a piece of land for a summer home in Peterborough, New Hampshire, a place so far away from New York and so distinct, it seems like yet a third country.

He likes to tell Sabine and others that he won it in a poker game in a musty bar in southern New Hampshire, but those who know him catch the coruscation in the eye of the teller.

⬥

He immediately falls in love with the plot just behind the house; the resemblance to the Black Forest is downright uncanny. Slowly, he begins to learn English so that he can fit in with these suspicious New Englanders. Three times over, he is an outsider here—as German, as Jew, and as transplanted New Yorker, though given his experience in the city, he can only laugh at this last. Over the next couple of years, he and

Sara make the New Hampshire home their permanent residence. He jokes that all he wants is to learn enough English to
turn up his nose at someone greener than he in town. The real
underlying motivation, though, is so he can read the presettle-
ment charters kept down at the archive in the town hall, and
learn the history of the land on which they live. It's a beautiful
tract, teeming with red oak and red maple, or *Quercus rubra*
and *Acer rubrum*, names like those of old friends. There are
also paper birch, yellow birch, and sweet birch on the plot,
not to mention a handful of glorious white pines the likes of
which New England is famous for. He practically expects to
see the king's demarcation on these last, for which, of course,
he'd have to, at least mentally, reprimand the king. He's fascinated by the impact humans have had here, the preponder-
ance of stone walls in the south on pastured land, the massive
logging of the White Mountains.

Nineteen thirty-eight is a lean year for a landscaper, as
Americans eye Europe warily, and guard their own pockets
accordingly. While he dreams of returning to Freiburg, the
extended silences of his parents, other family, friends, and former students make Germany seem more and more distant and
forbidding.

Then, on a September evening, the most powerful hurricane of the century rips through Peterborough almost completely unexpectedly. They have at most a couple of hours of
warning. Florida gears up for the storm, and then it is mis-
takenly thought to have gone out to sea. The Weather Bureau calls for a "chance of rain." By evening, Providence sits
under fourteen feet of water and the streetcars have shorted
out, setting off a ceaseless cacophony of horns. Schöner is
landscaping a house in north-central Massachusetts, and Sara
manages to get in touch with him. He tries to race home,
but the storm soon overtakes him, and he takes sanctuary in
a mill in southern New Hampshire. It takes him two days

to get home—roads are flooded, bridges out, the rivers that passed underneath having permanently changed course. Sara, having waited out the storm in the attic, is unharmed, but the house is flooded. By the time he arrives in downtown Peterborough, he's seen a lot of damage, but the sight of the steepleless church makes him stop short just where the traffic light used to hang.

First, he holds his wife tight, then he slogs outside to survey the damage in the plot. What he sees is catastrophe. Most of the red oak has uprooted. The red maple has either bent or snapped, plainly crushed under the falling oak or pine. The paper birch is almost all uprooted, bark strewn about like the papers of a raided library. Sweet and yellow birch, decapitated. The fallen logs lie like corpses to the northwest, where the wind came fiercest. Schöner can smell the lingering salt air of the ocean even though they're nowhere near it; it must be in the soil now, glacial till heavy with days of rain. As he curses the storm, then, he doesn't know whether to wave his finger up at the sky or down below, and so he does both. Knees sinking in the muck, he hears Heidegger, taunting, rejoicing in the destruction, the closing words of the rectoral speech: "'All that is great stands in the storm.'"

The storm, though, is forgotten almost as quickly as it came hell-bent through. The next day, Chamberlain meets with Hitler to negotiate over Czechoslovakia. Soon, Hitler will invade the Sudentland in spite of this meeting, and a couple of months later, the world will awaken to the news that Germany has invaded Poland.

❖❖❖

In the following year, the wood begins slowly, almost imperceptibly, to regenerate, forming a low, tightly packed canopy. The temptation is to clear the land, to try to get money for the logs, but 275 million trees have been felled in New England, enough to build 200,000 five-room houses. Market value goes kaput. Many of the trees have been too damaged to serve as wood anyway, and are only worthy to pulp. He convinces Sara that they ought not to try to clear the land, but allow it to be what it is, to become what it will become. He wanders the plot, hoisting himself over the many pits and mounds that have been formed by the felled trees, heaving himself over the downed wood.

For a year, he watches the red oak as it survives, but then passes away. The pine and the bit of hemlock are also down for the count. But then he notes as sweet birch, a novelty for him, clings to mounds and even to exposed rocks. Snapping the stems to release the soothing wintergreen, he admires its hardiness. And where mineral soil has been exposed in the mounds, of all things, paper birch begins to grow.

The fecundity of the plot and the number of species that survive amaze him. Working on the yards of the well-to-do, most of which were cleared of wood afterward, he cannot help but marvel at the greater richness and diversity on his own land, and the number of ways that it has managed to regenerate itself—through crown releafing and sprouting, seedlings and saplings alike.

But even more wondrous to him is the presence of new species entirely in the understory. They have sprung out of the pits and mounds as though they were just waiting for a storm to usher them in. One day, he discovers the *Epilobium sp.*, whose stem will eventually turn red and offer up a white flower. A library visit reveals that this is common in Finland, close enough to Germany to make him tremble. On another occasion, he stumbles onto blackberry plants. And best of all is the common cinquefoil, the glorious yellow flower he decides he'll pin in Sara's hair. He crouches with the guidebook near the ground before picking one, squinting and rubbing for the slight serration that will distinguish it from imposter weeds.

The day he plucks that flower, he decides to write Heidegger.

He is short but direct. He knows the chances of his words reaching Heidegger are minuscule. Nevertheless, he writes, wishing he and his wife well, asking where he now stands. He knows from some other Freiburg transplants with whom he corresponds that Heidegger resigned the Rectorate fairly swiftly in disillusionment, and has become seen as rather inconvenient to the Nazi cause at best.

In his letter, he includes a postscript describing the recent gems that he's turned up on the floor of his forest. He writes, "You know, Martin, it's strange. Trees have always defined the forest for me. I climbed in the canopy, because I thought that's where the best, truest view was. But in the wake of the Storm of 1938, I find that the little plants of the understory have become very dear to me, dearer than I could have ever imagined. I will not burden you with their Latin names, but I do urge you to take notice of them the next time you are out walking in the woods. Humbly, Schöner."

⸻⧓⸻

As the years and even decades go by, Schöner watches as the species composition in the forest changes radically. In 1948, pin cherry has shot up from impetuous seedlings, and red maple, white ash, and red oak, sprouted from stumps, rule the upper canopy. He sometimes thinks that if he looks hard enough, he will see the pin cherry grow another millimeter before his eyes. When he's not out in the woods, Schöner manages to keep in touch with his American Freiburg colleagues, many of whom have gone on to venerable careers, some returning to Germany after the war, others staying on, or returning elsewhere in Europe. Their numbers include Nobel Prize winners. As for Heidegger, Schöner learns that he has fallen on grave difficulties after the war, forced to defend himself for his apparent embrace of the Nazi program. His library, it is rumored, has been confiscated. Schöner pictures troops thumbing through the tree guide, seeing his handwriting.

Again, with this image in his mind, he writes to Heidegger, but again he hears nothing.

⟨◇⟩

Schöner drives to Boston for a copy of the May 31, 1976 issue of *Der Spiegel*. Heidegger has famously given an interview, to be published only upon his death. Its publication means, of course, that Heidegger has died. But it is as if he is still alive for the duration of time that it will take Schöner to read this interview.

He drives with the magazine on the front passenger seat all the way back from Boston to Peterborough, where he will walk out onto his property to read. It is only appropriate that his last conversation with Heidegger take place in the woods. By now, the pin cherry is gone. Gray birch has come and gone into decline, still here but weakened and prematurely aged.

Hemlock, dark latecomer, looks as though it means to stay forever, claiming even the floor with its dry red-brown needles. He can see, too, the trees from 1938 pointing northwest, even greatly decayed. Still, he finds a log firm enough to plant himself on as he reads through the article.

What does he hope to find? A personal apology? An admission that he, Heidegger, has wrestled in private with the facts of the matter of the Holocaust for the past thirty years? Has agonized over them? That he made a mistake? A grave mistake, one worthy of a dunderhead rather than what Schöner is certain is one of the most astute minds of the twentieth century?

If he expects any of these things, Schöner is disappointed. Heidegger explains his "brush" with Nazism. Or explains it away. Or attempts to.

On the rest, he is silent.

When Schöner sees the symbol at the foot of the column that marks the end of the story, sees that Heidegger has only a few words left, too few for what he must do, Schöner shuts the magazine.

Now, as he hangs on the walker and looks at the plot, untouched for over fifty years, he hears the Subaru sputter and the spitting of gravel that means they are pulling up the driveway to the house. It seemed long when he first moved here, because it was longer than any driveway he'd seen before, but by now he is used to it. In less than a minute they will be here. Soon they will be showering him with bundt cake, or framed pictures of grandchildren in formal attire. Beneath all this will be their agenda: to convince him to clear the forest, to make way for the future. He wishes he could explain to them why he can't allow this to happen, what the forest means to him intact. But at times like these, he feels like he can almost understand why Heidegger stayed silent right up to the end, why he found it so difficult to speak of a past in which he'd been at once king and fool. And he suspects that even now, he won't be able to say it, won't be able to name all those left behind— Lechenmeir, Schott, Fiedler, Tannenbaum, Kindler, Schöner, Schöner—parents, friends, uncles, aunts, students, teachers. Nor will he be able to articulate how this plot preserves them, how in it they preserve themselves, having risen up from the leveled earth like resurrected beings from the fallen heaps and mounds, risen in every conceivable way as none other than themselves.

Urban Planning:
Case Study Number Three

There is no room at the Manswer-Antoli, the city's epony-
mous hotel, but he's so accustomed to being turned away
that signs barely register. His boots, trudging about the city,
are somewhere on the far side of mud-caked, a thick-crusted
record of travels through floodplain and savanna, taiga and
miasma. He would do well to stop and borrow a chisel and
scrape them, lose some of that deadweight. But every time he's
about to do that, he thinks, Wait, maybe he could plant something in them—what, after all, is more precious than land? He
could grow vegetables—nomadic tomatoes, wandering water-
cress. He cannot tell whether this is a good notion or simply
hunger's delusional logic, so he bends down and tucks a two-
leafed twig into one of his mudbanked feet—for memory, so
he can reconsider when his mind is clearer, once he's rested.

The shops are closed for the night, grates tightly drawn,
those lacking grates sending out red alarm pulses at staggered
intervals. In their inaccessibility, objects take on heightened
desirability—a baguette that looks like it might regenerate
endlessly, a chest of drawers that promises to keep him company, talk or listen if he decides to unravel his own story.

For a city so utterly shut down, it is strangely alive, bustling
with pedestrians. After some of the places he's been prior, he is
most grateful for this heavy foot traffic, this to-and-fro. Whenever he thinks about dying, he reminds himself that when he

has pictured his own death in the past, it has always been him alone. Because nonexistence runs so counter to the spirit of such company, he feels protected by the crowds. So long as he can distract the part of himself that will decide to die, he reasons, it cannot happen.

And once he settles down, finds lodgings, gets a few bites in him, showers away the grunge, he'll revel in it like an anthropologist, a theatergoer, a bird-watcher, a flaneur in situ. In his current state, he knows, his mere watching will seem threatening, arouse suspicion that he is sizing them up for robbery and worse. Best to maintain distance, feign disinterest. Little stolen glances and peeks must suffice for now. The scarf of gauzy translucent red, trailing a woman who rolls forward with the certainty of a shore-bound wave. Two businessmen, mirror images but for one's mole, the other's suspenders. Boys with flatulent elbows and sharp whistles and spasmodic laughter.

Who knew Manswer-Antoli was so popular, so teeming with life? All this he would've missed if he'd heeded the warnings against coming here.

⋖◈⋗

Hours? Days? He can't keep track of how long he soldiers on, the signs all identical: NO VACANCY, CLOSED. If I could just rest on a bench, he thinks, sighing at the streamer of tape that seems to partition off each and every one, warning of wet paint. It would be worth anything simply to sit. A pair of pants—small sacrifice, that, for savory comfort, renewal.

Crouching to slip under the tape, he hears the policeman's piercing whistle.

"What'sa matter, can't read, buddy?" says the officer.

"I can," he grumbles, moving on. What civic diligence they abide by here! It's too much. As he shuffles off, he hears the officer's radio blasting staticky bulletins and glances back to see him shaking his head in obvious pity and disdain.

⋖◈⋗

Soon enough, soon enough, thinks the officer, watching as the man with the tiny tree growing out of his shoe hobbles away. It's not *his* job to inform him, obvious newcomer, that he is dead, that ghosts can never sit, never alter, but only walk the streets and boulevards ceaselessly, exactly as they arrive. *No, let him wait,* the officer thinks. *Let him wait while he still can for the shop doors to spring open like shutters on country villas, wait, as we all did once, for the aroma of fresh-baked bread to burst forth and fill the air.*

The Discipline of Shadows

Up on the chair, I reach for the ceiling and beat the vents, sending mold fluttering downward. Like some black rain, it lands variously on me, on chipped, yellowing tiles, on the paperwork fanned out over my desk. It speckles the latest budget, leaves a trail of powder on the glossy cover of the newest *International Journal of Umbrology*. It must be going into my lungs. I think about miners descending, invisible until the shaft collapses and the cameras swarm. Maybe, I think, this is what we need—some tragedy. Something more than mere scandal. More than Lew and his lawyer. More than the death of a department, which is like an animal, already limping, vanishing at last under the wheels.

I won't have time to change my shirt before the big meeting, and for a moment I regret this. After all, lawyers and trustees, the titled and brass-nameplated, will be there. Lew's "representation," all the way from Lower Manhattan. At yesterday's department meeting, the guy sat with Lew, hovering at the edge of my vision, a thick-browed smudge of pleated charcoal. Finally, I wanted to confront him. "Mr. Vadrais," I wanted to say, "at the end of a workday, when you exit Two Fourteen Pearl, do you ever pause to take in the shadows?" I felt them like a chill, then, those revenants of an older New York, strewn across the narrow, birdshit-encrusted streets.

But I held my tongue. He would've been mystified, and the rest of them would've all thought I was losing it.

The Department of Umbrology is located in the basement of Sackler Hall on the easternmost edge of campus. Our neighbors are the physical plant and Parking Violations. Students and professors of all ages huff by in three-piece suits and skimpy spaghetti-strappery, tickets in hand, excuses rehearsing themselves upon the tongue. Upstairs is the old Engineering Library (the new one, slated for ribbon cutting in September, a veritable suspension bridge with walls—it stuns) and three rooms the Theater Department uses as a sort of gulag for old props. There's talk of tearing the building down. The odds of our outliving it? In this economy? I ask you. A memo before the wrecking ball meets the wall is what I hope for.

At four full-timers and one visiting professor, we are the smallest department on the campus (not including the interdisciplinary ones, like Africana Studies and Foreign Languages). I'm sometimes asked to defend my department's integrity (and I mean this etymologically— no one, till now, has questioned our moral stature, only whether we ought to be considered *one*). Well, I muse, what about Foreign Languages? Are they "one"? Can we roll up all the vernacular, all the literary traditions, the Day of the Dead and Bastille Day and the notebooks of Dostoyevsky and *das Bier und Bratwurst*, and, by cramming them together under a single roof, make them *one*?

Immediately down the hall from my office is that of Dahlia Peterson on one side and Phil Abelard on the other, and then past that is the office of Lew Dorris, and then finally our visiting scholar, Alex Kuperman. Dahlia is our shadow-theater person; she thinks she's made it to Broadway and I'm not going to disillusion her. Her office, the largest, illuminated from within by Indonesian lamplight, ushers one into a 2-D universe of gauze stretched between bamboo poles, tables overspilling with the most ornate, intricately carved puppets. The room is always alive, CD player blaring gamelan or some mainstream fluff, students snipping and doweling away at all hours like child laborers, only happy, her Brooklyn accent wafting like fresh bagels down the hallway as she chastises them: "Not like that . . . Who taught you how to . . . Here, here." She's superficially abrasive but profoundly gentle, the students inform me—worked to the bone, by term's end they are putting on virtuoso epics of Bali, Turkey, or China, and in Advanced they Westernize, shadow-working their family memoir, slave ships with oars the luminous water pushes back at, streets that seem somehow paved in gold even if just variants of black, always, Marge Simpson makes an appearance, it's a running joke. Abelard is the one who's been here longer than I and grown way too complacent. Doesn't bother with office hours, hasn't produced an iota of scholarship in twelve years. Wrote his book about shadows in lit back in the day, but since he got tenure, it's been a handful of conference talks and *Easy Rider* in his swivel chair. Kuperman's fresh blood but wrong blood type—hasn't panned out at all. My hopes were high. A scholar of neonoir, he's actually produced a film you might've seen, *The Better Half*? So we've snagged ourselves a bona fide celeb. Too bad he's always on the phone with his agent—pair of Bluetooth pincers, one on each ear. He teaches on Tuesdays, and then I swear he slips out between the blinds, jetting back to L.A.; his weekends start Wednesdays. I won't miss him, nor will the students. He was a mistake—a case of mistaken identity, you might say, with no more interest in shadows than a rooster has in gold coins. But one door farther down is Dorris, our rock star. Astrophysicist, Ph.D. 1987 from Dartmouth, his long, frothy hair cascading onto ample shoulders, but don't be distracted—you'll need all of your cognitive faculties as he leaps from discussing what happens to shadows from objects approaching the speed of light to the tiny fingerprints left behind by the particles called muons. Then he unwinds by pummeling his way through some video game, sounds like a teenager in there, tearing things up, kicking through walls and mowing down Nazis. Like some home brewer, he even designs his own games as pastime. But no ego on him, no Kuperman. He pro*duces*, too—four reputable journal pubs in the past year, four! Unheard of. One in the *Umbro*, too, the mothership, damn him.

As for me, my work is much more mundane. Philosophy—the ontology of shadows in the history of thought, and given the postlinguistic turn, of course, how they're treated in language. Plus, I oversee the department. I've chaired for eleven years now and probably will till I retire or keel over. No one else wants it—can you imagine Dahlia, with her sextuple-jointed puppets, filing a budget or tracking postgrad job stats? She may talk like a Flatbush Avenue importer with her students, but she's a softy when it comes to the bureaucrats. I'm not crazy about paperwork but I'm orderly and never cowed, especially by some administrator with a diploma in something called "public policy."

❖

And hey, if Lew wants to cash in on his research so his two kids can go to their colleges of choice, can I blame him? He can even justify it morally—he's *making the world a safer place.* His algorithms will help snare terrorists huddling in the mountains of western Pakistan. Help rid the world of evil.

Not incidentally, they'll also make him rich, and in the meantime the terrorists will cover their tracks better, find alternate hideouts, go deeper, where their shadows, seen only by the walls, won't betray them.

Still, I don't hold it personally against Lew. With Edmund, it feels a bit more personal, more *Et tu*ish. After all, *I* recruited him, groomed him, saved him from the fate of a giant state school with its rows of clonelike cheerleaders and ambiguously mammalian mascot. Last time our eyes met, he ducked between buildings and I caught his shadow as it fluttered for a millisecond at the corner, as if hesitating. He was gone. *Cold shoulder* no mere figure of speech.

⟨⟨⟩⟩

In memory, I'm Edmund's age again, home for fall break. I sit my father down and tell him I've got an inkling of what I'm going to do with my life, and he looks at me quizzically. "Umbrology? The study of umbre*ll*as?" Impossible to know, then, how typical this reaction will be. Countless times I'll hear it over the years, even hear about ingenious designs from closet inventors, giddy for an audience. "No," I'll learn to cut in gently, "the study of shadows." (Always *shadows*, the vernacular, never *shadow*, though the semantics is hardly uncontroversial in the field; one either deems it substance or quantifiable entity and thus divisible. Each has consequences.)

My dad is far from the worst, though. From him, I never expected understanding. He worked with his hands, wiring buildings, whole counties. Worse are those who should know better, colleagues whose own disciplines get scoffed at as impractical—sociologists, literary critics, art historians. When *they* imply or even state outright that offices and funding and a fax machine are luxuries we aren't worthy of, it stings. We're a stone's throw from parapsychology, they'd have it; we're Sasquatch groupies, Roswell nuts. I much prefer the out-and-out jokers, such as the guy who showed up at one of our slide shows—open, as always, to the public—and cast a giant phallus against the screen, balls and all. Witless, yes, and yet my instinct was to invite him to one of my classes.

The thing I find least forgivable, though, is flatness. "Oh, study shadows, do you? Well, geez, how about the football team, huh?" Dwelling in two dimensions so much of the time, as I do, I shouldn't be rankled by this but am.

⟨⟨⟩⟩

It's not hard to pick us out: the vision always slightly askew, aimed downward or slightly to the side. We take on a certain look, a spinal kink, the price exacted in chronic conditions that demand regular visits to orthopedists, chiropractors, the town's Rolfer. It's not all bad—I kept crossing paths with the same violinist. Once we'd established the similarity of our ailments, she got me cheap balcony seats at the symphony, and Edmund and I, then on benign terms, sat there and reveled in the antic play of bows and horns across sheet music and against the performers' neatly pressed white shirts, with the occasional ricochet off the gleaming, chair-checkered stage. Of course, I enjoyed the music, too; without it, the shadows would have been of only passing interest.

⋘⋙

Leaving my office today, I sit in the parking lot, visor lowered, watching Kuperman's Impreza out of the corner of my eye. I'm not the following type—I've never pursued anyone in my life. But as chair, I'm the guy ultimately responsible if he's not in his office during the hours clearly posted. So far it's easy—I might just be sitting here exactly as I am, downing wasabi peas. I suspect he's off to see Dahlia. Their sparring, the way their barbs hook just slightly toward one another in meetings, betrays a secret history, a tryst. Case in point: he recommends a cinematographer friend as a guest speaker, she fires back that the lecture series is about the students, not *us*, he parries with "There's no rule that says they can't *enjoy* the talk . . ." And here my gut tells me this is all allegorical, that it's the bedroom that's on trial. The grapevine backs me up. While I generally frown on faculty flings, I can see it has added a few coils to Dahlia's step; maybe she'll get around to writing the article on shadow erotica she's been bandying about since the day I met her. I know Kuperman is using her for short-term gratification, probably plying her with promises whose shelf life is the term's end; I hope it won't leave her marriage wrecked, but beyond that, I don't really care one way or the other.

But I have to ensure Kuperman isn't in violation of the terms he signed on for. If he's contractually on campus x hours a week, whether he's schtupping Dahlia or playing cribbage instead is, frankly, irrelevant.

Now he pulls out and I do a slow five count before pulling out behind him. I get stuck waiting for students, one walking a bike, to cross at their languorous pace, and I'm sure I've lost him, but at the light, I spot the Impreza. I stay three car lengths back as we glide down Meadow and into the right-turn-only lane for Fessenden. He goes straight, not the way to Dahlia's two-family Victorian. A motel rendezvous? He pulls into the lot behind Sips and Swigs, and I, in turn, ease into what isn't a spot but a good vantage point. At first, I think I'm mistaken when I see Edmund Evans in boxlike glasses, frayed jeans, and loafers stride up and into the shop. There are several students who share his look, and Edmund doesn't touch coffee. And he can't stomach Kuperman, at least as of last time we spoke. But no, it's him, and they must be here together. I consider abandoning the car and strolling in but balk; three umbrologists in a coffee shop sounds like a joke, but can be no coincidence, so instead I squint at the semiopaque windows.

Edmund and Kuperman? I make out shapes at a table. An anti-Venn diagram—two sets whose overlap is nil, betwixt whose sensibilities runs an unfathomable chasm. Yet here they are.

I'd give anything to be able to listen in. Instead, I shovel several fistfuls of peas into my mouth, wasabi like a creeping flavor-shadow, until I hear a series of raps on my window and look up to see a cop pointing at the sign; he looks angry, personally offended. Nodding, I turn the ignition—I ignite—and move out. I'm running late for Intro Umbro, the first years, and if I'm not there, they'll leave.

I race in two minutes late, and there are jokes—"We were, like, whoa, is it a shadow holiday?"—and statements—"Bix was ready to peace." Bix, backup quarterback who can scramble and throw with equal ease, exquisitely diligent, takes the ribbing good-naturedly. I say, "It's a good thing you didn't. It's movie day."

"No movie today on the syllabus," they inform me.

"We're switching things around a little bit," I announce, fumbling to get the DVD in the tray. *He Walked by Night* appears on the screen, and I let the film do its work, just this once sans hand wringing about reducing myself to mere projectionist. I find a seat in the back, look on numbly. The plot is trivial, boilerplate police procedural, so I (and the students) can focus on the shadow elements. A deranged killer lurks in the sewers beneath L.A. There will be much to talk about. How blinds, noir's signature emblem, are magnified, splayed over walls and ceilings and clothing. How the black-and-white universe of the film itself dictates that shadows are more substantial than nonshadows, the latter appearing ethereal, impalpable. But I can't focus.

<hr>

Edmund Evans was a product of that flat America where the land reaches out like canvas under tension and the shadows stretch correspondingly—sparse, stark. I met him at some undergrad research forum, where he was going a mile a minute about some economic correlation he'd graphed up on a poster. His leg bore a giant cast, but he was up there on his feet and he swung his crutch like a pointer, explicating away to anyone who'd listen. I heard out his spiel and asked some question to show I'd been paying attention, and then I extended a hand, which he seized after awkwardly repositioning the crutch.

"Umbr*ology*?" he said, squinting. "No, I can't say I know what that is." In the next instant, he did something I'd never seen before: he guessed it. "Score one for Dublassi. AP Latin," he said, shaking his head. And in that single etymological grab was adumbrated a path, a future. He'd been set to transfer to another school for business, had already sent in his application. But what, he wanted to know, was *this* all about, and I could see hunger fleshing out into his face, his eyes, hunger after something that couldn't be found in any of his graphs or his econ textbooks, soon to be doorstops. His face let me know that right then he'd follow me anywhere.

⋙⋘

For each of us, of course, the shadow we fell for first. Reaching for our second or third drink at our annual conference's cocktail party, we kick off shoes under the chandelier, bask in the presence of the like-minded. Warily at first and then more boldly, we tell our stories:

— Regaining consciousness, the first thing that entered our field of vision was the shadow line of the very fence we came tumbling off, merciful as a missionary nun, leaning over us.

— The show *Mystery Science Theater*, with its silhouetted peanut gallery, sent us into spasms of laughter time and time again.

— In Arizona's Black Rock Canyon, hiking with a friend, we lost our way, and, thinking this was it, curled up in the slight shadow vestibule formed by the banks of a dried arroyo, conserving ourselves till awakened by the sound of the single-propeller and, without waiting for visual confirmation, stood out of the gulch and started to whip broad circles in the air with the shirts we'd already taken off.

— With our dad, we heard the crackle of Lamont Cranston announcing, "The Shadow knows," about to abort some foul play or nab some perpetrator.

And we wanted to know, too, whatever there was to
know, even without knowing what this might be.

Less dramatic beneath the sui generis sprawls the universal,
submerged somewhere in the collective unconscious. Who
didn't skip beside his shadow, marveling at it as an emperor
might his lands or a peasant his erection, this view of the aug-
mented self offering up just a whiff of omnipotence? But just
when we thought it gave us boundless control, our shadow
evaded us, hiding itself inside another or going its own way
(priming us early for love)? Like any boy or girl, I chased mine
up and down hills and on sunbaked pavement till I came tumbling, breathless, to my knees.

In truth, it began for me in a garden, a stolen kiss and hot
breath in the ear, a sundial with a gnomon of regal brass,
angled amid peonies and shrubs. I stood on tiptoes, arching
my neck to catch a glimpse of the face, rimmed with mystery
symbols, no number system I knew of. Just behind me stood
the girl I'd been told all week was my cousin but who, I'd
learned earlier that day, wasn't—it had just been a figure of
speech—and this discovery set free the pangs that resigned to
their unrealizability, I'd stifled all week long. Now I could look
unflinching into her pale seaweed eyes (brine on the palate),
and even study the two faint bumps in her plain white T-shirt,
partly shrouded where the shadow fell.

Maybe I already knew what a sundial was; maybe she explained it to me; maybe some adult came along to edify us.
Who knows; these things are as lost as her name. I was nine
and we were left alone, the two of us, while They toured the
mansion with Some Period of Furniture that held some fascination for them, and as I swung around, her lips caught
mine in the chill of the shadow. Would I ever recover? Is it
too transparent that a lifelong love affair (with shadow, not

her) begins here? Or simply unfathomable in this age that any love would last a lifetime, even one whose only constant is the peripheral figure?

⋖⋘⋗

What an obscure, tenebrous bunch we are. I've been relieved to find I am talking to a bryologist (scholar of mosses and lichens). I shake my head in time with the bluesy lament of the reprographer (connoisseur of copies and copying). I once skipped a return flight to spend the night with a woman who declared herself a pyrologist instead of merely a "chemist who studies fire" (and her brown hair indeed went embery in the dark).

At least the dictionary affirms that these exist. Others, more fledgling, more marginal, persist solely by the curatorial zeal of their adherents. I half-pity the neologist (novelty and newness across the board) and the spontanographer (doodles, sketches, and scribbles)—academia's stooges, her warthogs, creatures who persist because nature is decidedly not beautiful, who operate under some inner need, nuzzling up against anything that doesn't run away screaming.

⋖⋘⋗

Here are some tips if you are planning to apply to one of the five degree-conferring graduate programs in umbrology in the United States. Don't make any jokes pertaining to how you've always had a shadow. It's akin to writing you've always had teeth on your dental school application—simply beyond the pale.

Second, do your homework. Out of the five programs, two are primarily devoted to shadow theater, leaving three for strictly scientific study. In their defense, one of the theater programs is highly interdisciplinary, and they incorporate scientific principles into what they do. One, though (petrified of getting embroiled in another lawsuit, I won't name names), finds science anathema. They seem to think the shadow world ought to be kept as mysterious as possible, as ludicrous and untenable a position as that is in this era. Now—when we can explore the stars, sunspots and eclipses and shadow images on other worlds, those that asteroids lend one another as they hurtle through space, the six-thousand-mile-thick shadow that Saturn's razor ring casts on the planet's surface; now, when Lew Dorris can sit beside intelligence officials poring over satellite maps of Tora Bora, distinguishing cave from cliff, searching for the slightest hint of human presence—how can they believe such a thing now, of all times?

My last word of advice: Don't allude to Punxsutawney Phil or anything related to Groundhog Day, even in jest, anywhere on your application.

—◇◇◇—

It is not what the shadow tells us about the figure but about the ground that ultimately matters.

—◇◇◇—

It's become harder and harder to catch the interest of the undergrads in Intro Umbro. Thank God for video games. With Lew's help, I can strip away the shadows from fight scenes to expose how ridiculous and cartoonish their so-called virtual worlds are sans proper shading. And from there, I segue right into painting before they can object—first the *Mona Lisa*, so familiar that it might as well be a video game, the eyes tracking them as if they're being controlled by some remote joystick. I point out how da Vinci steeps her outfit in shadow, captures the sweep of her hair, dribbles it down her neck, pits shadows at the corners of her cheeks, forcing them to vie with one another, dramatizing the enigma of her emotions.

Next up it's Dolcinaux's untitled work, commonly *Paripurgferno*, (1774), that magisterial reinterpretation of the moment wherein Virgil admits Dante into Purgatory. Where Dante strips Virgil of his shadow, leaving his metaphysical status a mystery, Dolcinaux sends it back toward Hell, adding the likenesses of the shadows of a terrace and a sphere that aren't in the painting. From notebooks, we know that Dolcinaux believed Dante got it wrong, that hellish circles, purgatorial terraces, and paradisal spheres ought to have been combined into one, a sort of folded triptych of translucent panels. He didn't have translucent panels, so he did the best he could, his quarrel with Dante writ large here. If I've done my job right, some students are still awake by the time I'm done explaining this.

⟨◇◇⟩

In my usual spot in the library once, bleary after hours of staring into one book or another, I fell into a trance. It was as if something had pulled some of the ink partway off the page and it was hovering between the paper and my eyes. As I tried to hold it aloft, it struck me that the choice of black as the near-universal color of print was no mere convention, no mere appeasement of the eyes. My epiphany: Printed words were the shadows of referents. Things: rock, sand, onion. Ideas: carpool, justice, maximization, irrevocability. Paragraphs were composite shadows of the scenarios and subjects they captured: the overwhelming richness and messiness of the world distilled to bare, chiaroscuroed necessity. Sure, imagination, not eyes alone, was required in reconstructing the original. Yet in my carrel at that moment, I swore I could see the strand of beach rising off the page, shells strewn everywhere, jagged watermarks and slick seaweed pods, and could feel the onrush of surf, salt spatter, and greedy undertow, and I suspected I'd hit on something nontrivial. Newly awake and trembling with cold and not a little fear, I gathered my belongings and moved quickly past the unsuspecting undergrads, their heads buried in books, and exited. My manic gait mirrored the fervor of the conjecture: if words were shadows, then all fields were umbrology, all knowledge a strain of the umbrological, and all of us of a scholarly bent spend our lives peering at shadows. And what, then, did this suggest about the Bible and the Koran and the access they might offer to the sacred? In the distance were evergreens with what little snow they hadn't yet shed and the gangling deciduous trees with their intricate interweavings, neuronal branchings. I saw the agriculture complex with its various roofs covered with swatches of snow, then the purple bruise of a cloud bank unfurling across the sky, then the orange glow like something from another world, and then I tried to see before me a page, *the* page, with these words upon it. As I neared the parking lot, its blue signs with white lettering felt discordant, and I fell in among a crowd arriving for or leaving a game. There was a honk and someone leaned out of a car and yelled, "Ursula's not the whore, *I* am!" and everyone in earshot erupted in laughter. At once, my insight shriveled into preposterousness like a balloon surrendering, and I felt ridiculous, all the more so as I, too, was laughing along. I haven't returned to that idea since; maybe someday.

⟨⟨⟩⟩⟩

There was a woman once, though. A couple of flings but only one, really (I don't count my sundial maiden). Valerie stayed awhile—months. She got me to talk about things I never had, try things, foods—Indian, Tibetan, Moroccan—whose existence I'd had only a vague awareness of before. She took me out to a ball game, prodding me every few hitters with little quizzes about what had just happened. At museums, she'd take me by the shoulders and gently pull me away from the canvas, forcing me to take in paintings at a sweeping glance and describe how they made me feel. She made me carry her bags, restock her lip balm, sniff her slippers, all of which I have to admit I enjoyed. Together, we salvaged a dog, Saskia, from the ASPCA, gave her a home, and even cured her of the habit of peeing at the slightest jarring sound.

Val didn't even mind my endless discoursing about shadows, though she told me once she preferred rainy days because on them I looked at her more directly. She talked about us relocating to Seattle. Maybe there I could shed my strange "wandering eye." She only half-believed me when I insisted it was shadows I was watching askance instead of other women. Somehow my gaze would be pulled in the direction of the most stunning or scantily clad (so she claimed—I hadn't noticed), and later that evening she'd be sobbing or, as the months went on, brooding in ruffled distraction.

Once, watching her apply mascara, I pointed out that makeup was nothing more than the insinuation of shadows onto the face to feign the signs of youth. I said this as I might have to my undergrads—the type of assertion they'd record dutifully, and which every so often incited them to lively discussion and intellectual sparring—although afterward I have suspected that I may have meant to hurt her for some reason. At the time, her brushstrokes held steady. But a day later, she announced that nothing—no therapy, no medication, no aphrodisiac, no self-help book, no spontaneous trip—could bridge the gulf that lay between us.

⋖⟨⟨⟩⟩⋗

Rasmussen, president of the university, has staked out Intro Umbro and pulls me into an empty adjoining room after I dismiss them, shutting the door behind him. He doesn't bother flipping on the light. "Glenn," he says, appearing troubled, maybe slightly haggard. "I wanted to feel you out on this one. What's the mood? What is it going to take today with Lew?"

"Your guess is as good as mine," I shrug. "He has a lawyer. We're no longer communicating directly."

"I see." He mulls this over. "How can I sweeten the pot." It is more statement than question. I'm reminded anew of how unctuous I've always found him. Never a glimmer of interest in our departmental offerings, goings-on. Quick to pardon a plagiarist whose parents are paying in full. "Look," he continues, "I want to be fair to him, and fair to the university."

"Of course."

"There's one more thing, Glenn." His voice falls to a hush, and I can hear the din of students milling about between classes. "I've had some people contact me. Homeland Security. This is in the strictest of confidence. Obviously, this algorithm is, you know, really something."

"I know about as much as you."

"I don't know whether to mention Homeland Security to-day. I don't want to scare anyone."

Oh but you do, I thought. "That's entirely your call."

"Maybe I'll hold it in reserve." I can't make out his eyes in the dim light, can't discern whether he is waiting for some kind of response.

⟨⟨◇⟩⟩

My feelings about Book Seven of Plato's *Republic* are likely slightly more virulent than even the average umbrologist's.

"Motherfucking Plato," I was telling Lew Dorris one May. My best students were graduating and going on to Nantucket and New York, one to be an architect for the summer *hautes monde,* the other to serve as a loading-dock clerk. It was de-pressing. "Fuck motherfucking Plato. Far as I'm concerned, he can take it gangbang-style from Socrates, Glaucon, and Ade-imantus one-two-three."

Lew was a fiendish player of darts. We'd completed a round or two, and Lew's feather shadows were clustering around the bull's-eye, forming a penumbra, where mine were lost in floorboards and flopping miserably off a vintage Guinness pelican beak.

"Ease up, Glenn" is what he was saying. "Get one near the board."

"No, but I mean . . ." I stammered. "Take Plato out of the picture, look at what we get. Respectability, Lew, that's what we get. The respect we got coming. Galileo, motherfucker," I said. "Gali*le*o knew the value of a shadow."

Each time I squeezed a dart before the furrows I could feel in my brow, he'd shrink back, watching people in the vicinity nervously. "Glenn," he said. "If it isn't Plato it's someone else. People aren't made to love shadows. It's that simple."

"Screw that," I said. "We *are* made to love them. Hello? Three-dimensional vision?" Hearing myself saying it, I felt foolish: I'm going to remind *Lew Dorris* about 3-D vision.

"Glenny," he said. "It's the end of the semester. Take some time off. Go to Orlando."

I knew Dorris was speaking figuratively—he knew I had neither a family nor a desire to cavort with giant cartoon replicas. For a moment, it crossed my mind that roller-coaster shadow in Florida sun could be manna, the theme park itself a sort of Rorschach of America.

"Lemme ask you something, Lew," I said. "Thought experiment. Lessay you can go back in time and ya have the chance t'ssassinate Plato. You're alone with him, no one's looking. This is before he writes Book Seven, okay?" I felt myself growing more lucid in the act of speaking. In ten minutes I'd be puking in the alley behind the bar. "Do you do it?"

"Glenn." He shook his head.

"It's a hypothetical," I said. "Critical thinking, just like we ask our students, right? All of Western philosophy a footnote to Plato. Versus giving shadows an outside shot at r-e-s-p-c-e-t."

"You're drunker than you think you are," said Lew.

━◈◈◈◈◈◈━

But, you say, Plato's Myth of the Cave is the stuff of academicians only, any prejudices that it instills in us merely academic ones. You say there is no abiding denigration of shadows in our society, subconscious or otherwise. I, however, know otherwise, having felt the sting of discrimination firsthand. Most memorably at a ski slope this past winter, a gleaming December day, ideal conditions for shadow watching. By ideal (sorry, Plato, I'm stealing back that word), I don't mean only from a

weather standpoint; consider the slope itself, its perpetual ca-
reenings, poles and skis jutting against a bright scrim of snow.
Nothing surpasses a city street in summer, with its buildings,
awnings, pedestrians, cane-bearing and non-, cyclists with
mesh baskets and spokes, dogs tugging on leashes, three-card-
monte tables evaporating quickly as they were thrown together, shoulder-strapped bags, cradled melons. But still.

I was out on the slope, staring, admittedly. Had I been a
sociolinguist or a family-systems therapist, I might have holed
up in the lodge, pretending to read a book and taking in conversation all around me. You might think that after twenty
years of study I'd grow weary of shadow watching—*They're all
alike*, are they not? Yet I'm certain that only now, after these
decades, have they begun to yield up their secrets to me.

The ski patrol approached me, two directly, one hanging
back, American flags sewn onto their shoulders. "Hey, buddy,"
one said.

"Yes, sir."

"How are you today, sir?"

"Fine, just fine."

"We've had some people saying you've been here in this
spot quite a while. Doin' a whole lot of looking."

"Yes, that's right."

"You, ummm, waiting for somebody? Planning on skiing
today, or got kids on the slopes?"

I looked down at an absence of skis. The outlines of my in-
terrogators towered on the heavily trodden snow, stretching till
they struck the roofline of the lodge. Mine merged with theirs.

"I'm an umbrologist," I chanced.

"What's 'at you say?"

I started to give the usual explanation.

"That doesn't sound like a real thing. Is that a real thing?"
he asked one of his compadres, who shrugged and grunted.
"Well, look, irregardless, this here's a family recreation spot.

So I suggest you maybe find yourself an alternative viewing location." Then after a moment: "Sir, can you look at me now, in the eye?"

I let my eye climb up his torso slowly, nodding. He went on: "We've had some unsavory characters here recently, if you know what I mean, so we need to know that you're here to ski or with someone that's skiing, or you're gonna have to move along."

Skia—Greek for shadow. "Have you read Plato's *Republic*, Book Seven?"

His partner stepped in. "Sir, we're not gonna stand here and be mocked. This is a ski resort."

"I was under the impression it was a mountain."

"I'm gonna give him . . . I'm gonna give you one more chance to walk to your car."

As they escorted me, flanking me, with the radio-bearing one behind, I didn't resist, and it occurred to me that much of this could have been avoided had I simply invented, say, that I was blind.

❮◈◈◈❯

The morning Edmund informed me that next semester he was going to work with Lew rather than with me, I'd been daydreaming and had almost rammed into a stopped car that was waiting for some animal to cross. I'd managed to slam on the brakes, and my pulse was still pounding when I arrived at the office. Edmund slipped his news, then, into this strange pocket of relief.

"Well." I'd sucked in my breath, disappointment lodging somewhere down in the region of my diaphragm. "That's fantastic. And all the Greek you've been learning—you're simply going to forget it?"

"Never!" he said in mock horror. His tone pivoted, though. "It does make sense, though, doesn't it? You support the move?"

It did. It shouldn't have arrived as a shock. With the majors or even those with an umbrology concentration, I'm their first love, ushering them into the field. I do a little bit of everything in Intro, an exotic uncle with a seemingly bottomless bag of novelties, a living room vaudeville act. Once they've had a taste of the more advanced classes, though, steeped in one or another subfield, they *specialize*. Mostly, they move on, cordial to a fault—I get an occasional email, or they drop in to tell me about their thesis or gripe about how Abelard holds their papers hostage.

But I couldn't believe Edmund was sitting in my office telling me this; he'd practically lived there these past two years. As my research assistant, he had access to hundreds of pages that, thankfully, no one else will ever see. But he did more than track down references—he filled the margins with comments, netting fresh references from the Sargasso of mediocre scholarship. He'd spent hours in the scuffed, stained armchair, its foamy entrails pouring out as we talked about Pliny and Rembrandt and impossible objects and life, too, his ups and downs with his girlfriend, his mother's battle with depression.

It was little wonder he was destined to go with Lew.

⸰⟨⟨◇⟩⟩⸰

The meeting feels like a courtroom except without any designation of who's on what side. Empty chairs flank me. Rasmussen presides in gray vestments, sport coat and striped shirt and white tie with what look like spouting little blue whales. Lew sprawls, too-long legs jutting awkwardly till they're practically in the center of the room, Vadrais on one side and Edmund on the other, and then there's Amos Duffy from Mathematics, and Sue Gessen, a dean with whom he's chummy, and I wave to her. Next to them are trustees I only know from meetings like this one—though there's not been one exactly like this one. Next is Kuperman, and, sitting right next to him, Dahlia. The president looks jovial, or looks as if he's straining toward some Platonic form of joviality, and everyone else appears overly severe. Even Kuperman looks like he's been cast in a serious role in one of his movies; I didn't know he had it in him.

Rasmussen starts things off with a toothy smile. "We're gathered because we understand that you, Professor Dorris, have developed an idea here at the university that just might benefit all of us. So, essentially, seeing ourselves as pioneers of the twenty-first century, looking to ride out these tough times, we'd like to know how we can help you and help ourselves and . . . help our students."

His voice drones on and I pluck some wasabi peas out of the bag, the few that remain, loading them on my tongue like bullets. Then I am drawn to tug and pull at my eyelid with my nonwasabi hand. This makes his image double and appear to lean, like some aspect of him is bowing or trying to get out, and the tilted version exhibits a deference so foreign to his character that I can't help but find it amusing. I send him back and forth like this. The transformation continues, the head expanding and reshaping itself, tendrils coiling outward till he's no longer a balding bureaucrat, but a sort of shadow puppet villain in a demonic headdress, hinged at the joints, and I start to hear strains of gamelan as he makes his false-friendly pitch. A Demon-king.

Vadrais stands, now also swinging at hinges, stiffly made. "Mr. Dorris has developed certain ideas and, in particular, an algorithm that does promise to be lucrative. However, the terms of the offer you have made him are not sufficient to persuade him to authorize the school to . . ."

And then things start getting ugly. The Demon-king bristles. Pulling back, he increases in size till he towers over the entire room, a grim Gargantua. I think then that he might windmill his arms or soar through the air or double over into an elephant and invite the trustees to mount him and ride on his back into battle. His accusations fly like a downward volley of arrows at Vadrais and Lew, some sticking in the wall, some in the table, some hanging, tips embedded in Vadrais's clipboard. I hear the words "Homeland" and "Security" and murmurs sweep like electric current through the room. Vadrais comes to his feet, wielding his hand like a scimitar and throwing out countercharges—"coercion" and "neglect" and "red tape" off his lips like throwing stars. Again and again they come at each other, sometimes landing a clear hit, at others leaving us to guess from thrust velocity and the ensuing shudder. My hand is no longer on my eyelid; things just look this way.

A trustee jumps into the fray. "Let me be clear about this." He reads off a sheaf of papers. "There were research grants filed through the school? There was a sabbatical, no? In two thousand and . . ."

At some point I realize that it's me he's addressing, and I nod, since what he says is beyond dispute.

Now the Demon-king whirls to address me. I almost want him to appear paper-thin, as shadow puppets do in the instant they are reversing direction, the instant when the illusion fails. "My understanding is that the department is coming up for review, along with every other expense on campus. Times are tough. We think Umbrology would be much more likely to get funding if, as is the case here, tangible benefits could be pointed to."

Vadrais jumps in. "For the record, we don't think that the university necessarily has Lew's best interest at heart."

The Demon-king nods. "Maybe Glenn can speak to the integrity of the school. He's been here longer than . . ." He looks around. "Well, let's just say he's an institution at this institution." He chuckles.

The whole room is watching me and waiting. I see Kuperman, Dahlia, jobs hanging in the balance. Dahlia's, at least. But before I can answer, Vadrais jumps in again. "Lew's researched this, thanks in part to a very talented student of his who has developed a plan for a start-up." He doesn't gesture to Edmund, but we all know whom he's referring to. "Dr. Dorris believes the private sector is where he can make what he is rightfully entitled to. He has interested investors."

For some reason my gaze is drawn to Kuperman, and I catch the slight smile percolating over his face, the knowing glance he shoots Dahlia, and know exactly whose connections were used to get these investors. The expression is so subtle it would be hard to convey in shadow theater, exactly the sort of thing that makes it an art.

The look changes nothing. What I say is exactly what I would've said anyway. "Dr. Rasmussen, I'm afraid I agree with Mr. Vadrais. I don't think it is very likely that the school has Lew's best interests in mind."

━◈━

Afterward, there is the brief chaos that ensues when a jury pronounces guilt or innocence, the tumble on one side or the other of the high wire of fate. Formalities are discussed, the school not abnegating its pro forma right to sue, to which Mr. Vadrais only says, "Of course." And then order returns and we are academics who will sit together at graduation in a matter of weeks. In the hallway, Lew comes up to me, shakes my hand, and thanks me. "Glad you understand, Glenn," he says, adding, "You always supported me." Edmund is nowhere to be found.

━◈━

Later that week, I stand in my driveway watching a total lunar eclipse, one of the most dramatic instances of shadow imaginable. Most shadows happen in black and white. We live in a chromatic world; umbrologists can't compete. If shadows came in a lavish array, if they suddenly took on their casters' hues, I might be a rock star (think Strato-). As it is, I'm more like an erhu plucker from northern China, consoling myself with chilly, two-stringed beauty. Not that I would choose to go electric—I'm merely stating a fact about the world.

And another: Not infrequently, shadows do flirt with color, this being one. Because of how the moon moves through Earth's shadow, coupled with the light-filtering effects of Earth's atmosphere, the moon appears as bloodred as Mars. The cold metal of my car's hood yields a bit as I lie back. I want to shout through the neighborhood, pound on doors—rouse the mesmerized viewers of *Lost* (are they any *less* lost than the characters on the show?) and the compulsive checkers of email.

I want to share it with someone, but the street is silent. Others, out there beyond my block, must be watching this, too, but I can't think of anyone. For a moment I consider calling one of my former students—there are over a thousand, with one or two who stand apart, who might pick up warmly, wish to talk about things other than the eclipse, inquire how I am and ask after Saskia. I might take poetic license, borrowing the stories of some of my more illustrious colleagues about consulting with the designers of the game Goad, ("gonna make Halo look like Ms. Pac-Man"), about extra-tight security clearance while decoding maps, sifting for the anomalies whose discovery could forestall disaster. Something about this incarnation of the moon makes the truth feel malleable, as if it can be suspended without altering its fundamental features.

But then, I think, why not just be blunt—the department's on the brink of oblivion, and a tinge of black mold sits on my shoes from earlier in the week. I glance at it; in this earth-fed moonlight, it is nearly impossible to resist finding a pattern there, something that belongs and will persist long after I slip them off and head upstairs.

Urban Planning:
Case Study Number Four

It is hard to convey to you, who have never been to Ganzoneer, the comic futility that attends any attempt to walk there, due to the elasticity of her streets, walls, and sidewalks, which send the newcomer flailing and sprawling. If you are seeking to anchor yourself after a stretch of limbo, of water treading, of one of those aimless periods that life occasionally thrusts upon us all, go onward. You'll find nothing solid here, with the exception of the Old Quarter, where scattered vestiges of the former Ganzoneer remain, like the stalwart North Church, jutting upward as if slicing at the sky. Once, she was like any other city, hard concrete, all corners and edges, and residents will still go to that part of town every so often to rub their hands almost religiously against the gritty surfaces.

The rest of the city undulates underfoot in a sort of gelatinous mass—it jiggles. Most cities are ectomorphic; Ganzoneer is the consummate endomorph. Residents of nearby Vitmora go so far as to call her "the Splayed Fleshpot," maligning her central thoroughfare, Innapovna Street, as "Thong Blvd.," and adding further insult by pronouncing this "*bllllllllvvvddd*." This can be chalked up mainly to pettiness, since Vitmorans would rather slam their neighbors than face up to their own problems, which have driven the city's last three mayors to drug addiction, shameless promiscuity, and a gunshot wound to the medial-temporal lobe, respectively. Sure, Ganzoneer

103

isn't what most would consider graceful. Once one acclimates to her peculiar genus of motion, though, she harbors no shortage of loveliness; it wouldn't occur to her long-term residents to demean her with "jiggles," nor compare her to a beached cetacean. No, you are far more likely to hear them remarking on her sublime way of yielding to the slightest air current, the sensuousness of her rippling, the jaunt and jounce she lends to the most ordinary stroll.

The brochure *Your New Home: Ganzoneer* opens:

> Planning to relocate here? Great! However, please heed some advice from those who have preceded you here (and there are many). Your first days and nights (but especially days) in Ganzoneer can be disconcerting, reminiscent of the transition a box spring–mattress sleeper undergoes when s/he fulfills the lifelong dream of owning a water bed. It is highly recommended that those planning to move here, in fact, *sleep* in a water bed and spend a couple of hours a day on some form of trampoline or rent an inflatable "moonwalk" contraption for up to a month beforehand. Though this will not fully prepare you for your first day on the street, it will significantly reduce some of the initial shock. We do not recommend the "acclimation shoes" that some are selling (that go by "ganzies" on the black market), as these are based on altogether different principles and will actually make it *harder* once you get here, though if you are *not* relocating here, we'd opine they can be quite fashionable.
>
> Remember that YOU are mostly water yourself, and thus that the polymer-based proprietary hydropolylipidinous compounds that comprise most of the city's architecture are hardly alien to your own anatomical makeup. In fact, *you are more like Ganzoneer by far*

than you are like Paris, Delagotha, New York, or Raed-meon (unless you are a cement-, metal-, and glass-based sentient creature. In which case, Welcome, Cement-, Metal-, and Glass-Based Sentient Creature!). Become, then, more like what you are—where other cities, even those tropical ones beneath lolling fronds, offer up hard corners, horizontals and verticals at every turn, the re-sistance of straight edges, Ganzoneer offers you naught but embraces, caresses, bouncy, jubilant, TRULY TROPICAL moments.

Ganzoneer: Become More Like What You Are.

Emila cringes when she thinks of that catchphrase, when it catches her; the whole brochure hounds her line by line, in fact, though she reminds herself that she wrote it under tight deadline, under "snark attack," as she calls it, from Maypeath, her boss. That this voice—so distant from her own sensibility, so crass and patently patronizing, so transparently manipu-lative—that this voice nevertheless came from somewhere within her makes her shudder. Initially, she thought she could be the closet intellectual who just happened to pay the bills at the Bureau of Tourism—after all, they'd hired her on the basis of her credentials, right? She was overqualified, sure, and they all knew it, but she made extra sure her copy was unassailably down-to-earth, vernacular, employee-of-the-month-friendly.

And still, she'd hoped to smuggle in her thesis (sweet sub-version), which argued for a secret link between phenomenol-ogy and sociology, positing that the majority of crime, poverty, homelessness, and mental illness could be traced not to the heightened density of population, nor to anonymity, nor to materialism (these she argued against). No, the root cause was simple hardness, the unforgiving nature of pavement, from which blood, vomit, death, and grief are too easily wiped clean. It was that simple: Cities, like prisons, secreted their essence into your flesh, turning you hard as they were, perhaps not overnight but assuredly over time. She'd tried to spell it out in the brochure: "The steely resistance and determined glares that worked in other cities will not only disappoint here but will undermine your very intentions." Maypeath red-lined it, reverting instinctually to his mantra: "Focus on the positive." Thus Ganzoneer wound up a partly chewed gum wad, a sex-starved temptress—that, she thinks, is how in the end her brochure packages her city.

She remembers her own arrival in Ganzoneer: no water bed, no bounce machine, no special shoes, just a lonely twenty-four-year-old with dry light-brown hair, a degree in sociology from Vitmora's most prestigious university, and an attraction to the library that verged on the agoraphobic. Having gazed longingly over Ganzoneer from her cell-like turret for years, she finally had the opportunity to go there and test out her theory. Her first day was hellish, an experience she could only compare to seasickness, each step like being on a tiny deck in tumultuous open seas. She'd had no idea where to focus her gaze, the whole city swaying pendulously, and her along with it. Others seemed to negotiate the streets so easily, to glide with the swarthy ease of skaters adept enough to chase pucks, one another. When she fell the first of numerous times, instead of skinning a palm or knee, Emila felt herself caught in a series of tiny falls, an errant ball arriving slowly at inertia.

At first, she figured she'd spend a year here, then return to Vitmora, ready to shake them up with new ideas, propose they soften and slacken their own streets. But she has not found Ganzoneer immune to problems; they lurk just under the veneer of bounding joy and cartoonish delight. Liberation harbors a dark side. The Ganzoneerian handshake, limp and rubbery, often precedes betrayal, sometimes by mere minutes. Ganzoneer's columnists shift their stances daily, and politicians their positions hourly; one is scorned here for having a definite idea that one clings to for more than a week. Blood and the stench of poverty are as easily hosed off from these ductile surfaces as from more solid ones. And, in the end, the crime rate in Ganzoneer is as steep as Vitmora's or anywhere else's. Emila doesn't understand exactly why, but she senses something altered in herself after a mere eight months here. Bathing in the morning, she'll often find herself running the razor over her legs long after they are smooth, relishing the friction and pain, envying the hard, glinting edge, and even this envy has a certain palpability, that of things too long denied.

Planetarium

By the time I recognized Kevin Scully, "Skulky" to those who were enrolled in SAT prep classes, and "the Skull" to everyone else, he had already locked me in a mortal embrace. I extracted myself; it was him all right. Under the circumstances, there were good reasons to doubt it—I hadn't seen him in fifteen years. Also, I was dizzy and nauseous after steering the miles of switchbacks up the Going-to-the-Sun Road in Glacier National Park, and so I didn't trust my own perception of things.

I'd been going a little faster than I'd wanted to, spurred on by the cacophony of cries for the bathroom. The late-afternoon sun in the west seemed most blaring right at spots where the edge plummeted into oblivion. "That's *it*," I'd announced to my family, grinding the gas pedal into the floor. "No more liquids this week for *anyone*." Now, the rear floor of the rental car was strewn with discarded plastic containers and crumpled juice boxes, and every so often they spat their remnants. And the four of us, my wife and two kids and I, had been peeing like rats in a dialysis lab.

Scully hadn't followed me into the bathroom, but he must have seen me go in, since he was waiting for me when I emerged. Now I stood back and looked him over while my ribs decompressed. Once I was sure it was him, his elated response to me made even less sense. We'd been in the same circle of friends back in our New York high school, but what that really meant was that we had possessed roughly the same social rank, and we were therefore able to pick one another apart about evenly without either getting the upper hand. Another way of putting this is that we were separated by less than five points in terms of GPAs. Just standing near Scully made me want to shelter Emmett and Kelly, my two kids, from the cutthroat competitiveness that in many ways had defined me. He might have changed his outfit from a polo to a flannel shirt, and traded in his penny loafers for scuffed boots, but as far as I was concerned, he was still contagious.

"Those yours that were just twirling?" asked Scully.

"That's what we call 'windmilling.'" I said. "A new version called 'Indian windmilling,' to be exact." They were being Indians because we'd gone to an Indian museum the day before. They had been patient for about six and a half minutes while my wife and I had looked at pottery and masks and tried to point out things like the symmetry that Kelly had just learned about in school. But as soon as we looked away for a minute, Kelly had built a fort with brochures, and Emmett kicked it over, and she began to screech. I didn't explain all this to Scully.

Now they came out with my wife, Lena, and so I extended something in the way of introductions. Emmett grabbed onto Lena's leg. Scully got down on one knee and clapped mittlike hands over Emmett's tiny ones, as if he'd been getting holiday cards for years and was finally getting to meet him. When Scully released them, Emmett stuck one in his own eye.

"What did we say about that?" I said.

"Wha-ha-hut?" he whimpered.

"What did we say about putting fingers in eyes?"

"I don't kno-ho-how. . . ."

I absently told him he *did* know, but my attention was back on Scully now. Moving in height order, he'd risen slightly to greet Kelly next, and then made a sweeping mock-chivalrous gesture before rising fully to greet my wife. Around us, people called out to one another, milling every which way. I was trying to watch them all, like I might see someone else I knew, someone who could rescue us. Scully must've said something amusing—whatever it was, it made Lena smile. I smiled, too, and then the three of us made a big triangle of grinning. In his smile, I could see his chin's firmness, its compactness; somewhere over the years, his gelatinous fleshiness had melted away.

We made our way over to the display cases. In front of the crouching skeleton of a bear with a pinched, angular cranium, I hoisted Emmett up for a better view, but he started to kick, so I put him down. It was gift shop time. Scully was showing the kids something, lecturing them about bears, from what I could gather. I watched peripherally while glancing through a couple of calendars and coffee table books about Glacier and the Continental Divide. All the picture books were alike—they were all gorgeous, but who could stop to buy one when the real thing was right behind you? One caught my eye and sucked me in, though, about the Going-to-the-Sun Road: *The Pride of the Park*. That road had induced two main reactions in me. Yes, I was in awe of the engineering acumen that had created a fifty-two-mile (83.69-kilometer) road at a steady 6 percent grade through a forbidding mountain range between 1921 and 1932. But that awe had turned to queasiness as the air thinned out. My ears had stopped up, and I'd heard my own voice go reedy and remote. Now, glancing at pictures, the sensation came charging back, this time made worse by the bombardment of crowds, lines, and the steady clang of the cash register.

All at once, a lot was happening: Scully was chatting with the girl behind the register, Lena had a pocket-size book on wildflowers, and Kelly came jangling through with a set of bear bells. To Kelly, I said, "Okay, but I don't want to hear those the whole way down." Then, to Lena: "How many times will we use it, though?" Kelly began to moan, "How could there be no food here?" Lena shrugged and went to put the book back.

Immediately I regretted the words, feeling like they'd come from some machine and not me. I knew what this trip meant to her. I hadn't until we'd moved into our new, larger place in Brooklyn and unpacked photo albums that she hadn't looked at in years. In the midst of all the boxes, she'd stood in a state of suspension, flipping through the binders. I'd peeked over her shoulders, loving her for her gapped-tooth smile, her swimsuit, her stick with its impaled marshmallow, all against the backdrops of various rented campers. Her family had crossed the country a dozen times but somehow had never made it to Glacier. Then there were the college pictures—posing with the Outdoors Club at an elevation marker, even rappelling up the side of a cliff, something she'd done a couple of times. It didn't exactly fit into our lifestyle, climbing up rock walls, but every so often I wondered whether she resented having filed that part of herself away.

"You know what? Get it," I said.

"No, no, you're right. It was an impulse thing."

I went to pay for everything else, and Scully leaned over and whispered something to the girl behind the register. She nodded and handed me too much change, and then with a wink she said, "Not to worry—you got the discount."

"Thanks," I said hastily. My heart was pounding like in an anxiety attack. I couldn't wait to get out of there. I clapped my hands, rallied the troops. "Let's step outside, how 'bout? Get some of that mountain air, what we're here for."

It was a relief, that air, as soon as I opened the door. We descended the stairs to an overlook with a railing, and I tried to look casual leaning against it. And there was Scully, still with us, no intention of letting this be a fleeting run-in. He was talking to the kids, pointing. "So, the Continental Divide, huh? Place where the rivers flow in different directions. Where the weather systems change. Two *completely different* weather reports up here in Glacier, one east and one west."

As he held forth, he gestured toward the side of a mountain across the road. The air was clear, but in my mind it began to shimmer like those pyramids Lena and I had visited in Mexico on one of our first vacations. Striations of rock alternated with clumps of plants, making it look like something made, with stairs leading up to the flat top. Now I recalled how tawdry and giddy that trip had made us, how it had made us want to clamber up and strip in the Yucatán sun. When we'd gotten back to New York, Lena had announced that she thought she was pregnant, but then her period came along a couple of days late. We chalked it up to the water. Suddenly that felt like a long time ago.

"So *how* is it that you know each other?" asked Lena.

"Ah!" Scully laughed. "Class of '89, is it? I don't exactly think of myself as an alum of the illustrious 'Tompkins Tech,' but they did give me a diploma."

"Wow," said Lena. "Small world." She started explaining it to the kids. "Remember the school we visited, the time we drove by Daddy's old school and pulled over to look? Remember?" Kelly's "Yes" sounded dazed, and Emmett was curled up near the railing like the marmot we'd seen at one of the turnoffs on the way up. Kelly had singsongily dubbed him "Emmett the Marmot," and I was on damage control, since I'd been the one to point out the resemblance.

Scully said, "I do my best to avoid thinking about that place. And I do a pretty darned good job!" He laughed. Then, like he was about to embark with us on a private tour, "So . . . the Continental Divide, huh? Family vacation?"

"You guessed it," I said.

"How long you out for? I take it you're still in New York?"

"Six days," I said. "Not long enough. Then we head for Seattle to see their aunt and uncle, my brother. Then back in school come Labor Day, of course. She'll be starting the second grade. Emmett's going to be in nursery school. Yes, to answer your question, we're still in New York. We made it to the Slope, though," I said, and then added, "Park Slope." I looked around. The mountains made Flatbush Avenue feel like the Visitor Center's handicapped-accessible ramp.

"What about you," I said. "On vacation, too? Kids of your own?"

"Nawp, nawp." I heard his voice change a bit. Or maybe it had been like that before and I just hadn't noticed. "I'm here permanent. Live over in Kalispell, about a half hour from the western edge of the park. I run my own company, actually, lead adventure tours of the backcountry. Some fishing, some horse, some canoe. Heck, licensed in hot-air balloons, haven't had the opportunity to do much of that. And in my free time, do volunteer work in the park, trail maintenance and the like." He pointed back behind the Visitor Center. "If you've hiked the Highline, you've seen *some* of my handiwork: reinforced cable wire so you don't go tumbling. Just for heavy wind. Just in case." His smile was easy and generous. "And no kids," he said, holding up his hands, thick, muscular.

"Wow," I said. The wind was picking up. Somewhere around that moment, I realized I was going to have to reassess Scully here. What I mean is, he wasn't the guy I'd always assumed he'd become. I hadn't really thought about him over the years, but in my not-thinking, punctuated with the occasional thought, he'd become someone else. An engineer, like me. Or a lawyer. Or maybe gotten his M.B.A., gone into business. It was assumed. I didn't need to consult an alumni directory or Google him to confirm it. Maybe I'd bump into him at the twentieth, and he'd be Old Scully, "Skulky," junior partner at his firm, or head of Public Relations. He'd have a wife with a tan that you couldn't miss even under reunion lighting. Maybe I'd have a brief, drunken flirtation with her. He'd have a kid, maybe two. One of them would want to talk internship.

The guy in front of me quite simply wasn't the right Scully.

It was someone who had begun as Scully but whose life had diverged imperceptibly from Scully's at some point, two vectors departing from a single node. An old professor of mine, O'Connor, had explained this sort of thing best: "Shooting an arrow at a razor blade," he'd said, "and hitting it dead-on." I pictured O'Connor with his crazy beard, sketching it out while standing amid the chalk and all the equations.

"Did you say the Highline?" I said.

He pointed. "A ten, maybe twelve-minute walk from here to the trailhead. That's where the catch line is. If you haven't done it, I highly suggest we do. No pun intended," he said. Maybe my face showed reservation. He added, "Don't worry—it'll hold ya!" His laugh was puffed out with air, like an accordion. I'd kind of thought of Scully as being mildly asthmatic.

What bothered me most was not that I had to revise my initial impressions, but that I couldn't find any trace of the old Scully here, as if he'd been wiped utterly away. I wanted something—the grade grubbing, the carping about the special treatment of athletes on game days, the boasting about his dad's trips to Singapore and Hong Kong—that I could fix onto, attach to the guy that I remembered. And none of it was there. It was like he'd just thrown the old Scully over the side of a cliff.

"Hey, why don't we go check out that trail of yours?" I said. "Hey, kids, Scully helps to build the trails here in the park. He's like a ranger." I looked at Lena. "We can take a few minutes to see the trailhead of the Highline Trail, no?"

Lena looked a bit confused. She said, "These guys need food."

"Oh, I've got stuff," declared Scully. "They like granola bars? The chewy kind?" He offered a thumbs-up, and when I returned it, he said, "Wait right here."

―◁◇▷―

Scully handed out the chocolate chip and the peanut butter bars, and we set off through shrubbery and scruff. The whole family was chewing as we followed the trail through its downward dip, passing through a meadow. I'd pinned a compass to my shirt pocket, and now watched the needle bobbing in the general direction we were headed. We were surrounded by mountains—two to our left, one behind, and a ridge straight ahead. Above that was a giant pile of rock shards culled together. Behind it lurked a mountain that resembled a skyscraper. It felt as if they'd been designed by some architect, even the ice field mimicking a sheet of glass.

Lena was looking down, pointing to the wildflowers that dotted the grass with yellow and orange-red. She said, "Those are glacier lilies. That's Indian paintbrush."

Scully said, "Right you are. Pretty good for a bunch of city slickers." Kelly skipped off the trail and reached down to grab a handful.

Gently, Scully called, "Hey, you don't want to pick those."

She looked at Lena, who, in turn, looked at Scully, who shook his head.

"No, honey," said Lena to Kelly, pulling her by the sleeve back onto the trail.

Kelly looked like she was about to cry, and Scully leaned over, patted her head, and said, "It's okay. Just that the growing season here is real short, so our meadows are real delicate."

We moved together. I watched the backs of Emmett's sneakers, flashing red bulbs. Each of his steps looked like a potential stumble. We stopped to watch mountain goats on the side of a hill; they seemed unperturbed by the steepness, well over forty-five degrees. Scruffy, absorbed only by the next mouthful, they barely noticed us. "Yes, they're eating an early dinner," said Lena to Emmett. Then she turned to Scully. "It's amazing that they can walk up there."

"These goats love the extreme angles." He indicated this

with his hands. "That's how they protect 'emselves. Occasionally, they'll use those horns, too, mostly with one another. Sometimes you'll see them square off." His brought his fists together as he added, "Mostly the males, during mating season."

"Typical," Lena snorted.

Scully laughed, like she'd gotten at some secret about him. "There's one spot in the park, though, where there's a salt lick. It's up on the side of a moraine, practically vertical. They go crazy over there. All bets are off. You'll see males knocking females out of the way. Even kids are fair game. No pun intended." He smiled again, glancing at the kids. "Yeah, salt makes 'em go nuts. Heck, they've been known to lick unsuspecting hikers."

Lena turned to him, and she must've looked confused. He held up his arm, which was glistening, and said, "Sweat. Yum, huh?"

"Aha," she said. Then she started asking him a lot of questions. "Speaking of hiking," she said, "what are these hikes you organize?" She asked him about his adventuring, about backcountry camping. "The only way to go," I heard him say. She looked back and smirked at me, then said loudly, "I don't know about backcountry. Maybe when I'm an old woman. Getting him to take a week off to go car camping has been an ordeal." She turned back to Scully, and pretty soon I heard her talking about rock climbing and surfing. I'd forgotten about her surfing. For a moment, I thought he was going to put his arm around her, give her a consolation hug, slip her a brochure.

Now, no matter how I've depicted myself up till now, I'm not the type to backpedal from what's on my mind, even at the risk of ruffling some feathers. I listened, like I always do, staring at the little green patches on Scully's pack. But at some point when the trail opened up just a bit, I eased myself forward next to him so that we were in a line. "Scully," I said.

"I have to ask. What happened to the guy I knew from high school? This," I said, giving him a double solid open palm on the shoulder, "is all well and good. I mean, you've done quite well for yourself. But . . ." I paused. What was I getting at? "What happened to the Scully I remember? You know, the grade grubber, the guy who made a stink about the way athletes got coddled. The guy who used to tell us he would follow in his father's footsteps and beat the pulp out of the Nikkei. No offense, Scully," I added.

The wind kept becoming more audible as we neared the side of the mountain that had loomed ahead of us the whole way. Now his voice struggled to rise above it. I watched his hair blowing chaotically while he talked. "I always wanted to make it out of New York," he said. "Right from day one. I mean, I hated it—the goddamned Upper East Side." He snorted. "I didn't even realize it, though, for a long time. I mean, we all had it pretty good. Our parents all did a pretty good job of making us not see that there was a 'rest of the world,' if you know what I mean."

"I think I do know," I said. "But how'd you realize it? College? Ski trip? Class-five rapids? Smack your head and see the light?"

I watched him get this far-off look, but it was like he was straining to see something really close, peering through some bifocal in midair. "You know, of all things, I think it really had to do with the Planetarium Club," he said. "Did you know about that?"

"I heard about it," I said.

"Did you say Planetarium *Club*?" inquired Lena. She was trying to listen and pay attention to the kids, who were immediately behind us but fighting to keep up the pace, Emmett in particular. It was uphill after the initial descent. I figured I'd be carrying him at least part of the way back.

He laughed. "It wasn't really a club, exactly. Let's face it, not school-sanctioned. Not something I was exactly putting on my 'college transcript.'" As he said this the trail narrowed a bit, and I naturally fell back a couple of steps, so I was with the kids.

"Tompkins Tech," I could hear him explaining to her, "had a planetarium. In the school. I mean, that's the kind of school that it was. Some schools, I didn't know any at the time, but I'm sure they barely had books and chalk, but we had a planetarium. You guys ever been to a planetarium?" he turned back to ask Kelly and Emmett.

Kelly shook the negative decisively.

"Yes, you have," said Lena. "Remember the time we went to see the star dome in Manhattan? And, pumpkin, you went with your school."

"Sure, the old Hayden Planetarium," Scully recalled fondly. I was really glad that Scully didn't bring up going there to smoke weed and watch Laser Zeppelin, not with my kids right there. I gave him credit for that omission.

He went on: "Only problem was, from my perspective and that of several of my peers, the *only* way you could see the planetarium in *action* was once a year when they opened it up and showed it off on Open School Night, and then it was really mainly for the parents, and students were asked to 'make as much room as possible' for parents. So my *dad* and *mom* got to see the planetarium once a year more than *I* did. Then the other way you could get a gig in the planetarium was to take astronomy with Millert. Problem A: Millert's class was killer, a sure-fire GPA sinker. Problem B: Millert himself was *completely* insane. I mean, the guy used to spend half the class talking about how the Earth was eventually going to get swallowed by the sun, and how that made everything meaningless." He looked back at me. "Only Fettis could debate him, Fettis with his *Portable Nietzsche*." Now this was sounding more and more like the Scully I knew and sort of disdained—griping, judgmental, grade-conscious. I didn't know if I was conjuring him back or if he'd been lurking there all along, just waiting for an excuse to come storming out.

"So, the Planetarium Club—that was what we called ourselves, a bunch of us forward-minded individuals. We made a copy of a key to the planetarium—some kid whose dad was a locksmith. God, I couldn't even tell you his name just now."

"And you broke into the planetarium?"

"Broke into the planetarium," he said, throwing in "not a good idea" to the kids, as if he felt obligated. "About nine or ten of us. And not only did we break in there," he said; "we had ourselves a real sleepout there. Somebody—gosh, I think it was Carl—who's our valedictorian?" He turned around as he said it.

"That would be Brian," I said.

"The other one, then, the salutatorian. He knew how to run the equipment there like a dream. He'd been Millert's sidekick for years. Heck, he must've gone on to work for NASA. Anyhow, basically the two of us got the thing fired up, and . . . it was amazing. I can remember the first time. It was like nothing I'd ever seen before in my life. I'd been to the country only a handful of times. I mean, in my life I figure I'd seen at most a handful of stars, and suddenly just *splattered* across the sky were thousands of them, most beautiful sight. I mean, it wasn't like I didn't know what a star was, but honestly, I thought of them as being the little pointy things, like stickers you get for good behavior. I don't think I was the only one, either. I mean, Sammy Rusa—that guy who worked in his parents' 'restaurant,' which you know was a front, right? You think that guy had ever seen stars? Except when he got into a fight." He gave that barrelly laugh again.

"So you stargazed *inside* the school," Lena said.

"That's precisely what we did. And not just once, a few times. We had the complete getup. Learned to spot the constellations. Good for romantic purposes, heh. Told stories. Just like we were a thousand miles from the city, in the middle of nowhere. I remember I never wanted to leave that place. Knew I'd been born in the wrong place or the wrong time or somethin', knew it truer than I'd ever known anything."

"So what happened to it?" asked Lena.

"Guess. Someone took it too far. We were going to do it every month, was the idea. We'd even imitate the position of the stars across the sky; remember, this was a science and math school. But then one kid—*not* a rocket scientist, this one—decides he's gonna make s'mores, and tries to light an actual fire in a wastebasket. Freakin' idiot, pardon my language," said Scully. "Set off the smoke alarm. Duh. We had to clear out of there, which we managed to do before the fire department shows up. The next week, there's a new electronic alarm system on the planetarium door, like nothing you've ever seen. It's like Area 51, 'Closed to the General Public.' I doubt if even the parents got to see it again after that."

"How sad," said Lena. "I mean, there's something so innocent about what you were doing. It's not like you were . . . up to no good."

"Well, it wasn't entirely pure," said Scully. "We did everything—I mean *everything*—that you do while stargazing." Suddenly he drew up.

"This is it," he said. By now I'd almost forgotten why we were out here. The trail ahead hugged the side of the cliff for about a hundred feet. You could see the road below like an ancient riverbed. The bare exposure meant that the sides did not look so steep, because you could see if you slipped the several places where you might cling to a flatter patch if you slipped. But I thought that might have been illusion. Scully strutted out onto the ravine. He looked remarkably like one of those goats. I examined his cable. It looked like a bike lock that had been uncoiled and stretched out and every few feet secured to the rock. He gave it a yank. "It'll hold. Most of the time, you don't even need it, but it's there for you just in case." Emmett shied back, and Kelly looked like she wanted to approach it, like the cage of a dangerous animal. She put her hand out from afar. Lena had her hand on Kelly's shoulder. She reached for the cable and he pulled it toward her, but it did not quite meet, and she leapt back. You could hear the wind moving things, shifting rocks. "I think this is as far as we go, Scully," I said.

We began silently making our way back. Sure enough, I was lofting Emmett onto my back before long. In my mind, I started cross-examining Scully on how the drilling had been done to stabilize the cable, how the core samples might have been taken. I figured he probably didn't know the first thing about how it had been done. I pictured him aiming a drill bit at that rock and gouging it again and again. I pictured him flustered by my questions, trying to dance his way through them, or sidestepping and changing the subject.

For a while, there was nothing but the sound of our sneakers crunching gravel and thumping on dirt. Then Scully said, "So how come you never joined the Planetarium Club? I mean, you must have known about it. Carl, John Paul. You were friends with those guys."

I squinted. "I think I remember hearing something about it. But I don't think I ever got the word, the signal."

"You had," said Scully, "maybe you'd have cleared out of the city, like me. Maybe you'd have gotten a yearning for remote places."

"It's certainly possible," I said. "Then again, it's possible that I wouldn't have. You never know how something is going to affect a person."

"That much is true," said Scully, shaking his head, looking off again, like he was grateful anew for something. Suddenly, Scully elbowed me and said loudly, "Now wait a minute, you *were* there, weren't you?"

"Nope," I said. "If only I had been."

Lena said, "But then maybe you wouldn't have stayed in New York. And you wouldn't have met me. And you wouldn't have *these* lovelies." She patted the backs of their shoulders, and the pair of them looked up as if right then I was deciding whether or not to keep them.

We kept going up the trail, and even though I didn't want to stop, I had to put Emmett down. "You're getting too big for me to do that for very long," I said.

As if no time had elapsed, Scully said again, "You were there."

I denied it again.

He paused, suddenly, hands on his hips. "Well, maybe you don't remember."

"That doesn't sound like the kind of thing you 'don't remember,'" I said.

Lena said, "I would hope not."

We continued up the trail, and I could hear Kelly, bored by now with plain old walking, break into her little rhyme. It went, "Dah, dah, DAH!" sounds that kept almost forming themselves into words, but falling short. It sounded like a story that she was telling only herself. For a couple of minutes, it was just that and the rustle of our feet and Emmett's sneaker-flickers. We all fell into a rhythm. So it took me by surprise when Scully stopped short and pinched the flap of my shirt pocket, like he was grabbing for the compass, and said, "Come here for a second, I want to show you something. Just you." He called out to my wife and kids, "It's just an old Tompk tradition. I'll have him back in a jiffy." I hadn't heard that *mpk* sound in a long time.

Lena, her eyebrows raised, glanced tellingly at her watch. Kelly skipped in a circle, but Emmett stood forlornly. I shrugged to them. I said, "Be right back," then added, "Holler if you spot more mountain goats."

Scully led me just off the trail, through patches of scrub and taut branches. He was just a step in front of me. The crunch of scrabble and dry grass below and the hiss of the wind created two discrete strata of sound. He bent back a branch, a real gentleman, so I could pass. It snapped back behind me. As it did, I found myself on a narrow rock that jutted out sheer into space. In a Western, our horses would've had to rear back, whinnying. I aligned myself with the rock's width, what there was of it, checked my footing. The drop was precipitous. The Skull came out onto the rock, so he was facing me. Then, with his hands turned sideways, he touched my shoulders, so that the lower edges were resting right on my scapula.

I panted. "What are you doing there, Scully, hanging up a portrait?" I could hear the pounding of breath, as though one of us had just hoisted the other one up, right over the lip of the ravine.

He stared at me. "Admit it now. You were there."

"You're crazy," I said. I meant it.

He shook his head. "Why won't you just admit you were there?" He was all throat now.

"Let's just say I was, Scully. *Then* what?" I heard my heart-beat. "But of course I wasn't."

His mouth was tight. I could see the imprint of his tongue on the inside of his cheek. "I can't figure it out," he said. "It's not as if it's something to be ashamed of."

"On the contrary," I said. "I'm ashamed to have missed out."

His hands stayed wedged there. I couldn't tell whether they'd begun pushing down or whether my shoulders were rising, but either way I could feel little balls of bone against his thick fingers on either side. It reminded me of a building I'd worked on. Prestressed cables to offset unknown load combinations. And I zeroed in on that building. I became it, poised between evenly spaced twinges of pain. Under his flannel, the road looked so far away and weirdly proportioned that it could have as easily been up or down. Looking back up at him, I caught menace moving quickly like a sheath of cloud. I imagined him explaining to my wife in a calm voice that I'd fallen, somehow.

"You haven't changed a bit," he said with disgust. I sensed that he wanted me to defend myself against this charge, but I didn't say anything. He went on, "Okay. How about *I* don't admit to something. How about I don't admit I can see that you're the same fucking competitive bastard you were in high school?" I tried not to blink. "No? Okay, or that in less than a half hour I can see that your wife is only *some*what happy. No? Okay, let's say *neither* of us admits that if your wife goes on one of my tours, it's a good bet she never looks back?"

I held his stare.

At once he released me. The same hand that had applied a viselike grip to my shoulder now wrapped around and squeezed the other one, almost affectionately, you might have said. I half-expected to see Lena poke through the underbrush and point a camera at us, call out, "Smile!"—immortalizing us, buddies against the backdrop of sky. I looked at his face to see if he had registered the tremor shuddering through me. He'd already moved on, though, chuckling, shaking his head. "You really shoulda been there," he was saying.

—◁◇▷—

I was still trembling a bit later that night when we'd settled down at last at our campsite, in our family tent. The others were fast asleep. Scully was long gone. I didn't know if he'd ever get mentioned again. I doubted it, even though we'd eventually gotten a tourist to take a snapshot of us with him in front of the Visitor Center, before we shook hands amicably and parted ways.

The strange thing was, I *had* been there, in the planetarium. The very first night, along with the other nine people, except that there weren't nine others, there were ten others, eleven total, and I had been among them. Maybe somehow I'd been quieter, or less obtrusive, so that in his memory Scully had edited me right out of the planetarium, right out of existence. And the ultimate irony was that I was the one who'd been responsible for one of the most memorable moments of that night, a moment that no one who was there should have forgotten. I mean, if you were looking back at what deserved to stick from that night and what deserved to fade into oblivion, my contribution should have certainly gone into the "preserve" pile.

You see, I'd actually *taken* astronomy with Millert, and we'd actually gone to the planetarium on several occasions, and each time I'd watched carefully and curiously while he set up the equipment before he dimmed the lights, and when my eyes had adjusted to the dark, I'd watched him operate the console as much as I'd concentrated on the starry sky it projected. While everyone else was enthralled by simply seeing the stars, I, who was going to be an engineer, knew I was supposed to be interested in things like how exactly the equipment worked, how it functioned. And when we were lying there in the dark after we slipped in that first night, the sky at first looked okay, but it had to be said that there weren't a whole lot of stars. Not that most of the people there would have known the difference. But I knew, because I'd watched Millert run the show. I knew how it was supposed to look. So while others were laughing and calling out things like "Hey, that's my hand!" I'd spent about ten minutes or so adjusting the computer and switching the modes, just like I'd watched Millert do. I was surprised by how hard it was to actually control it, even though I knew it by sight, and I was getting frustrated, especially since no one really knew what they were missing. I almost gave up. But then I toggled a certain switch. Instantly where there'd been maybe a hundred stars, there now were thousands upon thousands. It looked like scarves whipping through a snowstorm, and you could see that the sky wasn't dark at all, nothing like the dim shroud we had all assumed it to be. I could forgive Scully for forgetting about this, though—it had been just an instant, and while there'd been a collective "Ahhhwwooh!" a few hoots and scattered applause, soon enough everyone had gotten acclimated to this new look and gone back to their business. Meanwhile, I had found a spot on the floor and lain back along with everyone else in the dark.

You might be wondering why I didn't just fill in this gaping hole, though, to Scully. I could understand how he'd overlooked me. It had, after all, been dark that night, and confusing, and even though our voices kept rising, mostly we'd tried to keep them to a whisper so as not to disturb the custodians, who even then were moving through the hallways like distant comets. And to be truthful, I'd never gone back, never really been part of the "Club." But all those factors aside, I'd been there that first night.

The real reason I hadn't divulged this earlier today was that for me, the significance of the evening had been bound up in the fact that there'd been a girl there. I didn't really want to think about her, and I hadn't much at all. And the truth of the matter was that I had never told my wife about her. Never. Though I hadn't consciously avoided telling her all these many years, I'll admit that I'd missed opportunities to tell her. And in fact, there was one moment from that night that came back with particular acuteness to me. We'd all had something to drink and something to smoke—Sammy Rusa, in addition to supplying the keys, had flipped open a flask of Jack Daniel's. We kissed, this girl and I, started to do some other things, and then one of us pulled back. I figured there'd be plenty of time; this was only the beginning. As that night in the school turned into morning, I found myself escorting the object of my affection downstairs toward the parking lot. We decided we'd go home for a few hours, or maybe go to a twenty-four-hour diner, revive over some coffee. At the top of the stairs that still looked like a possibility, even though by the time we'd made it to the first landing several minutes later, we'd both recognize that what she really needed was to empty her stomach of its contents and to be taken home, where she could slip stealthily into her own bed. For the moment, I had my arm around her and she felt good, though limp as a weed. She staggered and swayed on the steps, one arm on the rail and the other clinging to my shoulder. As we went down, she blurted, "These *stairs* are really a pain in the ass. Edgerton should get rid of these *stairs* and replace them with *stars*."

Edgerton was the principal. At the time, I thought that that was easily the most charming and witty and poetic thing I'd ever heard anyone say who wasn't dead and British. My belief in the sheer genius of the statement had carried over to the next day, as it would for years to come. I felt that it held tantalizing mysteries that I would peel away slowly. The next day, I approached her before homeroom, giddy with lack of sleep. But not only did she not recall saying the words that I had celebrated even while I half-slept, not only did she flat-out deny having said them at all, but she refused to talk to me at all, then or ever again.

And that's what I was thinking about as snores issuing from somewhere nearby faded. I could sense Lena, a patch of warmth there beside me, and then just beyond, in the vestibule, the kids, lying silent, their warmth more tightly circumscribed. I sat up, unzipped the tent, and, quietly as I could, ventured out. At a picnic table, I gazed back over the silent campground. As my eyes began to adjust, the scattered domes appeared strange to me, like some sort of village had sprung up here, tucked into the wilderness. And then I had the idea that within this village, each of the houses could have been a miniature planetarium. Even as I thought it, I recognized this for what it was: a fanciful notion. Yet I must admit it stirred in me a momentary satisfaction. Not the kind I get when I'm the one who's able to solve a particularly thorny design problem, one that's stumped the room; no, this was something else entirely. I sat there and shivered and watched the tents gradually resolve themselves, becoming mere tents again, hunkered down under the vastness of the sky. Then a pummeling wind came at once from all directions, and all I could hear was the thrash of canvas, flapping, rippling, and, almost inexplicably, holding fast.

The Gendarmes

A loud banging noise was coming from my roof, and it wouldn't let up. I kept glaring at the ceiling and waiting for it to cease, but nay—crescendo. Finally, I stormed outside. Sure enough, an entire baseball team was up on my roof, *again*—gloves, bats, a catcher in full tools of ignorance. In lieu of a baseball cap, each wore the signature blue headgear with yellow trim of the French military police. The catcher was the only one properly attired.

"Hey!" I said. "You're playing baseball on my roof."

A squat, wider man with a brazen mustache caught a crisp throw from third base, which I couldn't see but assumed was on the far side. He spat tobacco in my general direction. "Yeah. Thanks."

"That's my *roof* you're playing baseball on," I said.

A lanky fellow, no more than eighteen, looked down. "And a mighty fine roof it is."

Squat Mustache added, "Got some loose shingles over here between second and third, what our shortstop tells me."

"Yeah?" I said.

"You could be looking at a lawsuit," he said. "I'd get those fixed."

"Who the hell do you think you are?"

"We're the Gendarmes," said one, sleeve outstretched with child-showing-off-diorama pride.

Just then a sharp foul ball took a harrowing turn, ricocheting off an oak trunk and toward my head. I snared it. There as a collective gasp from the roof, followed by a shout of "Out!" or *"Oui!"* from somewhere over my kitchen, from a slight hump of an umpire.

I examined the baseball. It was a ball like any other, only around the stitching it read *"For Rooftop Use Only. Danger: Do Not Use On Grass. Potential Combustible."*

I looked up.

"Explosive, eh?" I asked.

The players began to look at one another nervously. Then Squat Mustache called down, "We don't talk about that. Traditional league rules. Just don't get chlorophyll on it."

"And redundant," I continued scornfully. "'Potential. Combust*ible*.' Wasteful, just wasteful." I shook my head disgustedly; nothing infuriated me more than redundancy.

I scanned my yard, which was, as it had been when I woke up that morning, covered with grass. It was wrong that a ball could hurtle at any moment and erupt into flame. At the same time, I knew that that was precisely what I wanted to happen, what *would* happen next if I allowed my instincts to hold sway. To protect us all, I tucked the ball into my pocket and began a frantic shimmy up the side of the house.

The players gathered and looked down with gasps of alarm. "What are you doing?" they cried out in patently fake French accents, shaking accusatory fingers, the big brown digits of mitts well-worn from use and exposure to hundreds of hours of midday sun. I planted a foot atop an outside light, grabbed a shutter, and hoisted myself the last few feet via a gutter.

Having never set foot on my roof, I little expected it to be covered with veritable pampas of artificial turf. And a baseball diamond, molded to the contours of the house, was shimmering in the now-fading daylight. There was also a cupola, which was inaccessible from inside my house.

"Okay, boys," I said, grabbing a glove from the pile underneath the handwritten *EXTRA*, and pounding my fist into it.

Gingerly, I made my way to what I guessed was second base. "Let's play ball."

They stood around looking sheepish, staring down at my roof, which, I could see, as the squat man had indicated, was in clear need of repair in places.

"What are we waiting for?" I demanded.

Finally, one mumbled, "We don't really know how to play." Another chimed in, "That's why we're up here. So people can't see that we're not actually playing."

"So what *are* you doing?" I asked.

The Kid, as I decided I would call the eighteen-year-old, led me over to the far side of the roof, the side I hadn't been able to see. To my shock, there were animals in cages—pigeons, a lemur, a raccoon with a clear case of alpacatitis of the testes. What I had mistaken for an umpire was in fact a squirrel. There were also video screens showing nature documentaries from the 1970s, the kind with voice-overs and saccharine music, muted. There were two buckets. One, filled with peanuts and Crackerjacks, said *Positive Reinforcement*. The one next to it, labeled *Negative Reinforcement*, teemed with a leech-cauliflower salad.

"We're scientists," admitted someone wearing a badge that read *Pitcher/Spokesperson*. "We're conducting an experiment." On careful inspection, I could see that the word running down his pinstriped uniform was *Scientists*, not *Gendarmes*.

"And the nature of your experiment?" I asked.

"We're trying to teach animals to grasp the concept of extinction," said Pitcher/Spokesperson. "We're tired of having to bail out endangered species. It's high time they learned individual responsibility."

"Hmmm," I said. I thought about it for a moment. Their intent was benign, if not downright noble. I was used to scientists who just wanted to advance knowledge for its own sake, a cause I despised and attempted to undermine whenever possible. This, however, was worthy. It would mean less work for my grandchildren, who, while purely hypothetical right now, were likely to inherit nothing and, I was certain, bearing even a handful of my genes, would require decades for soul-searching instead of worrying about the environment and such.

Then it occurred to me. "Maybe they can be coaxed into playing our national pastime."

The team members looked at one another in confusion. "*America's* pastime," I said, realizing that some were still half-pretending to be Gendarmes. Lips curled as they strained to read one another's reactions to see if it was okay to embrace this idea.

"What better way to teach individual responsibility than *that*?" I said, grabbing a bat and carefully releasing the latch on the lemur cage. I explicated the sacrifice bunt, which I figured the animals, or, as I dubbed them, "the rookies," would be doing a lot of, at least till I could instill in them the importance of off-season conditioning. I didn't realize it at the time, but I had a thing or two to learn from *them*, too.

A Box of One's Own

A guy started carrying a box around the neighborhood one day. Not a small box, the type swaddled in clear tape and addressed with scented marker; no, this was a great strapping thing, cardboard limbs flailing akimbo from a cardboard torso, defying its carrier to heft it without tripping or colliding with a wall. It was like the guy was about to give birth, unable to see his own feet, while also blindfolded. I'd seen the pregnant prancing in maternity blindfolds before, and it made me nervous, it made me cringe, I tell you.

After seeing him parading around like this up and down the sidewalks for a week or so, I confronted him. "Hey, buddy, so what's in the box?" I figured he'd already been spoken to; I figured he'd have a set answer by now, maybe three if he was smart.

A snarl. "Do you really care?" It was the box that spoke. The man wielding the box kept going, his trajectory not unlike that of a rickshaw operator with dementia. I followed a half step behind, like a piece of toilet paper stuck to his foot. As I thought this, I looked down—sure enough, a piece of toilet paper was affixed to my foot. I removed it, deploying a forceps with a special toilet-paper-from-foot-removal accoutrement, which took a mere half hour to assemble and but a half hour to disassemble, and thoroughly eradicated the least trace of the toilet paper in only fifteen minutes. It didn't just yank it off—nay, it vaporized it and scorched the bottom of my shoe, too, applying with a gleeful flourish a gloss that would ensure that future toilet paper scraps would think quadrice before attempting to stow away from bathroom tile onto my sole.

I spotted Box Man coming up the landfill feature known locally as "the Molehill," comprised of tens of thousands of moles that had been surgically excised from their source—cheeks and derrières. Those who desired to graft a mole onto their visages knew they could always rely on this reservoir of protuberances, as well.

Now I was ready for him. "I *do* care," I pleaded as he got close. "I really, really do."

The box sputtered but then responded as instantaneously as though our conversation had been continuous.

"What is it that you think you care about, exactly?"

"I do not *think* I care. Yes, I think. And I care. But notwithstanding your skepticism, I do not think *and* care in a single semantic swoop."

"Harumph," said the box. "You're the last person who would know what you care about. And, in any case, I can almost guarantee that you do not care about what is in me. What you do care about is seeing what you can't immediately see, what's concealed from your vantage point. As soon as you see what's inside me, you'll cease to care and will wish to discard me like any piece of cardboard that isn't ruggedly constructed with such Euclidean virility as myself." With this, it began to do the box equivalent of flexing, bending its flaps, making its corrugations ripple outward.

"How do you know if you won't show me?"

"I will not relent," said the box. "Narrative structure would dictate a gradual withering away of my defenses and a climactic divulgence of the contents of my secret interiority. But I know all about narrative structure. So don't even try it, buddy."

I had started out being intrigued by the man behind the box. I felt I'd been distracted by the box itself. If only I could pry it away from the hands that bore it around, slice through

it with an X-Acto knife or set it aflame just long enough to
out the box bearer. I checked the forceps I'd used earlier, but
I hadn't splurged for the flamethrower or any Deluxe Features
at all, having been down on my luck at the time due to the
legal fees expended in settling a court case with a maimed
courtesan.

There was only one thing to do. I needed a box of my own.

When you are not in need of a box, the prospect of snar-
ing one appears piddlingly easy and straightforward. Boxes
abound, this world a surfeit of boxes. Packages fling themselves at you; in a pinch, you could scoop out the Styrofoam
peanuts, feed them to the nearest lemur, and keep the box. The
concentration of cardboard rivals that of atmospheric oxygen.

And yet, when bereft of a box, in a non-box-possessing
state, the simple procurement of one becomes a staggeringly
difficult obstacle, as I was soon to discover. I went to sources
that I was sure would land me a live one: a moving company,
a department store, a company that sold ready-for-school di-
oramas over the Web for obscenely lazy children. I figured I'd
order a "Washington Crosses the Delaware," rip out the Father
of Our Country, the Popsicle-stick oars, and voilà. I told myself I'd be doing a good deed, since some kid would actually
have to do work.

Not so fast. They'd been bought up by the world's fastest-
growing confetti concern, which ground up offbeat items—
yachts, chocolate bunnies, erotic Victorian curios—and pressed
them into little flakes for those disenchanted with mere *papier*.

"All the luck," I lamented. Then I found a box lying outside
on top of an orange rind atop a juniper bush, which was itself
straddling a gin mill. I didn't hesitate—I grabbed it, steeping
my senses in its ablutional aromas.

Now, embracing my own box with the desperation of a man
who wants to show off his fox-trot with his wife at a ballroom
dance in order to impress his mistress who is fox-trotting with

another man only to find that his mistress's lover has invented a whole new variation called "the fox-gallop," which is faster, more rhythmically impressive, and just plain groovaliciouser, I approached the original Box Man on the path.

By now, though, box toting was rampant. Everywhere you looked, there were men and women carrying boxes, boxes carrying men and women, and, most of all, boxes carrying one another, having done away with the middlemen, along with the appetites, petty jealousies, and other inconveniences that had gone with them. The box I was pursuing, I realized, was no longer the one that I had set out to find. I heard a chorus chanting, "This End Up! This End Up! This End Up!" getting closer and closer, but my view was occluded. And then it happened: I was swiftly inverted. Just like that, eye-to-eye with an ant, a divot—holy rhythm.

How sweet they felt, then, that first time it rained, the dolorous globules, reaching my head only after caroming off the long-suffering bottoms of my feet!

Internodium

Our talking is a kudzu of carotids in which we lose our marbles. Hours later, they tumble out as we are snoring, awakening us one at a time, hard little tumors we flick underneath one another. By morning, we lie like border states whose boundaries are rivers, anomalously straight, canals funded by nature.

⸻⟨⟨◇⟩⟩⸻

When I get nervous near you it's like a utility forms and hits a whole town with its too much. Everyone goes shed 'n' attic and unearths devices: those they need, those they never use, those borrowed and never returned, those they wish they'd borrowed and could thus return, those they don't recognize, those whose uses they can't fathom, those double-barreled ones that lend skulls cold spots, those too flimsy to withstand unearthing, those that served as stunt doubles for other devices once, in their heyday, those they don't really need. But want. Among them: electric utensils, rodent rotators, epilepsy inducers, oars, spooling agents, laminators, pompadour replicators, run-on detectors, vaginal dredgers, mechanical fins, metronomic innards, palate ticklers, religious spatulae, hissiphones. Those that look burned but not flammable. Those that come off synthetic yet overripe. Those for pulling, for turning, for penetrating, for twisting and more. Thanks, we say, blushing, thanks. What they do with them is done, and then they are put gently back into their slots, slid onto the hooks and rafters, and eventually I can meet your gaze once more.

><⊗><

Next year starts my stint as anthropologist on that island where relationships and existential quandaries are thrashed out in small talk, and any mention of the weather or the pop diva's latest gown makes the strongest rack with weeping.

><⊗><

Even the tolls adjust on our approach. You catch them trembling and think it a trick of light. Whatever we hand over, coughed and culled from cushiony crevices, is always "exact" and "change," and still you clamp down, silent as mile markers, on one bald coin.

><⊗><

Whatever else we are, we are surely a beard that has convinced its owner to stop shaving. How long? No longer do we even notice the Unabomber comparisons, the razors orphaned in the snarl.

Urban Planning:
Case Study Number Five

Write when you are starving. Write when you are sated. Write in the throes of eating—find a way, free up a hand between bites, intrachew. If all else fails, invent a new writing implement, half pen, half fork (to think the spork anything other than a mild innovation shows a paucity of imagination); then sweep a bite into your mouth, pausing only briefly before nose-diving right into the midst of your ongoing sentence, the one you left hanging between a dependent clause and an independent. Now, at last, the acts of eating and of writing have fused for you into a single four-pronged gesture, as they did for me long ago.

Truth be told, what food I have now makes a fork useless, barely holding together on the tines. Nowadays, I eat with my hands, manners be damned, though once they gleamed like a new set of steak knives. Who the hell would I try to impress, now, in this bombed-out husk of a building under a crumbling roof, sky streaming in through strung-together sheets of tar and salvaged Sheetrock, funneling water when it rains? Who will I impress—the occasional vagrant who wanders in, having sniffed out a human presence? Or the dark-eyed urchin who comes late afternoons in his second skin of tattered rags? Every day I set aside a few morsels for him to dissolve against his palate.

Sometimes, watching his frantic chewing, I pity him—he'll

never know what food can be. Yet at times I envy him for what he hasn't known—pumpkin bisque lapping against an atoll of salsa, steam rising from fresh-torn coriander *brioche au brocciu*, rivulets of mango waiting beneath like buried treasure. He won't know braised lamb shanks you'd swear were fruit, nor the quivering tangle of Singapore noodles, at once soft and crunchy, nor sesame chicken that winks with a thousand knowing iguana eyes. He'll never witness the birth of *naan*, warm and glistening and mottled with birthmarks. He won't know the translucent green of cabbage drizzled on sushi rice, nor the bolder greens of draped asparagus, nor the snarling green of a cauldron of wasabi. He'll never burrow in the darkness of elk roulade stuffed with morels, nor come face-to-face with duck confit brindled with chilled open figs. He won't know the suppleness of shrimp reincarnated on the tongue, nor the squid whose toughness demands that you chew with attention, a bracelet or belt. He won't know the way smoke's essence can penetrate polenta right down to the plate, nor ginger's habit of loitering at the surface, forgotten till you trip over it. He'll never know the golden, salty saxophone solo of a *jiaozi* dumpling, its scent nearly palpable as it makes its way across the room.

The siege has been on so long, it is no longer front-page news, barely news at all. Every commentator in the world has already weighed in, and, nothing having changed for the better part of a decade, the world has, quite reasonably, moved on. Olympics have come and gone, and we no longer send athletes (we were known for water polo), since even if they were able to slip out and get there, how could they compete against those who are well rested and fueled, mitochondria rippling in their cells?

But you have to imagine Vassilonia before this siege laid waste to us. When you look at us now, skin-and-bone strays, you'd hardly know how cherubic and jaunty we were once.

God, we relished nothing more than walking off our meals in the fading of daylight. To walk through the city during its heyday was to navigate a thick, aromatic fog, the very air a front of flavor punctured by pungent crosscurrents—"Ah," you'd say, "Galvin is jacketing his prawns in shiitake again . . . or is that Devon experimenting with saffron? Both?" You'd bump into someone you knew and all would belch, one at a time like cars at a four-way stop, and they'd try to guess what the others had eaten—such were good manners, then. People were innocent, dressed differently (rounded, flaps and slits to aerate, exuding formality even on days off). An unfathomable gulf divides us from that time, makes it so hard to believe that people were *people* then, moving about in three robust dimensions with vivacity, coughing and wheezing, chortling and flirting and kissing and *eating* above all, eating and eating and eating, doing so with the greatest conviction, with vigor and savoir faire and newlywed lust lavished on food rather than flesh: At the morning's first, semiconscious stirring, they ate, midmorning ate again, midday and midafternoon, twice in the evening, inventing names for meals—*argent, vespens, efferzeti*—mixing and matching dishes from far-flung corners of the globe, things too loosely assembled to be called dishes, flinging spices blindly into the waiting maws of pots, sometimes checking the label afterward, the stovetop a welter of activity, a percussive clamor, the cook whistling or gossiping all the while—unthinking, careless, saucy. They needed no justification for their indulgence; food was the cornerstone of Vassilonian existence. *Our* existence—I remind myself, "this people" was me.

Even in the thick of company, though, I always ate alone. Part of me, at least, was inveterately, metaphysically alone.

⊰⊱

It started, Vassilonia, as a faceless, generic city, a seat of colorless commerce and bleak industry. It was during a precipitous downturn in the economy that the restaurateurs, calling themselves "The Fearless Nine," banded together and formed a coalition, deciding that it would no longer be feasible for people to eat out in the foreseeable future unless urgent measures were taken. Led by the mustachioed visionary Antonio Corrido, they vowed that rather than shutting down or waylaying pedestrians with pleading offers of cheap meals, they'd feed everyone as long as they were able through the crisis. After all, people had to eat, and why not well? They gambled rightly—the dollar may have been worthless paper, but that summer and fall the earth yielded up a particularly bountiful growing season, and there was a general sense of ebullience. Soon the number of restaurants had doubled to eighteen, and not long after that there were dozens, as people caught on to the fact that the industry could somehow remain just slightly to the side of the mainstream economy, which itself was already starting to recuperate.

An ethos began to take hold with unspoken rules. Don't try to compete with your neighbor—don't try to one-up him on his most popular dishes, steal her secret recipes, mimic their decor. Be different, strive for uniqueness, and eventually people will line up at your door. If offered the choice between Cerignolas and Luganos, it is human nature to choose one type of olive on Monday and another on Tuesday, but if faced with seven brands of Kalamata, they'll gravitate toward one jar and cling to it. Hence, you had to be nonredundant. This ensured that you could get not only Chinese but also Mandarin, Szechuan, Guayadongian; not just Indian but Navratan, Gujarati; not merely Moroccan but that indigenous to the town of Tafroute; the cuisines of Tasmania, Ganzoneer, Tibet, Raedmeon, Argentina, El Salvador, Vitamora, and Morrisania were all readily available.

Moreover, you would not eat, yourself, at your own establishment except on rare occasions. No, you had to go out, sample the city's wares, pump money and life into the economy, or else you were thought stingy, provincial, haughty. What little money you'd save by remaining in your own dining room would pale next to the loss in reputation. The phrase "eating at home" in the vernacular came to refer to masturbation.

And you could always tell a Vassilonian by his or her conversation above all. They were perpetually talking about food, reminiscing about a great meal—never about whatever they were eating at that moment, no matter how splendid, aromatic, and memorable it was. That would be for another day, another meal. Facial expressions, little gasps of delight would have to suffice to compliment the chef, who, after all, might not even be there—he might have already slipped out to eat at another establishment, replaced by the next shift. Always, the conversation at the table revolved around great meals of the past. It was only in this contrast—between what was now being eaten and what they'd eaten in the past—that they made sense of taste, for flavor, it was assumed, only existed as a set of contrasts. Trying to describe what was right now on your tongue was like trying to cup the present in your hands— invariably it would slip through the fingers. Certainly there were philosophers who offered alternative theories—that, for instance, our brains were equipped with a universal template that enabled them to assemble complex flavors from simpler, more elemental ones without any effort or training. Still, the theory of contrasts predominated, maybe because people were by then so attached to the delectation of endlessly sifting and comparing their experiences.

Were we fat? We were by no means a lean people. Yet I'd wager we were in no worse shape than many others who ate with far less frequency. What we consumed was fresh, chewed with vigor and aplomb, every bite maximized. To this day, I can't eat rapidly without the chastising voices of an older generation—"Slowly, slowly"—echoing in my ears, as if presaging a day when food would become so scarce that it would become necessary to eat at escargotian paces.

When I first heard the term *foodie*, I laughed. Were we not all "foodies"? Equally amusing is the nation that chooses the "melting pot" as a metaphor; over the ensuing decades, Vassilonia leveled all of its nondescript office buildings and replaced them with giant replicas of pots and pans, bringing forth a magnificent skyline, with its crown jewels, the Collander Building and, of course, the Pepper Mill, whose luminous glow at sunset I won't deign to describe. Of course, all are gone now, scrapped for weaponry or, more recently, rusted over and mottled with verdigris, dark domes where scrawny dogs take refuge.

Where, you ask, did we get all of our ingredients to make such copious servings? From near and far away; nothing was actually grown *in* Vassilonia, and for this oversight no one can take responsibility but ourselves. You have to understand that our tourist trade was off the charts—even lodgings, aside from the homes of residents, fell outside city limits, there being so little room to spare. Yes, there were businesses that weren't restaurants, but all converged in one way or another around food. Clothing boutiques were geared around dressing for a particular cuisine—you could don authentic garb from any culture, or pair an outfit with your food (a delightful striped marzipan dress), or simply "dress for a mess," as we put it. And I must say our red-light district was far more risqué than anything you have elsewhere, whipped cream and chocolate fudge being fine but rather blah when you can find yourself glazed in amandine, or sprinkled with lemon-infused coconut shavings, pepper-cantaloupe chutney, and beyond.

A bit of a caste system, it must be admitted, began to emerge, with internationally trained chefs at the top of the hierarchy, followed by sous-chefs, followed by shopkeepers of all sorts, who were roughly on par with waiters, and below that dishwashers, necessary but never given the respect they deserved. Our mayoral elections consisted of great cook-offs, open to the public and swelling with waves of raucous cheering, which typically swept one candidate to a clear victory, though once or twice we needed to resort to ballots. And, of course, there were the critics, a rising class of academics who, it must be said, never learned to cook themselves, only to depict and analyze the dishes of others. The emergence of this intellectual class stirred a certain amount of resentment among Vassilonians, who nevertheless took great pleasure in reading aloud the most eminently quotable ones, and considered their writings to be a worthy contribution to world literature.

Among them was the legendary "Maz"—no one knew his true identity, as much as people tried to figure it out—were these his initials, or a shortened version of his name, some code, a tag à la a graffiti artist? Many of the critics were known by their faces and recognized, but Maz eluded any certainty about his identity. He'd write about meals he'd had months before, which was still practical because at that time restaurants simply *didn't* go out of business, and he'd make the writing so vivid it was as though he was still digesting. So he was impossible to trace. Legend had it that he was a shape-shifter, too, that one day he'd come in as a cowboy trucker, hunched over in stiff dungarees and heavy shades, and the next as an elderly woman with varicose veins dripping down her legs.

❖

The collapse was, looking back, as inevitable as it was sudden. It started with a wave of food poisonings—terrorists, cost cutting in the refrigeration industry to save a few bucks, a mass hallucination, no one knows. What does it matter? The bubble had burst. People stopped going to certain establishments. No one died, but toilets could be heard flushing throughout the city all night long for days, alternating with ghastly retching sounds that ranged from alto to bass. It was a horrific week and it passed. Yet, for the first time since the Fearless Nine had forged their pact, a general wariness seeped into everyday life. I remember it well—people stopped meeting one another's gazes. Exchanges of belching began to be frowned upon. Certain venues were avoided, spoken of in hushed tones. Tables sat empty. The critics, in turn, lashed out, as though they'd been holding back a grudge for years. Better scrutiny of food sources was needed—did anyone have any clue where these things were grown and by what sort of people? Were they out to get us? The critics' pens didn't leave Vassilonia unscathed, either, as they accused their own of rampant nepotism and double-dealing, targeting refrigeration moguls and oils barons. Some asserted that this newly exposed vulnerability meant the city was doomed. This incident had only made people sick, but when would the next one be, the one that would wipe them out, leaving them in the grotesquely preserved poses of Pompeii's citizens?

Head Chef/Mayor Needlebaum came down hard on the critics, as any political figure left dangling in the wind might. He centralized control, clamped down on the borders. Of course, the tourist industry that they'd always relied on was badly damaged, too. Then the growers struck back. If the first case was a fluke, the second one was frighteningly deliberate, a retaliation against the smear job they felt they'd gotten in Vassilonia's media and at Needlebaum's attempts to micromange them afterward. It had been a bad growing season, too, and some say that it all was merely an expression of their rage at forces beyond human control. Either way, it was trouble. The tanks moved in this time, not from Vassilonia. (Tanks? Ha— we had grills on wheels, running on biodiesel.) If Vassilonia couldn't control its own borders, ensure the safety of its own people, not to mention that of diplomats and expats, then other, more capable nations would.

At first, they attempted to occupy, but this proved

impractical. Their soldiers came in with their bland tinned rations, and we fought back the only way we knew how, with spices we'd stockpiled for generations. Hot sauces, so far off the scale of Scoville units that the word *atomic* wasn't mere hyperbole, found their way into their meals. Prunes that seemed to explode in the intestinal tract. Glass noodles containing actual bits of glass. We were able to beat them back to the border within a matter of weeks. But knowing that our ultimate sources were outside, they ringed the city and froze any incoming traffic. We exhaled collectively, went back to life as usual, waited. Figured this was merely the first of several retreats.

They never came. Here, then, we remain, almost a decade later, turned inward, having exhausted our once-plentiful reserves. Some of us who know the older epics, who see the murals and remember the tough times from which we sprang, retain a modicum of hope. But there are reasons for despair, too. Already there is rumor of cannibalism in some quarters, though if I know my fellow citizens, it will be unlike any cannibalism ever witnessed: the bodies prepared in fiery sauces that have been hidden away for years, garnished in artichoke hearts marinated in many-pressed oils, sprinkled with tarragon and sage culled from a window box, with side dishes of pâté whose richness reveals decades of fine dining.

Me, I write. Though I've made this rind of a building my base for the past few weeks, I'll move again, as I always have. I don't sleep in the same place for long. And one day, maybe I'll slip across the border. Maybe I'm Maz, or maybe I've just studied his columns long enough to have usurped his name and style as my best bets for survival. For now, I bide my time and vie with the four- and three-legged for scraps. I still can't bring myself to talk about the food that's in front of me, no matter how simple and crumblike it is. Instead, I walk the length of an endless table of memory on which reside the imprints of the thousands of meals I've savored, each having done its turn on my tongue and fading to a spectral place, flaring up momentarily in words and then passing briefly, if I've done my job, to your own buds. These memories—more, even, than my city, my writing hand, my life, even my sense of taste itself—are what I fear losing most.

Runaroundandscreamalot!

SIR PLAYALOT! reads the long sign across the front. It is a cold, rainy Wednesday. This is where Pete brings her on cold, rainy Wednesdays—you might say that this is The Place to Be on Wednesdays of a chilly, precipitation-ridden disposition. His weekday with Sasha, and every other weekend. Not the most conventional custody arrangement, not that Pete has researched the History of Custody from top to bottom, but because Bethany fought for a teaching schedule where all of her classes clump on Wednesday and had to go all high noon with the dean about it and him working out of the apartment these days when he works at all, he figures it's the best arrangement. So here they are.

Sasha disappears into the series of semitranslucent tubes that form the "crawlbyrinth" that must cover about a quarter of the surface area of the place. He exhales—it's been a long morning, rain never a boon to parenting. It feels like the gutters are funneling through him. He turns toward the woman nearby, who is watching what must be her son. The boy is Asian and she not evidently so. On a chalkboard the boy's drawn a dragon that you can actually tell is a dragon, and he is young enough that this is noteworthy, unless the dragon was there to begin with and he is just coloring over it, in which case his achievement is far more modest. Either way she is dirty blond and wears formfitting jeans and a tight black petticoat, and he senses that she wouldn't mind talking to him, either. They have not actually smiled at each other but have presmiled.

Her son inverts the chalk and begins a series of stabs at the dragon, yelling, "Die! Die!"

"Hanh, Hanh," she calls out—he sees the kid's tagged his name in giant letters next to the dragon—and she shoots Pete a look which he interprets as "Respect me in spite of and possibly a bit more for my son's crazed rambunctious streak?" And he tries to shrug and nod in a way that conveys "Hey, just us parents in here, all figuring out this parent thing together." Since becoming a dad he talks less and gestures more, and he wonders if this is the case for all parents, too fatigued to form words but able to speak volumes in a shrug, a twitch.

Rain pummels the roof, concentrating, it would seem, directly above his head. With weather this grim and his apartment's disarray, it was a no-brainer to come here after he swung by to get Sasha at half-day kindergarten. Her second week—everything still so new, the hermit crab still known as "the crab."

It's irksome that Sir Playalot! doesn't have more to offer. Months ago, they exhausted the snail slide, the light-up sound-off hopscotch courts, the crawlbyrinth, the mini-mini golf course, the plastic castle, the climbing web forged from high-tech materials (from a local company—Pete recognizes their suspension bridge logo; he knows a guy that works there) with just enough give so that they can dangle without drooping such that Pete himself clambered up and would've stayed on if Sasha hadn't started screaming because her braids, the ones her mother'd tied that morning, were coming, in the unconscionable way of things done distractedly, undone. Like he'd minored in the braidal arts.

If Pete were in charge of Sir Playalot! he'd do things just a tad different.

He says as much to Hanh's mommy, what the hell. Not

solely because he sees that her T-shirt exposes if not her actual nipples, then at the very least a brassiere that implies nipples in the sense that boarded-up windows in a building strongly indicate poverty or the aftermath of a fire.

"Oh yeah?" She laughs. "What exactly would you do?" Her tone—part conspiracy, part challenge—feels like a gift.

"Do you want the short list or the long one?"

He glances toward the register, making sure that Tru, the irrepressible Trudy Renfro, won't hear him. He doesn't want to impugn either her business or her humanity. No doubt she opened the place partly out of the need to put food on her own table, a motive with which Pete can wholly identify, and partly because she loves kids and parents and knows that in this community their options are limited, have been since the toxic glaze was found slathered onto wood at the playground, glaze that, however pretty it made the wood—and make no mistake, this was a playground that made out-of-towners slam their brakes, risking the minor fender bender for the prospect of giving their kids the opportunity to hone their playing muscles there—was leaching onto children's bodies as they were sliding and monkey-barring and playing video game tag. To this day, one could forgive but not forget the local headline, a single glaring insult-to-injury typo: LEECHING. The playground, after sucking bone-dry a bond issue that'd already had neighbors nearly in fisticuffs, remained fenced off. Thank goodness Tru had cut the ribbon on Sir Playalot! just a month later, rushing in to fill the void.

What would he do differently?

Better yet, what would *Angus* do differently? His brother would look at a place like this like a shark set loose in a shad tank.

"For starters, I'd rename the place Runaroundandscreamalot! I mean, look around." It's what he always calls it with Sasha—not like he came up with that on the spot or anything.

But she smiles, so he rolls with it. "And that castle? A little bland, wouldn't you say?"

"How would you spruce it up?"

Spruce—what a lovely word, all gum and old-growth forest. "Okay," he muses, trying not to betray how much thought he's given it already, that since the first time he came here that it was no longer an adult video shop, he's sort of been redesigning it in his mind like "Sim City," one of the exercises Angus has taught him to keep his mind sharp. "How about a moat? One filled with little balls or something squishy you could dip your feet into. Or keep it simple—water. And a cave of some kind. Who doesn't love a cave? With stalagmites, stalactites, and perhaps some Paleolithic paint so that Hanh"—he thumbs toward the lad as if he's known him since utero—"can throw up his best bison." What else? "A zip line, maybe just a small one that goes from here to—oh, you go deal with that."

Hanh has seized cardboard bricks from a tearful blond girl. Mom materializes at Hanh's side, laying hands on the bricks and efficiently guiding them back to their rightful owner. She choreographs an apology from Hanh and then directs her own to the girl's mother in a manner so unnervingly familiar to Pete that it reminds him he'd better check on Sasha.

The crawlbyrinth looks kind of like a greenhouse in which human children are being cultivated. It is not quite big enough to get fully lost in. When he and Bethany were still married, he'd been in a corn maze with her and three-year-old Sasha, and they'd gotten completely disoriented. You think corn is wholesome and don't think about getting seriously lost, the same way you don't think about corn syrup as pulverizing the liver unless you find yourself listening to NPR a whole lot. Unless NPR becomes your best pal-o. Remembering that maze, he recalls Sasha starting to stamp and grimace, and his growing certainty that they weren't anywhere near the exit, and how it appeared to repeat itself like low-budget animation, the corn starting to look ominous and spiky. Thankfully with the crawlbyrinth you can see in and out, which is nice, but you still have to figure out which tube goes from A to B, and it's not like he can go and rescue her without a great deal of contortionism, and he's not sure Tru would be A-OK with him traipsing atop the contraption. Luckily, he spots Sasha from the edge, but less luckily, she is chasing some boy, who looks like he is past the enjoyment stage of their tête-à-tête.

Pete crouches, remembering how strange the acoustics of these plastic catacombs can be, and he's about to dive in even though he's not sure he can squeeze through the turns, but then he simply bellows her name and his tunnely voice must have found its way through because he can see her make her way toward him.

As he waits he wonders what he'll say next to Hanh's mom because probably rattling off more revamping schemes will seem both egotistical and daft. Maybe he'll chortle, "Well, it looks like both our kids are bullies!" But no, *bully* is charged, like *terrorist* or *sex offender*, and he doesn't want to label her son, just as he wouldn't want anyone to label Sasha. Even if it might be accurate—there are, are there not, bona fide terrorists and sex offenders, and so, too, the universe must have its portion of bullies and he suspects Sasha might be one. He and Bethany can't for the life of them figure it out—her hair is Bethany's auburn-brown, her eyes are his, and the nose phases between the Nanas', but when it comes to behavior, the nucleic acids throw them for a loop. Just last week a boy got a lesson in gravity off one of those dome-shaped metal structures at recess, not a banner way to start kindergarten.

He's always considered himself an "identify the cause, then troubleshoot" kind of guy, but when it comes to Sasha, all that's out the window. He'll just take the solution, thanks. But the divorce! Wouldn't it be nice to just point to the divorce and be able to say, "That's it!" like collaring a criminal out of a lineup?

But it's more like global warming, a lot of disputation about the root causes. Because the truth of the matter is that the bullying predated the divorce. It started back in play group, with the inescapable reality that Sasha was brute-factually larger than her peers and, unless adults intervened, could rearrange reality quite handily. There were plenty of things she couldn't do, but running headlong at Samantha Crisp or extracting Ben Mulcahey from a swing were not among them.

She sounds asthmatic when she emerges. "Da . . . ddy!"

"What, honey?"

She grabs him and starts to pull him toward the hopscotch. Oxlike, she gets him off balance and he actually stumbles a little bit. He regains his ground, reinstates proper Dad-mode. "Hold on, hon. What was going on with that boy in there?"

She's breathing too heavily to answer right away, or she is exaggerating to not have to. "That . . . boy . . . was . . . the . . . monster . . . in . . . the . . . maze. And I . . . was . . . the maze . . . solutioner."

By now, the boy has been flung like a dishrag over the shoulder of his equally diminutive mother. The monster is a mewling mess; the maze solutioner is . . . funny, cute. He'd like to tell Bethany about this, but she won't appreciate it coming from him. He says, "It's time to go apologize."

"Why, Dad?" she says, and for a moment his heart breaks, because her panicky expression evinces that she knows she's done it again.

There was a time when the postfight debrief would've been more of a hearing, more nuanced: "What happened? Are you sure she did that? Are you sure he did that?" Now he's gotten lazy. It's easier to just say "Sorry," to hoard responsibility even if it ought to be shared. Sasha's gotten used to it, too, he knows. He sees how quickly she dons the expression of guilt, as if it is the most natural one in her repertoire, her default.

Spotting Hanh, who's flailing crazily, he observes, "That

boy's going through a rough period, isn't he?" He sounds like Bethany, he realizes. But euphemism feels sweet on the tongue, and he can see something ease in Sasha, the frogs on her feet no longer resisting.

"Why is he doing that?"

"I'm not sure, honey. We'll go see him afterward." He brings her over to the maze monster, whose mother has the frazzled look of someone he thinks would say, when asked, that she loves being a mom, just not today. "We wanted to apologize," he announces. "Sasha?"

But she is twisting, still studying Hanh. "Sasha, do you have something to say to this boy?"

"It's all right," says Mom. "We needed to go anyway," says Mom. She is dangling her son and whispering to him and squirting liberally from the Sanitizer, the superhero that Tru has set up with Purell so that it glops out of a hole cut out of his rippling, muscular chest. From his mother's shoulder, the boy stares placidly at Sasha like he is observing a ferocious animal through Plexiglas.

"Sasha," Pete tugs her arm. But they storm off. "We're sorry!" Pete calls out.

Maybe, he thinks, going over to commiserate with Hanh and his mom will be the best bet. Maybe if she can see another bully up close, it will be like *Scared Straight*. It will be like holding a mirror up to her, and maybe he can use her budding inner Narcissus to send a message.

"Would you like to meet Hanh?"

"Hanh?"

"Hanh," he says, as if he's an old college buddy of his who's just showed up.

They stroll over. Hanh is lying on his back and his muscles are all scrunched up, so that he looks like someone on television who would lift and then eat a car. "Well," Pete says. "Looks like the weather's got everyone bent out of shape."

"I actually thrive on this weather, I think," she says.

"Oh yeah?"

"Yes. I'm a rain forest girl. The Pacific Northwest, Bolivia. I like rain. I just have to figure out how to make it work with El Crankodillo. There are more negative ions in the air," she adds. "Or positive ions. Or something."

"Ah ions." It comes out as one word, black-and-white, whereas hers are akin to the Matisses he sees in this video game he's been playing. He tries to picture where Bolivia is on the map. Again he channels Angus. "We'll put the rain forest in that corner."

"Deal," she says.

He sees the needle glint of an opportunity to go deeper than this joviality. "What brought you to Bolivia?"

"Fungi. The study of."

"Mushrooms," he says, immediately thinking that insiders probably don't call them "mushrooms," that maybe using the word *mushrooms* is like calling someone "colored" or denotes a telltale amateurism, like the way someone who doesn't know much about Mexican food like his parents will always order crispy beef tacos to be safe.

To his relief, she echoes, "Mushrooms."

He almost tells her about the time in college that he and Ethan Mellor took shrooms and wandered off into the middle of the woods and emerged in the midst of a gathering of Revolutionary War reenactors and he became convinced that all of the post-1700s history of America that he'd experienced was a strange dream. Even afterward, when the shrooms wore off and he was no longer shaking his head at Ethan and repeating, "No, man, you don't understand, it was a fucking revo*lu*tion," and he'd returned to his senses, he'd felt as though he understood America in a profound new way. It is one of his better stories. But is this not the worst thing he can offer to a woman who calls them "fungi," i.e. to treat mushrooms as self-indulgent fodder for the antics of his youth?

Instead he nods. "What about them?"

"Well, a lot of traditional cultures have used them for thousands of years. And so I work . . . worked to ensure that those who cultivate them get adequate compensation, don't get duped by pharmaceutical cretins. Pardon me if you're in Big Pharma."

And if he was, he thinks, watching her crescenty lips and her bosom's pertitude, he'd turn in his resignation that day. The truth, though, is that he avoids even the over-the-counter stuff.

"Nope, nope. My brother and I are inventors. Entrepreneurial spirits."

She looks intrigued or skeptical. "What are some of your projects?"

"Well," he says, "We're sort of on the hunt for our next big thing. Not *the* next big thing," he adds. He's towing the Angus line here; his brother believes fervently that an ill-chosen pronoun could stymie them, set them back decades.

So as to not sound like he's totally full of shit he starts to tell her about the trail surface–simulating treadmills with six pebble-and-root distribution settings. Sasha and Hanh have both hoisted themselves up on the countertop in the kitchenette that partitions the "grown-up" nook from the rest. Hanh is playing with the coffeemaker, which is one of those ones with the little bullet-train-to-landfill cups. He's examining it like it like a toy whose features he hasn't mastered yet, trying out every button. Meanwhile, Sasha scooches on her stomach.

"Make mine a dople espresso, please, Hanh," says Pete.

She's grinning as she scoops Hanh up, and then he is kicking and screaming again, while Sasha observes, hands on chin, all Bethany in her expression of cool fascination with the nutty things people will do that are counter to their own interests, although maybe Hanh actually has a winning strategy here, maybe wants out; maybe Hanh doesn't want his mom talking to the strange guy, the funny funny guy that puts a smile on her frowny-face.

"I think we're going," she says, as collected as though she's delivering some rare Bolivian creature right there on the premises.

It's only after they're gone and he's left with Sasha that he realizes that to him she is only "Hanh's mom."

Post the usual wrestling match with the car seat, as they drive away, he says, "Do you know what Hanh's mom does?" as if he's known her for years.

"What?" asks Sasha.

"She studies the mushrooms."

"Oh," says Sasha. "Yucky."

"In the rain forest," he adds.

"Is it close by?"

"No," he says. Then he corrects himself. "She did that be-fore," as if he knows the exact time line of her life. "In a past life. Before Hanh."

"Before she came to the Runnedalot place?"

"Long before that."

⊲⊰⊱⊳

The last few times Pete and Sasha were here, the place was already Sir Playalot! (it's supposed to be a play on Sir Lancelot or Camelot, or both, you see—the letters are shaped like little castle bricks, with flags jutting out of some of them and even, upon close examination, images of children in cute chain mail poking through between the turrets and—well, here his me-dieval architectural vocabulary gives out). The time before that, it was an adult-video store, and Pete was horny as all get-out. Veritably in heat. And his hankering at the time was most particular—he was seeking blow job footage (not foot job blowage). The blow job, the grail, the thing he didn't get from Bethany, even though, as if to taunt him, she was an utterly oral person, always chewing or licking or even sucking on something that wasn't him. Now, as he makes his way around the space, he can remember, vile though it is, exactly where each aisle was, the one that held interracial videos, the one that was devoted to amateurs and teens, the one for thirtysomethings, the aisles set aside for "gonzo," whatever that was, and the fellatio section, right where now there is giant whale beanbag, like someone's sick joke. It is as disgusting as though a child was murdered here, the bones interred beneath the ground, he thinks. But he also thinks about the irony of it all, a thought that passes through his head sometimes, which is that people are obsessed with the very thing that makes children but which is the very thing that they/we must keep from children, and isn't this very funny, that we protect them from it more zealously than we'd protect them from seeing a shoot-out. Sometimes he thinks this is a really profound line of thinking and at other times he thinks this is tied with a bunch of other ones for the Most Mundane Thought that's Ever Been Thought.

❖

Pete has learned a few things while being, for all intents and purposes, unemployed for the past eight months. Such as that which makes something spam is in the eye of the spammed. He knows that emails promising obscene sums are ludicrous and fake, but after pawning his Rickenbacker and amp and some tools to pay his electric, and putting on practically all his garb at once when his heat got turned off in February, he finds himself deleting them less reflexively and aggressively. Their reek of desperation makes his own feel less dire. And while he is moderately well endowed, he can only imagine how those penis-enlargement pills announced by various other emails fall—like manna, missives from the divine—if one is literally in possession of a pin prick. Spam are like weeds, i.e.

the name we bestow on whatever we deem a nuisance. Since Bethany vamoosed, he's developed an appreciation for dandelions. They've got shitty PR, a lowly reputation, but that doesn't make them any less vibrant than daylilies or orchids or anything else. A couple glasses of dandelion wine with the industry execs and you'd be singing their praises, rubbing yellow circles on one another's chins.

It will turn around, he knows. People will want to buy high-end copiers again. It's not like he sells fax machines or anything. But in these times people are sticking it out with their lumbering old Xeroxauruses. He barely even gets to the second level of features in his spiel, doesn't get to live-demo the faceup assembly, do his whole "Let's grill us some content!" demo, watch their collective cringe when his greasy spatula meets the glass because they don't know the grease is fake. Almost never does he make it to the Toner Challenge anymore.

⊸⟨⊗⟩⟩⊸

Angus had always believed he was destined for bigger, and Pete still looked up to him, in spite of how the whole reality show thing had gone to shit. So *Obsession Swap* hadn't been the breakthrough crossover sensation that the execs were hoping for. Did that make it any lesser a concept? It was awesome to watch the guy who collected military models go clubbing and see his sequin-enveloped counterpart bidding on a mounted Northrop T38-C Talon. The point was that Angus *did* stuff, shoved his foot in many a door. He pitched to the guys whose Hancocks came preprinted on checks. Could he pay Pete back? Did he owe child support? Nay and nay. But it was only a matter of time before his ship came in, sails billowing. Angus—and by extension Pete—was really counting on the thing with the energy drink to come through. Balls to the wall, Angus had marched straight into the corporate headquarters of his favorite energy drink–producing company. The bastards would probably get rich off him, but that was cool, because he'd sue and get his share that way if need be.

"You just *gave* them the idea?" Pete asked him.

"You sound like *Dad*," Angus fired back. "What do you take me for? Do you really think I just handed it to them complete with little fluttery bows?" He placed a digital recorder with its little dangling mic on the table and pressed PLAY. It was a little painful to listen to—there were awkward silences, and Angus's suit pocket, where the recorder had been hidden, was loud, the fibers outspoken, drowning out some crucial parts. But the gist was clear.

ANGUS: Do you know what I find to be the biggest problem with energy drinks nowadays?

ENERGY DRINK EXEC: [uncomfortable laugh followed by hard-to-discern response] . . . would that be?

ANGUS: That they bring you this artificial energy from outside your body. It's like the same as the oil situation with the Middle East.

[Energy Drink Exec laughs, as if not quite sure whether Angus is serious or not.]

ANGUS: Hear me out. Consider that the body isn't all awake or all asleep. What happens when you sit in an awkward position. Like this?

ENERGY DRINK EXEC: Whoa. Okay, I get your point. There's no need to—

ANGUS: Don't worry—I'm fine. I do yoga. Anyway, this is just a momentary position. The point is that in about five minutes, my leg is going to be fast asleep. The rest of me: wide awake. See where I'm going with this?

Energy Drink Exec: I might, but isn't that just an expression, a figure of speech? I mean, no offense, but your leg isn't *literally* asleep.

Angus: True. But it could be. Imagine if there was a way to sort of lull to sleep certain parts of the body that you weren't using and redirect that energy elsewhere. Imagine if.

Energy Drink Exec: Right, but the only way I can think of to . . . [sound quality muffled here] . . . anesthesiologist . . . costly . . . malpractice . . . invest in . . . any health claims whatsoever.

Angus: Man, how's the air down inside that box? Let's transcend western twentieth century—notice I didn't say twenty-first century—medisick for a moment here. Know anything about the yogis . . . Nepal . . . altitude sickness . . . carbon monoxide poi—. . . natural anesthesia?

Energy Drink Exec: Look, I can appreciate all the time and effort you've gone to and the sheer . . . I don't know, crazy ingenuity that you've shown. Those are definitely qualities that we are looking for here at—

Angus: Right, look, I'm not looking to get on the bottling line. I'm talking about an idea that's going to revolutionize the *industry*, understand. We're—

Energy Drink Exec: I'm afraid I have another meeting in a few minutes, I'm going to have to ask you—

At this point in the transcript, the fibers began to scream and there was something in the background that might or might not have been scuffling.

Angus snapped the tape off a bit sheepishly here. "I could easily edit this out, but this is only for the purposes of courtroom evidence on the off-chance that they go off and develop a product and steal my idea."

—<><>—

Anytime Angus and Sasha get together, Pete gets nervous because Angus is the exploding supernova of creativity and Pete more akin to a minor planet or a major asteroid in the Angus-verse. He's paranoid that after Angus leaves, Sasha will be like "Who are *you* again?" But the reality when they all hang out is far different, as if Sasha and Angus are on the far sides of an awkward chasm which if not the size of the Grand Canyon is at least a midsized canyon. When he picks up Sasha, he will sometimes avoid mention of Uncle Angus because he is afraid she'll beg and plead to see him, having outgrown her father like one of those shellfish that ditches its shell at the first sign of cracking. Sometimes he'll ask her if she wants to see her uncle, a test. "Nah, not today," she says. Maybe Angus is too out there, too weird. Maybe they butt heads too much for the alpha position because of her own headstrength.

Angus, he supposes, could be seen as a kind of an idea bully. Let's say that Pete wanted to play pirates and Angus wanted to play Rooftop Apocalypse. The latter won out every time. If Pete was lucky, Angus would allow him to don an eye patch or deliver his lines in a vaguely piratical vernacular. Angus had this charisma, too, so that it wasn't just with Pete that Angus reigned but also with the neighborhood kids. When Pete read the Great Brain books, he knew for a fact that he was J.D. and Angus was Tom, though he sort of felt that Angus could have benefited from a bit of Mormon discipline, something to balance out his largely-unchecked power.

The legends have it that their father was a genius in his own right. In his time, he'd invented a new kind of pickle that was, to the best of Pete's understanding, inside out, and tried to start a company that would soundscape people's homes. There were others, as well. None of these ventures came to a good end.

It seemed as if Angus had picked up their father's ingenuity, while Pete had inherited his patience and gumption. Everyone could see what a shame it was that these traits had been doled out to two distinct sons. Really, Angus and Pete's father's ultimate invention would have been a way to combine Angus and Pete. If you took all of Angus's schemes and Pete's persistence—his willingness to drive hundreds of miles just to show off a fancy new copier feature, to get down and boogie with the toner cartridge with a flamenco dancer's passion and flourishes, a cumulonimbus of toner dust kicking up all about him, which he'd then proceed to mop up with equal precision, although segueing here into more of a waltz—combined with his diligence as a dad—the methodical child-support payments that trumped the need for hot water, his front and centerness at every parent-teacher conference, his good sportitude in being sole dad at the Thursday playgroup and the steady stream of birthday soirees and so forth, you'd have an unbeatable amalgam, Superman and Batman in a single body.

Needless to say, it didn't work that way. Instead, Pete and Angus stagger around like severed halves of a whole. It's like that parable about the blind men and the elephant, except that the blind men are right after all, they *are* all petting different things, and it is these disembodied autonomous quarter-elephants that are blind, too. And let's face it, having these traits combined into one hadn't worked out for their dad to begin with, so maybe it wasn't meant to be. Maybe crossing Batman and Superman is an evolutionary dead end, a nonstarter, an übermule.

⬷⬦⬦⬵

If Pete were looking to hop into another relationship—and let him be clear that he is not—he could find worse places to go than Sir Playalot! It is impossible to justify coming here when the weather doesn't necessitate it, and yet he wonders what would happen if he were to become a regular, whether he'd find himself striking up conversations with other regulars. There aren't all that many options for things to do with kids in this town, and so you will see the same four or five parent-kid units in successive places—the library for story hour, the make-your-own-pottery place, and this. Everyone is aware of what the place used to be, before the building burned down in a suspicious fire—nobody wants to suggest that in this family-oriented community there is a nonnegligible market for porn, no more than anyone here would use gasoline for anything other than filling up their car or lawn mower. But still. A SWAT team of forensic anthropologists wasn't exactly called in to survey the aftermath and sift through the evidence. The owner of the adult store lived off in the city, and those who worked at the Inner Emporium were quickly rehired to work in the new stores that went up in the minimall.

Those new stores are morally unassailable—a high-end coffee shop (all organic, or "organical," as Pete refers to it after Sasha), a carpet import store, a portraitist and podiatrist (oddly enough, side by side, so that one must pay extra-close attention or risk comic encounter), a couple of therapists, a standardized-test tutoring center. Pete contemplates what it would be like to work at one of these stores. It would be tolerable, he decides, if you rotated—on Monday, you serve up lattes; on Tuesday, you unfurl some carpets; on Wednesday, you are spitting out rapid-fire logic puzzles to overprepared high school sophomores and underprepared law school applicants. But to go to any one of these places day in and day out? He's lucky, Pete is, that he gets to travel all over the place for the copiers, that he's not penned in. But it's not luck, it's choice. Or is it? These days he's been looking at the scant classified ads every morning, staring at the same ones again and again. How long will it be before he swallows his pride, untucks his chin, and marches without shame into each and every one of these stores with a stack of résumés (copied, at least, for free)?

For the next few Saturdays and Sundays and Wednesdays, Pete hopes for another rainy day so that he can maybe see her again, the woman. Hanh's mom. Mrs. Hanh. Ms. Hanh-Beatrice-Kaminski-Thorunsson. Her name could be anything. It seems only right that the world should present her to him again, with or without Sasha. For he doesn't need Sasha, right? Surely they can make conversation without the safety net of kookily endearing, incorrigible kids. He tries to find her on-line. Maybe she is a famous researcher. But typing in the name of their town (and the neighboring ones) and *fungus* and *Hanh* isn't very helpful, although he learns some facts about athlete's foot and that Hanh is a Vietnamese name.

In an effort to meet destiny halfway, he takes himself places he wouldn't otherwise. He dredges up outfits that haven't been dry-cleaned in eons, takes them in. If business picks up, he could need them as soon as tomorrow. Plus, he's pretty sure the woman who works there is Vietnamese. If only they could get past the nuts and bolts of garment-readiness dates, he might be able to ask her about life in Vietnam, which could be interesting in its own right. Beyond that, he explores various veins of intrigue, actual or potential—in antiques, in tchotchkes, in cheese. If only there were a mushroom specialty shoppe. Maybe he ought to venture out into the woods.

Of course there is the chance he'll bump into Hanh with Hanh's strapping, chiseled, blithely successful dad. "Is that Hanh?" he'll say. He'll introduce himself regardless. Might even slip him a business card—nobody gets a lifelong vaccine against the need for copies.

He considers walking back into Runaroundandscreama-lot!—his official name for it now. But she's a woman of the outdoors, one who gravitates toward dampness and moisture and earth, not plastic and titanium and artificial bricks (yes, yes, all bricks are artificial, he knows). He could get in touch with Bethany, volunteer to take Sasha for extra days. It would be good, he reasons, for both of them. But the arrangement they've worked out is running smoothly enough that they oughtn't to break it now. Bethany's a rhythm person.

The next four Wednesdays are among the sunniest on record. They're so transcendently temperate, he can't even justify going to Runaroundandscreamalot! for the air conditioning, which he's not even sure if Tru is running because he talked to her about it once and even though it can still get hot this time of year, she puts it on only if there are a certain number of people there because it costs a lot to cool a space of that size, and there probably wouldn't be enough patrons to warrant it. Back when it was an adult store, he could remember, it was intensely air-conditioned and he thought this was sort of a poor business decision because being cold was, was it not, a bit of an anti-aphrodisiac? He didn't think he'd ever seen goose-pimpled flesh in an X-rated film, although he can imagine that there's probably some small subset of people that get off exclusively on goose-pimpled flesh, for whom smooth skin is decidedly lacking and who have to take hot showers rather than cold in order to get their passions to simmer down. Such folk would've made good company this past February. If he is not careful with his finances, they will make good company this coming February.

⊷⊱⊰⊶

Most of the time, Pete is okay with being on his own, but on occasion he misses certain things about his life with Bethany and Sasha. How Bethany would fan out his mail on the table like the plumage of a gaudy bird. Or the way she would hang up pictures of both of them equally, a true champion of photo democracy. Bethany even included Angus and his parents, and even his disreputable grandparents got some mantel inch. The picture of him and Angus at the beach (they are dripping, and cowlicked Angus looks like he is about to pancake Pete's sand castle, which he is, but he also has his arm around Pete) won pride of place. They are so young, so grinful, Pete's glasses so clunky, Angus so handsome, and Pete too, if you take the time to really look. Now that picture lies somewhere in storage. Most of all, he misses sneaking in to steal glimpses of Sasha after dark, her lungs working without any mechanical tricks, her macaroni-shell nostrils pulsing just slightly, and he'd known at once, then and still, where the word *breathtaking* came from. Always in these tiptoed forays, he was certain she would awaken, but she never did. When she stays over, he'll still rise, creaking, off the foldout couch he sleeps on so she can have the bed, watching her puffs of CO_2 invisibly make their way into his room.

⊷⧓⊶

Mrs. Dobbins, Sasha's new teacher, sends them an email reminder about their fall conference, which Bethany relays to Pete, also calling and sending a text. Pete would've been there early, though, grateful for an excuse to get up first thing and slip into a newly perm-pressed outfit. Sasha, too, is smartly attired. In a sour-apple-candy green dress, she looks older to him than maybe she ever has, and she's wearing actual shoes with laces and socks, not froggies. It's a bit shocking.

While they wait, Pete sips coffee loudly to fill the morning void. What did he and Bethany used to talk about? Before Sasha, that is, because post-Sasha they talked, he realizes, mainly about Sasha.

"How're classes looking?" Pete tries. Sips.

"Egh." Bethany shrugs. "Approaches to Society is packed. They should split it into two sections, but . . ." She makes a motion that indicates money that is not there. He waits for her to ask about how Society is treating him, but she spares him from having to sputter unwarranted optimism. He looks around. The floors are freshly burnished, and though the school year has barely begun, already there are displays on the life cycles of plants. He looks for Sasha's handiwork but can't pick it out. No dandelions, either.

What, he wonders at times, was his relationship with Bethany ever all about? What did they spend those endless hours discussing? He wants some transcripts, or one—he can extrapolate. But he can't imagine what that one would look like. Did they talk about quirky coworkers? Immigration reform? Guano-zany relatives? His projects with Angus couldn't have met with much more enthusiasm then than now. By whatever freak course, though, those conversations led to Sasha, and maybe that makes it all worth it.

Bethany chats away with another couple who have arrived early for their slot. They yammer about a mutiny on the school board and who will chaperone the class trip to the apple orchard, both of which he was unaware of. Playdates are being tentatively scheduled through the end of the decade when Dobbins steps out to relieve him from this purgatory. Ushering them in, she offers Pete and Bethany diminutive plastic blue chairs, set awkwardly close, while setting Sasha up with blocks on the other side of the room.

Dobbins has her act together. Possessor of a snazzy tablet, funded no doubt with taxpayer dollars, she summons up a spreadsheet and flips it around from horizontal to vertical.

"This," she says, "is a breakdown of the behavioral and learning objectives that we're going to be focusing on this year. Although I've split it into yes/no, keep in mind that it's still October."

"So there are likely to be a lot of nos," says Bethany.

"Not *yets*." Dobbins nods.

Sasha is stacking up a storm, leading Pete to want to say, "Are you seeing this?", point out her architectural prowess.

It's a really good class overall, Dobbins continues, a good mix, balanced, and without making eye contact with Bethany, Pete suspects that they are thinking the same thing.

"And *her*? Individually, I mean?" Bethany asks.

Dobbins drops her voice. "The kids are just finding their places, figuring out what to pull out of their knapsacks in the morning, learning my quirks. Sasha can be territorial. When she wants something, it's 'What do I have to do to get that?'"

"So, really independent?" tries Bethany.

Dobbins squirms, as though Bethany has reached over and tried to jam the words in her mouth. "That would be an overly rosy picture to paint." She taps one corner of the tablet's screen with her pen, and text pops out. "Let's see. She had some difficulty with the directions on the corn-husk puppet project. Oh, and she didn't bring in something orange or yellow, which was fine—we had some things here, but she seemed to really want a classmate's basketball, and when Sasha wants something . . ."

Bethany looks mortified. "I felt terrible that day. We had a yellow blanket her grandmother made, and it got left—"

Don't, don't," says Dobbins. "There are good signs, too. Great with the crab. Self-directed for extended periods. Exhibit A." She indicates the Amazing Stacking Girl. "And copying numbers and letters . . ."

At the mention of "copying," Bethany looks as though one or more disks have spontaneously herniated, shoots Pete an accusatory look. Not only pushy but her forte is *copying*—her father's legacy and vocational fate pitifully intertwined. Pete shrugs, and there's a crash from the other side of the room. They all look up, struck by the noise, its timing.

"Especially consonants," declares an unfazed Dobbins.

⋙⋘

When he bumps into Hanh and his mom again, it is at the Halloween parade. Pete has been joking that he is a high-dpi replica of himself. Sasha is a Gypsy princess. Bethany completely got her ready but then had to go teach. "On Hallow*een?*" he said in disbelief, as if it is a sacrosanct holiday, during which the holding of classes was inconceivable. The upshot is that Pete gets to march with Sasha, and when he spots Ms. Hanh he's sure glad Bethany couldn't make it.

"Hey, it's Hanh!" he yells to Sasha, as if she's been asking about him nonstop. "Remember Hanh?" She's scratching her head, probably only to shake out the Gypsy glitter that has glommed there.

They make their way over through the crowd. Hahn is a stingray. He looks pretty realistic, his tail rendered out of something spindly and sharp, maybe a coat hanger wrapped in fabric.

"Awesome costume, Hanh!" he says, giving the kid a high five.

"And look at you, a darling Gypsy!" Hanh's mom says.

Sasha backs away shyly and conceals herself behind Pete's leg, and he feels a pinch of shame that they have merely dressed Sasha as the latest developmentally appropriate gender cliché instead of being, like Hanh and his mom, fiercely original. Unless, of course, there's some popular cartoon stingray out there that hasn't been brought to his attention yet, a goofy but irresistible stingray who is always getting into trouble for poking everyone inadvertently and gets exiled or saves the reef from some external environmentally devastating force, skewering nasty oil riggers and winding up a hero, domesticated and garlanded within the undersea community.

"Sasha, you remember Hanh and . . ."

"Ariana." At last.

"Pete," he says, relieved, wanting to write it down but not needing to because it seems obvious now that this *has* to be her name. He adds, "Sasha's not usually shy. Honey, what is this?"

A woman Pete remembers from playgroup calls out to him from the crowd and makes her way over. He can't recollect her name, but the daughter is Esther, and now there's a beet-faced being in a carriage, but Pete can't quite tell whether it's a boy or a girl. Esther was always shier than Sasha, retreating, you might say, and secretly when they'd go to playgroup, he was proud that his own daughter was more a risk taker, attaining greater altitude and veering near but not in the road and every so often taking things away from others. Esther still looks prim and proper, her costume expressing her essence sartorially. Pete can never remember the names of any of the parents, but it doesn't matter—like the owners of sports teams or music producers, they barely exist.

"Esther, are you a completely elegant lady?" he asks in his sweetest Dadese, and she blushes, nodding, and for once he's said exactly the right thing. Now Ariana introduces herself to Esther's mom and he gets the mother's name and then loses it because he's focused on Ariana's lips, and then comes the blare of megaphone. The parade lurches forth, past the tiny Unitarian church and the giant white-stuccoed Presbyterian church, which for some reason makes him think about the person who painted it and, in turn, makes him wish that he had a job like that, lobbing fresh glop on the side of something, anything. They go by the Montessori school, hang a right at the world's smallest graveyard. The whole time, he and Ariana are talking, and every few minutes she has to grab Hanh and retract his stingray barb from someone, a ninja and a robot and a belligerent carton of orange juice. Sasha, meanwhile, has bonded with Esther and the two of them are skipping along like lifelong playmates. This affords the chance, kind of, to actually talk to Ariana. She and Hanh live in those new Riverbelt Apartments. She moved here to be with a boyfriend, whom subsequently she left. Hanh, she adopted from Hanoi before she met the bf, and she has no qualms about raising him alone. Right now she is working at the vintage clothing store, hence the fantastic fabric that comprises Hanh's stingray suit.

In turn, he finds himself touching on his own struggles—the divorce, its effects on Sasha, that it's tough to get seed money these days if you're starting up your own company. A tough time to raise a child, no easier for a brainchild. He says this as if it is true for him, not just Angus, and in the marching he starts to believe it, no more dubious than skeletons walking and zombies shuffling. An older guy, a bird-watcher, dresses every year as an obscure bird; this year he is the Mauritius fody. They stride next to the high school and in an age-old town tradition the older kids are there also in costumes, more grown-up costumes, a slew of boy-wizards and some wit who's a blackberry bush except sporting the handheld devices in lieu of plump, juicy berries.

They get so wrapped up that it takes Sasha to wander back and point out that Hanh's protuberance is completely tangled in Esther's skirts, and she is struggling to pull away. Esther's mother says sharply, "Can the parent or guardian of this sting-ray please remove him from my daughter?"

Pete rushes in, still high on conversation, swirling, something real, like he's just been gathering morels, communing with fecund things of the earth. He steers them to the sidewalk, out of parade traffic, kneeling with hands on their shoulders. "It looks like we've got ourselves a situation," he announces. "These stingrays," he says, patting Hanh on the head, "have been washing up near the shore and bothering—not bothering, *bumping* into swimmers. And these lovely ladies in their fancy old-fashioned swim outfits have been getting hooked on these stingrays. *No*body's happy about this, right?" He can see Hanh's eyes through the flaps of brown vintage fabric and Esther's expression, and the crazy thing is that they're buying into it, nodding along like he's an emergency marine biologist, there to rescue them. Hanh pulls back with a rip, causing Esther to cry out, and Pete says, "Yikes! Those stingrays *can* cause a little damage."

"But no blood, right?" Ariana's joined him at kid level. And the kids are disentangled, Esther leaping into her mom's arms.

Esther's mother gives them a withering look as she pulls Esther away. No thank you, no nothing.

Ariana says, "See what I told you?" to Hanh, but she and Pete are unable to contain themselves at how uptight Esther's mom is and, by extension, Esther, although the girl was kind of a good sport about it, the more Pete thinks about it.

This time, they exchange information and agree to get together for coffee and, as Pete puts it, "to discuss the stingray situation." She leans in and whispers to him, "You handled that really well." In the car on the way to her mom's Sasha says, "Was that Hanh's fault or Esther's fault or nobody's fault?" He realizes that she was taking it all in, and while he might be lying he doesn't feel guilty when he says, "You know, that one, I think, nobody was to blame."

⟨◇⟩

That November, they start getting together for coffee. Hanh is in afternoon kindergarten, and Pete splits his days between a couple of not-yet-expired contracts in the area and Angus's latest projects, as well as getting really adept at the game Docent, which involves leading tour groups around a museum where the works of art come violently to life and do things that might occur in an anxious art history major's nightmares. He's reached the *Guernica* screen, which is basically like an animated version of the painting, unlike some of the earlier ones, which are more liberally embellished, such as Botticelli's Venus having laser-beam eyes. The cool thing is that you actually learn a tiny bit about art and leadership while you are playing.

But to say that he'd rather be talking to Ariana is the understatement of the century. She's lived not only in Bolivia but all over—New York, Nepal, Oregon, a year in Austria. Places he has seen on television, places he assumed he and Bethany would travel one day. Ariana's been a model, the main squeeze of a sommelier, raised reptiles. He's about to ask her whether she's worked as a docent, but nixes the impulse.

She's been almost married herself twice—once he backed out; once she did. Such balance! After the second thing went up in smoke, she decided she wasn't going to wait anymore and started looking into adoption. At first, she planned to adopt a Bolivian child—she'd visited an orphanage or two while she was down there—but the restrictions were massive, the laws byzantine. As in adoption in general, especially for a single woman. If she'd wanted to adopt from Korea, for instance, she'd have to have been married for three years. Hanh was almost two when she brought him back from Hanoi. The conditions there were far from terrible, but she suspects he may have witnessed some troubling things. He's supersmart but loud and fast, and he has these strange impulses that she doesn't understand, can only speculate where they come from.

"I always find myself picturing his parents," she says. "I wonder what I was doing at the very moment she started her contractions. At the moment she signed the papers to hand him over."

He's never thought about it, what it would mean to give up Sasha entirely. It seems inconceivable. He could give up Bethany, but as for Sasha, this hand, the one tilting this mug, he'd lose first. He wants to tell her that being assured you are the genetic parent of your child doesn't clear up all the mysteries, not by a long shot.

Yet speaking of mysteries, something peculiar takes place when Hanh and Sasha hang out—they play so harmoniously, slipping in and out of costumes and roles and letting the other be when needed, it's uncanny. It's like Sasha is Hanh's long-lost twin. Ariana invited them over one Saturday, and the kids were off playing in Hanh's room, and there was such a stretch of quiet that at some point Pete and Ariana broke off, stood in unison, and raced upstairs, bracing for the worst. When they opened the door, Sasha was frozen, balancing some sort of lizard on her arm, Hanh stroking its back. The lizard's stillness made it look like a toy, and when it arched its neck, and its tongue darted, he was convinced it was the world's coolest toy, something Angus would come up with. Back downstairs, they tried to fathom what strange forces were at work.

"Spells are being cast," insisted Ariana. "Who is she, and what has she done with Hanh?"

"Her 'Please' and 'Thank you' without me holding up billboard-size cue cards?"

"The dregs of his Halloween candy? The sixty-forty split?"

The first time Pete and Ariana kiss, they are alone together in her apartment, Hanh still at school and Sasha with Bethany—but they both glance toward Hanh's room. It's usually so placid in there that it takes conscious effort to remember that they're *not* there. It gives her a chance to remind him she's not looking to move too quickly. Not with her track record; not while she's still getting feet planted. That's quite okay by Pete, who isn't exactly ready for anything precipitous himself. Without the ring, he still feels a touch naked, occasionally still reaches for Bethany in the night. Once he got up and went to where in his little apartment Sasha's room would've been in relation to their bedroom in the old house, and he stood there, staring at his closet for untold minutes before recognizing where he was. This is something akin to the disorientation he feels as he and Ariana kiss.

—◦◆◦—

Of course he can watch Hanh for a day while Ariana has a chance to go to an all-day conference on mycopharmacology, "(Much) Room for Growth." Why do they hold conferences in the dead of December? he wonders. Same nonsense goes on in the copy industry. The conference is just an hour or so away, and she *could* try taking Hanh, but she's got a couple of interviews lined up. Hanh is fine with spending the day with Sasha and Pete. As long as it's not too much of an imposition.

"On the contrary," says Pete, "Sasha will be ecstatic."

Already he is imagining the greatness of the day he will provide, one that Hanh will look back on fondly decades hence. He'll buy new art supplies, a simple yet award-winning board game. He'll have to charge these items and may still be paying them off when Hanh is reminiscing, but so be it.

He's just added puppets to the list when Angus calls. Forget the energy drinks, Angus says. He's got something more pragmatic, something where they won't have to rely too much on scientific breakthroughs that might or might not be nigh. "Vacation Redux," he calls it. He doesn't want to reveal the essence of it until he is over there in Pete's presence. "Just like you wouldn't propose to a woman—or, I suppose, in this day and age, a man—over the phone, you wouldn't propose a business plan over the phone. Not one of this till-death-do-us-part magnitude, certainly."

"I've got Sasha today," Pete says.

"That's fine. I'd love to see my li'l niece. In fact, we'll get her input on this one. It'll be perfect. She's part of our target demographic. As in *every*body!"

"I'm watching another kid, too," Pete adds.

"Well, well, well, Superdad," he says. "One not enough for you? Got to be like Dad and have multiple balls in play at once?" Their father had played sports like tennis, Ping-Pong, even baseball this way, with two and upwards balls at a time. He called it "multiball," and introduced this way of playing to colleagues, neighbors, prospective investors. Dripping with sweat, he'd call the boys in and give a little speech about how beneficial it was for dexterity, mentally and physically strenuous and thus rewarding, not to mention more in keeping with the way the solar system operated, with its host of comets and interplanetary bodies.

"I'm in a relationship," Pete says. "It's her child."

"I see. Have I a new niece? A nephew at last?"

"It's just for the afternoon."

"Look, man, I really need you on this one," says Angus. "We'll make it kidogenic. Take 'em sledding. Run through a simulation with them. Be a bro. In the truest sense."

—◇◇◇◇◇—

Ariana drops off Hanh that morning at seven. Freed from a puffy red snowsuit, he is still in pajamas and at least half-asleep. Sasha herself is wide awake and glued to a cartoon, but every few minutes Pete overrides her objections and switches to the weather. They're watching a storm, and Ariana is reluctant to leave at first. She makes a call and confirms that the conference is on. Should she go? Of course—she has a pair of interviews set up, and maybe this is where she gets out of the vintage clothing shop and back to what she's capable of.

Pete has everything set up. Not only did he give the place a thorough scrub right down to the grout, he's set up activities: a drawing station, a Jenga tourney, a ministage consisting of an old storage crate and some plywood and drapes. A pair of sleds lean up against the wall in the hallway, ready to plunge forth. Angus calls again; he's running a little bit late, and again Pete tries to dissuade him from coming. Having the situation at least semi-under-control, he desires none of the volatility that Angus inevitably brings.

"Be there in a half hour," says Angus, and Pete thinks, Fine, we'll put you to work, at least.

Sasha and Hanh are drawing their fave planets—Saturn and Jupiter, respectively—when Angus arrives. It's eleven o'clock, precisely. The power goes out exactly thirteen minutes later, the number 11:13 burning itself irrevocably in Pete's mind. They wait for things to come back on, and when nothing happens, Angus asks, "Ya got any flashlights or anything, bro?" Pete scrambles, looking around. All his preparations for naught—what good are immaculate tiles when you can't see? Angus steps out, says he's going on a quest. While he's gone, Ariana calls. The conference is a complete bust, the grid knocked flat from Essex County to the South Shore, flights into Logan either canceled or delayed. She keeps apologizing and repeating how stupid she was to go, and he keeps reassuring her. The kids are great, the kids are fabulous, the kids are all right, remember how they are with each other? We'll be fine, he tells her. After he gets off with her, he remembers to call Bethany, too.

Angus comes back with candles and matches that he's sweet-talked from Pete's neighbors. Lighting a couple, he insists that Pete hear out his business plan.

Hanh whimpers, "Where's my mommy? I want her."

"Just a minute, guys," Angus says. "Let's do this storm right, eh? Whip up some hot chocolate like the Aztecs did. Electricity? Pshhht. I don't care if we have to use cold fusion."

They pull out every blanket Pete owns, and Pete cuddles in with Sasha close, holding Hanh's hand with his free one. Angus, meanwhile, has retrieved a dry-erase board from his trunk and set it up, in the flicker of candlelight, like they are all in some Neolithic cave boardroom together, kids and adults alike. It might be as bad as February was, but it isn't nearly, because he's not alone. Sasha asks whether the hot chocolate is ready, and Angus tousles her hair. "Just listen up first." VACATION REDUX, he has written at the top. "So . . . when you want to take a vacation, you plan it out, right? Figure out the itinerary, go to a tour guide or a travel agent. Take the kinks out, et cetera. But what's the worst part of any vacation?"

The kids and Pete shiver-shrug.

"When it *ends*, of course," Angus declares. "'Vacation Redux' is the service that makes sure it *never* ends. We store your pictures, sit down with you and help you relive the memories. It's multisensory. We're not just talking about inflicting slides on the gaybors." Pete's neighbors, the ones Angus procured a candle from, *are*, in fact, gay, though how this is relevant under these circumstances—burrowed in these blankets, trembling on the couch, teeth jerkily percussive as they ride out his rant—is ultradubious. "We'll figure out what your favorite dish was on the trip and make it for you to the chef's exact specs. We'll bring on smells—lake aroma, eucalyptus, you name it. We'll have sounds. The blues you heard down in N'awlins? Or let's say you went to Maine. Heck, it will be like there's a loon in the room."

"I'll say there is," chatters Pete.

⬥⬥⬥

That afternoon, they decide to venture out to try to find something warm to eat, someplace warm to sit. The car, to begin with. The moment they step outside, it is disconcerting, the rain-rattled ice, the air a shell of silence punctuated by the continuous sound of branches cracking and hurtling downward. The trees are crystal, spruce and pine tipping, top-heavy, as if a film of them is paused in mid sway. With every light gone, afternoon feels like evening, with night coming on. Down into town they drive. It's ghostly and grim. The heat has come on in the car, and Pete creeps at a steady five mph. Ignoring Angus's impatience makes it easy to tune out the line of cars behind him. Screw that, not with just one but two (three?) kids in the car. Even the gas stations are all out, silent. The one that's open has a line of cars stretching an eighth of a mile up the road.

"This is *nuts*," says Angus. "Pull over anyway." He runs into the minimart, returning with crumbled Lorna Doones; they've sold out of water, flashlights, batteries, wood, hot chocolate.

"When did we arrive in the Third World?" Angus scowls. "Good thing I'm the King of Exact Change." He offers Pete a Doone.

"Maybe for the kids?" Pete says.

They can see lights in the distance, and Pete heads toward them. A single string of stores on the main drag has, through some fusion of fluke and dumb luck, managed to keep its juice flowing.

"Run . . . a . . . round . . . and . . . scream . . . a . . . lot!" shivers Sasha. She used to not be able to say it. Maybe the cold makes it easier.

"What's that?" asks Angus.

"It's a place we go," explains Pete. "Where we first met Hanh, actually. Remember, guys?" He eases into the lot, jam-packed with cars, like the site of a rock show.

"And here's the thing," Angus says, to him the ride merely a temporary hiatus in his business proposal. "Let's say the vacation didn't work out. Let's say you got food poisoning from the raw oysters the second night. Well, then you get to decide whether you want to relive it or—what *is* this place?"

They pile out and go in, enveloped by the light and the din. Familiar faces—lots of families, sharing their horror stories, laughing, rolling their eyes. Tru Renfro is in her element: running around making coffee and tea and decaf and cocoa. Kids are playing in their jackets, moving around, keeping warm. Pete gets them on the beverage line as if it's just an ordinary day and he's brought the kids here. Once he feels them settling a bit, he turns to Angus.

"'Vacation Redux'?" Under ordinary circumstances, the idea might have seemed slightly eccentric, like most of his brother's notions, noteworthy for its sheer audacity. Like it was not a good idea unto itself but in a slightly different world it would've been. With some tweaks to either the idea or the world. But here, with half the town gathered, trying to stay warm, keeping their chins even, it doesn't seem like even a decent one. It seems demented.

"What do you think?" says Angus, tapping Pete on the shoulder. "Can we say 'Best Concept Yet'? Can we say 'What time do the banks reopen?'"

Pete's catching more people he recognizes now. Martin Feldspar from Baldis Tool Rental. He greets a mother he remembers from playgroup. He's looking around for others.

Maybe Mrs. Dobbins will be here. He's got one arm on each of the kids, leans down. "If we get separated," he says, "let's meet right next to the snail slide." Then he turns to Angus. "I don't think people *want* to endlessly relive their vacations," he says. "I think they want to go on new vacations. They want to get back to work and make enough money so they can have a single vacation, just once, with someone they care about. And then they can relive that, sure. *In their minds.*"

Angus looks a bit stymied for a second, like a boxer whose chin just got grazed. "Kids, what do you think?" he says, dropping into an eye-to-ear squat with Sasha. It's the closest he's ever seen Angus get to her, reminiscent of when Pete destingered Esther on Halloween. But Pete had been comforting, hadn't he? Angus looks slightly scary. Hunkered into this awkward crouch with his fiery sideburns, he looks like some clown that the place has hired for the day to keep the kids entertained, but who will cause about 5% of them to wet themselves. "Do you like it when vacation is over? Or do you want to go back, keep your vacation going?"

"Keep it going," says Sasha. Hanh shrugs. If this is his vacation, he wants it over ASAP.

"This is amazing," Angus says, regaining his feet. "We've got it all set up. A ready-made test audience, here. People of all shapes and sizes. Kind of white and middle-class, but let's face it, who will be availing themselves of this service anyway, right? What did you say the name of this place was again?"

"Runaroundandscreamalot!" says Sasha.

"Yeah," says Angus, that glaze in his eye, one Pete can remember seeing, but not for a lot of years. It was when he was going to do something bold and fiendish, like in Rooftop Apocalypse, right before he doused Pete's shoes with gasoline and set the match alight. He starts to wander away, and Pete watches him break into a jog, weaving between the clumps of people. He's headed for the crawlbyrinth—but no, he's stopping at the castle, sizing it up. He misses the moment when Angus is in midair, but next thing you know, his brother is hanging off the side by one arm like some kid. At first this is amusing, and Pete taps Sasha. "Look at Uncle Angus. What is he *do*ing?"

Sasha starts laughing, and others are beginning to take notice.

"Attention, attention!" Angus is shouting. "People of Runaroundandscreamalot!"

"Wait here," says Pete to Sasha and Hanh. "I'll be right back. Wait together?" They nod solemnly.

"Patrons, regular and under today's inclement conditions, of Run-around-and-s-*cream*-alot!"

Jesus, thinks Pete, in a headlong race toward the castle now, the crowd parting for him. Everything has begun to happen in slow motion. He sees Tru Renfro coming from behind the counter, sees her bafflement at this latest disturbance, somehow sees in her eyes in that single instant that she feels that she's opened up her establishment to the public under these extreme circumstances, that this storm could be the thing that keeps her in business, keeps her alive, keeps her from the fate of an adult-video store and of the storefronts on Main Street, stores that had been there for fifty years, stores that still sold penny candy, stores that had opened with the bluster of youth in beniger times, selling fashionable things when fashionable things seemed like necessities, seemed important, when everything that didn't seem to matter anymore nowadays had, but all that matters, as Pete can now see on Tru's face, is that she keep them all warm today, and that's what matters to Pete, too—that he keep them warm. And here's this lunatic, flying from the battlements, cupping his hands and yelling "Runaroundandscreamalot!" The people are restless and cold and confused, plus there are too many of them, and on an ordinary day it would be a fire hazard, a dozen codes violated, and people get trampled under conditions like these, do they not, the smaller ones can die, and there are a lot of small ones here. Next thing he knows, Pete himself is leaping onto the castle, tackling his brother, grabbing at him like he grabbed that stinger, with that same urgency, knowing that he has to silence him just this once, has to seize the upper hand. Down they tumble into the guts of the castle, the inner sanctum where he's watched Sasha play plenty of times but never had occasion to go. They clutch at each other, grunting, and he feels the spittle fly hot at him from Angus's mouth as his brother curses, sees the bulge of his flaring eyes, their wild longing, and he pulls Angus at last into the embrace he's always wanted to throw around him but never has.

Urban Planning:
Case Study Number Six

The city that was in denial that it was a city had a weekly farmers' market that ran through late fall. It drew farmers from miles away. They had to drag their wares on the subway or through gridlock. The central plaza went from its pigeon-molt weekday self to a Saturday-morning bounty of fruit so bright and burnished it seemed to exhaust the light around it. They talked of the harvest, traded tips about fire blight, and muttered obscene things about those who took free samples with no intention to buy. One man made puppets of his potatoes and was at once a big hit. At the end of the day, they all packed up except the pigeons, who strutted and churred amid the fallen toothpicks and cheeses and relish.

❮❮❮❯❯❯

The city that was in denial that it was a city called the sky-scrapers "mountains," its giant central train station "the Butte," its industrial waterfront "the marshlands," its spindly bridges "land bridges," its vacant lots "the ocotillo patches," its sewers "the arroyos," its sidewalks "eskers," its elevated trains "cutbanks," its skyline "the tree line," its brownstones "brown stones," its city hall "the Glacial Erratic," and its mayor "the Fungus Gatherer from Between the Hills." Commuters, craning their necks in search of any sign that their train's lights were coming closer, sighed and reminded themselves that they were, after all, dealing with a terminal moraine. They glanced

occasionally at their watches, which they stopped short of calling "the sun."

❦

The city that was in denial that it was a city went to a support group for other cities with similar problems. Only they
weren't the same problems at all. One city was dealing with
overcrowding, another with a crime wave, bodies bloating
harborside. Another was shutting down factories like crazy,
its 'stacks no longer spewing. The city that was in denial listened patiently to the other problems, eloquently delivered,
but when it was its turn, it stood up. "Look," it said soberly,
"there's been some mistake. I simply don't belong here. Y'all
are great . . . fabulous. You"—it pointed to the nonspewer in
particular—"haven't danced your last two-step. Any of you—
we could grab a drink, catch a late flick. But at the end of the
day, we must part ways, we going back to our endless starry
sky, and you . . . well, we are glad to send you a postcard of
our starry sky." The starry sky was the two, three, and four
o'clock shows at the planetarium, which they'd dubbed "Old
Hoag's Field."

❦

In the city that was in denial that it was a city, they used the
expression "sweet hickory borne on the wind" often, but most
of all on days when the wind was carrying southeast from the
waste-treatment plant.

❦

Under a weird sky in which silvery pollution had congealed
into a solid concavity, the city that was in denial that it was a
city caught a glimpse of itself one day. For the first time ever
in its existence, it was confronted with its gridlines, its fuming
drivers, its onslaught of suits and ties, the dirt-encrusted blankets of its transients, its grayness, its dearth of smiles, heard
its Ornette Coleman horn bleats and medley of languages
and saw its garish mannequins and spattered canvases and its

sleek triple jogging strollers and acres of paper. There was a silence as a citizenry entire gaped. The stock market, aka "the livestock market," ground to a halt, and even the taxi meters knew to freeze. After a while, a fog started to creep, then roll in off the ocean, shrouding everything. The collective exhalation (which took several minutes) was powerful enough to sate ten thousand hickories, carrying enough of their scent to make cities hundreds of miles away weep.

Pocket

My father is semiporous. Even now that he's been fully disassembled and the schematics rendered in a dizzying cross section, he remains largely unknowable to us. Once we spun tops in the shadow of his rocking chair, which turned out to be an optical illusion triggered by the elaborate arrangement of pieces of wood that did not resemble a chair whatsoever when gazed at directly, and why why would he do such a thing the same question we asked every time we gauged his charged breath for negative ions not excluding alcoholic ones or caught him slipping sawdust from his pocket into the meringue. Oh, his pocket. Plural: Pocket. Not pockets. Pocket—like deer, like moose. His coinage. I can hear him rage still at those times when, still young, we threw an *s* onto the end; I can see his flaring hair and contorted features dappled with benday dots like a comic-book villain as he came after us. Other than that, an unstinting pacifist mostly occupied with his many pocket. The fatal gift of the multipocketed vest one year started it; we could only watch wide-eyed as his obsession mounted, first with the stashing away of wrapper detritus clip coin oil subsidy paperwork in existing pocket, then the construction of new pocket, pocket stitched lovingly and then stapled hastily and then merely outlined in Sharpie, "Home of Future Pocket," unceremonious groundbreaking followed by new pocket springing up like housing, whole subdivisions eventually, Pockettown, the continual fractionation of slottable space, eat your heart out Zeno. Infinite places where things could be lost and found, places where things could stay hidden and accrue scruff, fuzz, and legend, places where things could fester, mold, and potentially molt, places a person could go lost for years, the only trace a rivulet of sardine juice spilling down the smooth side of a shirt they wore but a single time, unless, that is, you count memory.

_____

(1) Pockets are like subway cars—profoundly democratic, messy, jumbled and crammed. Silver bracelet rubs elbows with snot-fed Kleenex and clings to its strap.

(2) I borrowed a friend's coat and then he moved to Florida, so it is mine now. But it is pocketless. Sometimes I flail like an infant at the sides as if that might conjure them into being.

(((()))) If the string theorists are right, the universe teems with hidden dimensions; pockets abound. To make even a single new one, then, is to play at being God.

Altered Native

1. Crossing Tahiti off his itinerary, Gauguin heads instead for points north in his gambit to ditch civilization. The more his mind has lolled in the tropics, the more convinced he's become that the languorous heat, syrupy voyeurism, and ornate adzes will merely reiterate Parisian clamor and clutter sans the solace of steaming coffee and *pain*. Greenland—now *that* promises true primitivism. Shifting ice tetrahedrons, shuddering rumbles, and terns' glancing landings will translate *nature morte* more exactly than gaudy mangoes.

2. At Sennelier, he stocks up on paint: first the *blancs*, *de Troyes, de Lunare, de céruse, d'argent, crème, ivoire*, and then some *rouge* and *marron*, and even, in case there's some verity to the name, *vert malachite*. He procures wool skeins & the least imposing harpoon he can find.

3. Arrives tremulous in port of Nuuk, a longhaired French bohemian in a cowboy chapeau. For months, he has scrutinized salt form from his table's edges, model clumps and ice glares he built to apprentice himself. Still, the real ones nearly blind him. Blinking and muttering profanities, he catches laughter from sources he can't tie a line to. All this numbness, and yet these sting. From children, the three-pronged

bombardment—stares, jeers, and a single snowball—fazes him only till his eyes return. He imagines they are critics from the Sorbonne and doffs his hat with a contemptuous flourish.

4. Dinner with the governor. In awe of the plushness of the quarters with which they've provided him. He struts his title of "painter in residence." The commissions will surely start rolling in. *Any day now.* He writes as much to Mette, to whom he is still wedded, making sure to include a special note to Aline, favorite daughter, his *maman*'s namesake. One day he intercepts whispers about a meat market. When he inquires, his hand is made a map by calloused fingers, but at the appointed hour, parting the beads, he finds naught but putrid piles of fish. He purchases one so as not to offend and wonders if he can render paint from their oil, the metallic glow like souls still hovering around their corpses.

5. It's not too hard to find revelers to gambol with under midnight sun. What Impressionists could do with this light; what Vincent would do with it! This long hair, he thinks, must go—it freezes stiff, like his brushes. But no, he catches himself after a swipe with the paint-flecked razor; how impetuous, what madness to bare his scalp to such conditions. Commissions, too, have frozen, leaving his strokes brusque and scattered. One morning, he decides he's a Shiverist, an offshoot of Pointillists, but by afternoon he retracts it: too derivative of Seurat and "his damned dots." Which to learn—Danish, Norse, or one of the Inuit tongues? Wavering, he makes sentences from slats of each and is permutatively misunderstood. Regaling the locals with stories of his time in Copenhagen, he never

knows they've pegged him as a Danish spy. Behind his back: "Gauguile."

6. Nauseated by niceties, he trades his lavish room for a turf hut—lean, gray, away from the heart of town. The light is relentless, it finds him, harasses him, and yet he can't cease thinking of dark skin buried under textile strata. A centimeter's exposure here is the purest coquetry.

7. Nuuk has too much of the waft of Copenhagen; he must find the prelapsarian, the primordial. This hunger and a kayak bring him to craggy Kangeq, twelve kilometers distant, the Giverny of the late Aron von Kangeq, a painter, an Inuit master, he decides. He makes it his business to see some Kangeqs. *Mon Dieu!* Is that walrus attacking the nude woman or is it performing cunnilingus on her? Is the man at her side attempting rescue or cheering both on? Returning to Nuuk, he will allow himself to be tutored by this *tupilak*, will in short order produce his own *Manao Tupapau*. Which will shock Paris more—the girl whose nubility he makes no attempt to obscure, or the hooded walrus looking on, big death longing for little death?

8. Missing his bidet, he nonetheless learns to crap with gusto and hitch up his trousers with native dexterity and aplomb.

9. Nightly he falls skin to skin with one or another non-Mette, some as young as Aline, though the numbers aren't spoken. It is the layers of heat, also without number, from outer to innermost that he most wants to capture in paint, and where he feels acutest failure. Other failures, those as husband and father, are only

temporary, he reminds himself; one day he will re-
unite with them.

10. Darkness gradually usurps all. He works in the hut
but dreams an igloo of Sistine proportions, alighting
on a ladder like Michelangelo to fresco the underbelly
of snow. Disoriented when he awakens, he staggers
outside. The moon and stars collude in faint illumination; his *blancs* have ceded to various shades of dim.
He should've brought *gris* but it will take half a year
to arrive now from across the ocean. To think months
ago he shunned light, hid from it! The pictures of
Mette and children that he's propped up around the
room along with his own paintings: often he cannot
make them out.

11. Still he paints. And paints and paints. And carves and
carves. Canvases rim the room: *The Little Dreamer*,
The Man with the Ax, the sprawling *Where Do We
Come From? What Are We? Where Are We Going?* He
surveys this last from right to left: an infant in a fur-
tufted *amauti*; at center canvas the tree of life, its
trunk an upthrust seal, with an Eve who reaches for
an apple bitten as yet only by frost, and across the
left he has captured three afterlives: Agneriartarfik
lush with berries and caribou, Noqumiut for the lazy
hunters, sentenced to a diet of butterflies, and lastly
Agelermiut, where the seasons barter their features
back and forth. It is, he knows, a masterpiece.

12. He decides carvings will not be his legacy. To heat he
burns some, burns others to work by.

13. Blowing warm, clear crystals to lithen his brushes, he
knows with certainty he's stumbled on paradise.

14. Puking blood, he fancies himself Viking warrior rather than syphilitic artist.

15. Over a century later, museumed, his works make spectators unpleasantly cold. Some say, "We should go someplace warm." "Starbucks?" "Tahiti!"

16. Into his Creeping Glacier series, fronds of South Pacific green keep slipping like shards from a neighboring universe. These, plus the nipples and pubes he barely conceals under walrus hide, yield countless hours of talk for critics and prudes.

Urban Planning:

Case Study Number Seven

The City in the Light of Moths

The projectionist's heart broke as the spool of the film he was screening snapped, sending a thousand frames rocketing through the room. But no, we are skipping over crucial moments: the groping for scissors; the hands, known for steadiness, atremble; and a last look through the thick glass before the lunge. The first cut missed but the second connected, and then he'd watched the life exit slowly, like some enemy combatant dying in his arms, so close he could taste its breath, watch last prayers sputter on its lips.

He'd imagined innumerable iterations of this, foiling terrorists and rescuing his block—no, the whole city. In his imaginings, they charged in in ski masks and released the radioactive xenon that glowed inside his projector, or forced him at gunpoint to put on their radical film, or one where the screen would go blindingly bright at some point, scorching every retina in the room as if they were all standing at White Sands, unprotected, followed by a sonic boom that would shred their tympana. His fantasies expanded and contracted but inevitably wound up with him as the guest of honor at some gala, Inez's thin fingers entwined with his own under the table, "*Wesssss . . .*" engulfed in applause.

Now he gazed down into the theater that stretched out

below, "the canyon," they called it, as if it had been shaped by wind and water and time, the backs of heads anthropomorphic rocks. The rocks were looking back up at him. Instead of irate cries, an eerie silence welled up, a thin veneer over a thousand sighs. He could win them back, he thought. Some down there knew him, some loved him, maybe not in the way he loved Inez, but still, the word suited. It would take, though, a move as boldly restorative as this was destructive, and as he glanced down he could see the film was even now tumbling into the room like floodwater.

⋖⋐⋗⋗

Wes was required by law and by the powers vested in him as a projectionist to get another film flung up there as soon as possible. An audience in the lurch, *in cinemus interruptus*, would grow restless quickly. Uncountable other films commanded the sides of buildings for twenty miles. If he was lucky they'd pick themselves up and march out, grumbling and shaking their heads, some to return never, none happy. His wall might get its first mark, and Hatcher would rail at him: "Wes, what were you thinking! This ain't the boondocks. The Historic District. Diplomats, power players. At a debut, no less."

But darker possibilities loomed. The rowdy, the addicts—all it took was one or two, plus swirl in a couple of drinks—who might come right to the door, and let's say they began pounding and yelling about tearing him apart limb from limb? He gripped the scissors tight. It wouldn't be the first time a projectionist had been treated to vigilante justice. Technically outlawed, such violence was, but judges tended to look the other way, as if they themselves were watching a film on the wall opposite. Case in point: that dude over in District 4.1.5.E who'd twisted the lens so that the film was flipped on its side, but still, these things happen, except that out of spite or obstinacy or simple boneheadedness, he'd refused to fix it, sinking deeper into his lip's curl when the boos and hisses reached fever pitch, and then when they'd yanked the bench slats out of the pavement and torn off the iron rests for battering, he'd still refused to right the film or even admit any wrongdoing. When they'd finished with him he'd been rearranged so that it was said that from that point on he would look at the world ever sideways.

Wes had always blamed the projectionist, but now he felt a shudder of empathy. Things happened fast. He thought of the opening of *The Wild Bunch*—lazy western town, women and children parading and singing down the dusty street. You knew it was about to be bad, but not how sudden and thick the blood would spurt. He reviewed his options. Under normal conditions he could change a flat in under a minute. Its seal broken, the emergency reel would hold him till he could get to the archives, and he had another film to change down the block, but he still had thirty-eight minutes to get to that.

But he stood paralyzed, stunned, not even sure whether he'd just seen what he thought he'd seen. Maybe he'd conjured the whole thing? Had that even been Inez up there?

<><><>

Inez came home exhausted every evening these days, eyes bloated and hair mussed as she slipped past him into the tight apartment and made for the couch. Her stockinged feet pointed at where some ottoman ought to sit as she swigged her cognac and Coke down to the ice in the imitation snifter, while he sipped coffee and geared up for his own shift. No, she didn't really want to talk about her day. No, nothing was different, nothing she could pinpoint. They were putting her on more projects, true. She was competent, had proved herself, and now they had her editing like three or four things at a time. She had to work through lunch and mind her crumbs at the console. She stayed late. This was how things happened, how you got shunted up the ladder. It was happening. At once she was editing a documentary about people obsessed with hats, a murder mystery about a surgeon whose twin brother has slain him and taken over his office, and a comedy with indie leanings about anarchists in love.

Such gear switching was inseparable from what she loved about the job, what she loved about Palamoa. Why they stayed—born there, they'd been suckled alike on celluloid, barely blinked a blink without a film in their peripheries. ("Film," went the song, "you long, blinking train.") Till he was three, Wes had fallen asleep each night with *Mothlight* flickering against his ceiling: semitranslucent red-pink wings that burst into petals and veiny leaves and ramifying shapes that then broke apart into a red-pink snow, all of it fluttering above him gentle as a blanket. *Brakhage*, the incantatory name of the filmmaker he'd later learn from his mom, just as he'd learn that she always knew he was asleep when his cries faded and she could still make out the faint crackle of silent film wending its way.

Hard to picture Inez as "Julia" then, hard to picture her milking and bailing, sidestepping shit amid the grunters and lowers on her family farm in what were then Palamoa's outskirts. She still rose early. Everything else had shifted: Now where her farm was were the cineburbs, and Inez turned heads (human, not livestock) in stunning strapless things and camisoles you had to study closely to tell if you were seeing through them, while the handsome barn, a five o'clock shadow of paint peel, had itself made an appearance in several films. As kids do, she'd plotted escapes—New York, Ganzoneer, any elsewhere—and somehow gotten sucked right into the city's center.

Once Palamoa had drawn ships and sailors eager to reverse scurvy and celibacy, rushing headlong for the inland markets, for memories and paid oblivion. While they got off their sails got replaced: The Palamoans redid ships from top to bottom, but it was sails that built her, giant factories attiring ships in blaring new canvas. Today's waterfront shimmered, lobster boats sharp-hued, whitecaps whispering of depth, but for the cameras, really. Wes and Inez, like many young couples, lived out by the factories, taking advantage of the laughable rents and cheap eats. As they walked past the old buildings, they could hear the outsized machinery churning out screens, and a figure of speech had it that you could still cross an ocean with a Palamoan sail.

—◈—

Inez must have seen things as malleable to infinity. Why scrub plates and ruin skin, when, with a slight rearrangement, you could put their dirt-bedeviled state at the front of the reel and their squeaky virginity at the end? Something like this must have been her thinking. How else could she justify such blatant neglect, like she couldn't see the piles she was leaving, the clogs she caused?

Wes cleaned up after her in those early days, not begrudgingly—since it was *her*. And it was a novelty to him—he'd always prided himself on his disheveledness, his clothes creases that blurred into rumples, scornful of those who cared about such things. He was gawky and had to duck under low-hanging doorways; his glasses were scratchy, and he projected for parties and knew where to score if he didn't already have the substances you wanted. He was a hipster. His tattoo was unique. It ran up his right arm, like something in Sharpie, a hunter done in a few strokes, sneaking up on a bright red bison. When he showed it to Inez, she traced it as if she might feel the pigments.

"Is it static?"

Wes had smiled. It looked static, all right. The renderer, a friend from the art school Wes had dropped out of, had done it seamlessly; even Wes couldn't tell where skin became screen. He twitched and she gave a little gasp as it activated, and the hunter pursued the bison, who snorted comically twice and then ran into a cave. The skin blacked out until, with a blast from the hunter's torch, light returned. The punch line was the bison posed against the wall of the cave, holding preternaturally still, blending in perfectly with the paintings of animals already there. It was gorgeous, actually, this last scene, worthy of the Lascaux artist him or herself.

"Wow," she said. "Play it again, Wes."

After he did, she pulled up her own shirt to reveal hers, not animation but black and white on the center of her back, her family's farm somewhere off in the country done as a home movie, retrochromed to look older than it was, her grandfather holding up a fish, languorous cattle in a field. It was tasteful, and the bump of her spine, jutting in the middle and stretching the screen in odd places, only added to the charm. It made his feel like an amateur sketch. Everyone had heard the stories about tattoos jarred into motion in the act of lovemaking, the lover helpless to turn them off, and he wanted this, now, to be the case for them, and, reaching out to caress the bump, he could see her tattoo refract onto his fingers, felt himself connect to her then, something that could still happen, then.

<><><>

And now he took deep breaths and strategized as to how to buy himself some time. Stress he was used to . . . they'd cut back—the economy, everyone hurting, probably inevitable if you could play reality backward as he did sometimes just messing around in the booth, but regardless, positions had been cut, and now Wes often did the work of, by his calculations, his gripe-boasts to Inez, two or three men—he says men even fully cognizant that there are fantastic women projectionists, Daniella Riordan, need he say more, though it wasn't all that common, convention no doubt instead of anything deep down in the helices. Say "projectionist" and, as with "doctor," the synapses summon up a male.

He's no doctor, of course, neither the prestige nor the pay nor, indeed, the malpractice, though they treated him and the

M.D.'s and the shrinks as equals at the mandated trainings on cinaddiction. He still wasn't sure where he stood on the controversy. Nervous systems so enmeshed with films that they were *needed*? Ask him before that party and you might've gotten a different answer. Some artsy guy whose name he can no longer call up goes to a film-free party and gets stuck in the bathroom—don't ask how—and in there he just goes haywire, hyperventilating and rolling on the floor. When they pry open the door, his eyes are husks of glass, face flaring red, and his fists—these he'll never forget—clenched so that his nails leave indentations in his palms. Random frat boy makes the mistake of suggesting he just have a drink and chill out. It takes six to pull the addict off him, face bloodied, and to drag him out to the quad, where something is showing. In minutes, he's calmer than a monk. Before that Wes'd been 100 percent sure it was all mind, but the single incident brought matter neck and neck. It was a weird thing culturally. You could still joke about it, but a growing number got classified and wore the wrist chains and took offense if you made light. Still, that's what the emergency reel was for. By law and as a precaution, he needed to get something up there, and so, for the first time in his career, he reached for the bright red wheel.

⊰◈◈◈⊱

Wes and Inez stayed in spite of what the world had to say about them, how it typecast them, the Palamoans—gluttonous image ingesters, perpetual dupes, back floaters in a lotus sea. Get a few drinks in her and Inez fired back, a side of her that drew him originally. He loved to sit back and listen: *Yeah, navel gazers and deadheads, like you're not going to find those everywhere? Come on, could we possibly be any more* dis*illusioned? We gaze at more navels—see more, experience more. Innies? Outies?* (She'd lift up her own shirt at this point to reveal her own adorable outie.) *Tonight if I want to I can see a film about gay Indians or the sex lives of Mongolian sheepherders. I mean, everywhere people* *eat, shit, fuck, and live their little lives, but we . . . we live across history. We know elsewheres.* He dug that she really did want to learn about all of those things, then, at least.

In soberer states, she'd extemporize about how Palamoans knew exactly where the cogs of illusion meshed and where the seams flickered by undetected, how life could be adjusted with the efficiency a tailor takes to a suit: a few seconds trimmed here, an inversion or two, a telling juxtaposition, voilà. Other cities may have known the wrath of monsoon and hurricane, but in Palamoa it was film, film coming down in torrents and pouring onto cutting-room floors, and it could unleash as much havoc as a force of nature, could sweep you away if you weren't careful, leave you stunned and shell-shocked on your porch, wondering what had hit you. If anything, the Palamoans were consummate realists: none of that romantic crap for them, no waiting for rescue, no delusions of being on some grand hero's journey. Their only deity was the mise-en-scène, the frame—the smudgy/hyperlucid/eclipsed/doub/led/fickle frame—that ushered in and closed out, made for happening and nonhappening. The line between abject cowardice and awe-inspiring courage might have everything to do with the frame and nothing at all with your heart. But, Gunther might have posed, what if you were outside the frame? Did you even exist then?

⸺◈⸺

Inez could talk a streak, but for a while she shared her innermost thoughts only with Mervich, Henry H., who'd attained some celebrity with Reintegration Therapy, taking the splintered, shattered heap that contemporary life foisted on you and making you whole, gluing you back together. *Guy's all the king's horses*, Wes had thought. The treatments, from what he could gather, involved cooking and consuming a steady supply of veggie burgers sold by Mervich himself (they looked like Martian rocks) and taking long, hot baths. Mervich was a millionaire and was seeing Inez thanks to one of her work connections. But she swore by him. That went on for several months, and then one day his fees shot up inexplicably. From that day forward, Mervich's name was non grata around the apartment, and Wes wondered but didn't pry, sure she would share when she was ready, but that was never to make it into the frame.

⸺◈◈⸺

"Into the frame"—yes, metaphors froth in his consciousness up there in the booth. Things can get slow; once he's seen the feature for the fifth time, even at a remove—muffled audio, twice reflected in the double-paned glass—his mind does some odd turns. So, for instance, the give-out reel and the take-up reel move at the same time, but never at the same speed or in the same direction. When the film is starting out, the front wheel spins rapidly backward, and the lower one advances slowly forward. As the film progresses, they switch roles, so that by the end the lower reel is zipping along and the top one has slowed down. But there's that moment—an instant, technically—the absolute midpoint, when the reels, spooling in opposite directions, must be, laws of physics, rotating at the exact same speed. As that instant is perceived it is already gone. The screen betrays nothing; only the one in the booth could know.

And isn't this he and Inez? In mind and body, they occupy almost separate realities. When she is working, he is sleeping in or running his errands, and when she gets home, he's headed out the door to project. Hours later he'll stagger in, hopped up on cola and movie candy, or maybe his late-night perambulations have brought him to a peaceful place and he can simply steal under their sheets and listen to her breathe. Only at extremely rare moments are they precisely synchronized. And even then, opposites in so many ways.

Who, he wonders on occasion, is the one in the booth?

⟨⟨⟨⟩⟩⟩

The projectionist's nightmare: *He is not in the booth.* Well then, the booth—who's manning it? The film running, the booth empty. Where is he? Mired in vague dream coordinates. And the film is hurtling toward its end, which he senses, viscerally as you might intuit the imminent death of a loved one many miles distant. Shit, shit. Running and running, he can't get there, anywhere. The booth stays empty.

⟨⟨⟨⟩⟩⟩

In a snap, he was no longer in the booth, the emergency reel up and doing its job. He'd already lost part of his audience, but a sizable number were sticking it out. He'd always wondered what the red reel held, secretly hoping it would be *Mothlight*. It wasn't—it appeared to be a history of film and the city: scene from *Cinema Paradiso* where old Alfredo rotates the projector's beam out into the square. Voice-over: "... *which some would call Palamoa's moment of conception.*" Cut to: workers hammering sail on a mast. Scratchy jazz, herky-jerky motion. The stilted quality of a flip book, its charm. Talk flanked by quaint quotation marks. Pleats, dames.

"Thanks for your patience!" he called out, stepping onto the floor. "A first time for everything! Please enjoy the show while we work out the technical difficulties upstairs!" Should've been wittier, he thought, should've been Wesser, called the backup reel "the reserve grapes," thrown in some innuendo about the busted sex scene. He was still way out of sorts, though. Anyhow, he could already see them sinking back into their benches, settling into a story that they could never get too much of.

But instead of returning upstairs, he slipped away, crossed the street, and ducked into a hidden alleyway. He felt the liberation of a kid playing hooky. On the next block, something epic, Russian, wintry was showing, and beyond that? It was a fun house, only a fun house asked of you a single mind state, that peculiar to fun houses, whereas Palamoa demanded a continuous pivot, a peering into the pockets of life as they turned themselves inside out one by one. The films were free, of course. It had been written into the city charter at the Dimming. They'd never charge their citizens—what next, tax their moonlight, nickel-dime them for the evening breeze?

That breeze, faintly briny, buffeted him along now as he walked. As a teenager, he must've covered every block at least once. Ever revising his route, its logic. He'd do this time-travel thing, careful not to repeat any era, meandering through history decade by decade. Chaplin bumbling around inside the house teetering at the edge of a cliff in *The Gold Rush* → the dank, misty tunnels below L.A. in *He Walked by Night* → the binocular dance of voyeurism of *Rear Window* → *The Apartment*'s sadlovely rows of corporate futility → the stills at the peerless opening credits of *The Wild Bunch* → the purple ambush at the close of *Vagabond* → *Pulp Fiction*, any scene, really, but most of all the car, the car, the car → *City of God*'s featureless roof rows, sizzling tempers—he could gallivant over a century, cover the planet in a single swoop. If he timed it right he could hit most of his favorite scenes. It felt like being on a jet plane and watching a continent pass underwing—desert, mountains, lake, city, coast. Going in reverse had its own pleasures, and if you picked your route wisely you could find your way back to the Lumière brothers and Muybridge's horse levitations, which felt akin to catching a glimpse of the big bang from the Hubble.

Usually there was no method to his travels beyond serendipity and his nose, free-floating in the zero gravity of visual possibility until something caught him and held him in thrall and denuded him of time and place. Sometimes hormones overcame him and he'd find himself down by the river amid the blocks of warehouses no one had bothered tamping up the paint job on. Xtown, where the moans and grunts, feigned and surely some genuine, of couples and threesomes and be-yond, would've carried for miles but were mercifully drowned out by the sweeping sound tracks of less prurient walls. The streets here, darker, cloaked the pedestrian in anonymity, but once he'd spotted one of his teachers there, a Mr. Youngman. Youngman had nodded but said nothing, as if to suggest some shared understanding, some masculine code, though from that day on they averted eyes in the halls.

Past Xtown sprawled the Memorial District, a veritable city unto itself. Here they showed solely home movies of the dead, and it was transfixing simply to stand here, taking in snippets of life, candid moments—a steaming blueberry pie outheld, a frilly bikini making its beach debut, gentle ribbing about an old clunker. Only the wealthy got their own walls; for most, an hour if they were lucky, and you learned to time your pay-ing of respects, developed a fondness for the spirits who shared that brick space with your loves. Visiting his own dad's four-minute, thirty-seven-second wall, he'd been struck at various times by:

— his dad's gangliness as he held Wes aloft at the beach and did voice-overs of some encounter between Wes and a dauntless gull

— how even in this joy his expression was sad, as if he knew

— though they never spoke, the mourner who came after him, a woman whose age he could never place, who'd lift her black veil only in the blank seconds before her own father or husband came on, then lower it immediately after, like a curtain

— the awareness that the moths who'd brought him such comfort as an infant had been dead, allowed to live again only as long as the film played

— the notion that one day the Memorial District would
run out of walls

Now he crossed in front of some fire-spitting cyborg that appeared to be taking on a meteor shower with its fists, and he
was filled with a surge of pity for the genre junkies, strung
out on one block, the ones who OD'd on these sci-fi films
nightly, or who dieted on a steady intake of chick flicks, or
those who pitched camp on Lynch Row, imbibing *Mulholland
Drive* for time umpteen (by sheer repetition it would come
to make sense and ordinary vision go bent and surreal). Even
now he would cross midstreet if he got too close to the hor-
rormongers, their eyes fat with blood like sated ticks, their ears
echo chambers of screams, their skin scabrous. They looked
like they'd come right off the screen and would keep coming at
you. A bit wiser than his teenage self, he realized that many of
them scraped by as extras by day and just didn't bother strip-
ping off their makeup.

That you could live here and know only your own kind,
rarely venturing beyond your own neighborhood . . . it amazed
him, peripatetic who assumed that the city was sprawled out
for him, a thousand gifts waiting for his tearing hand. Nowadays, he shuttled mainly between two booths, but at his core
he was promiscuous, wanting it all. With films, that is; no
such temptation with women, eyes for Inez alone, minus the
occasional glance at a union meeting toward Daniella Riordan.

⋖⟨⊗⟩⋗

No question this walkout would cost him. His job was probably history. Maybe he could plead with Hatcher, but likely
not. At the intersection he paused at the "Don't Walk" clip
with renewed appreciation for the footage of the guy waiting
at a corner, his comical watch consultation and eye roll. More
than a minor celebrity, "Don't Walk Guy" was an existential
hero. His "Walk" counterpart, who burst blithely into the

intersection, was tougher to find abiding human connection with. When his clip came on, Wes simply crossed.

No, there was no going back. The very thought should have been terrifying, maybe a little exhilarating, but all he could feel was numbness. No longer was he that teenager. He wanted the allure of what beckoned around the corner, but he could only feel Inez's image behind, before, around him, her pale body, expansive, folded over edges, rooftops, fire escapes, exposed from angles that only he and a couple of others had ever laid eyes on. Till now.

He rehearsed what he might say, tried out lines. "If you'd only told me . . ." "One nude scene, no big . . ." "So I'm a stepping-stone . . ." "I *feel* . . ." "Fuck . . ." Outrage felt warranted but pointless. Saintly understanding rang hollow. Blood pounded in his skull. Maybe what cinaddicts felt, withdrawing. He felt his mental screen fracturing: It split, splintered—quadrants, ninths, shards. In one corner he had her by the wrist, in another stared her down, insouciant in the face of her confession; in one they were *figuring things out.* In one scene he entered, drew, and fired three bullets into her chest and watched the sheets absorb her blood, and in another he let her discover him screwing Daniella Riordan in his booth; in one he was loading his stuff onto a moving truck and in another he had her hauling hers up and in another she was weeping and begging forgiveness and in another she was even now with *him,* the other one—another begging—he who'd been visible mere moments ago on his own screen, a place as intimate in its way as his bed, and Wes recognized him at last, some producer she'd introduced him to once. Now he replayed the scene, foreign shadows slithering across her body's dunes, but this time his own entered and intervened, and she clutched at the sheets in the universal gesture of the caught, and the film went on with him in it but he couldn't see what happened next.

⬦

He needed a blank wall. A wall without image was a wall wanting image was a wall potentially anything. A wall was a screen was naked was stripped down was calling, calling for colored ions to dance up and down it, lick it caress it make love to it. Behold the naked wall. The wall without image, rare enough in Palamoa that it bore an element of eros, like women's flesh in Muslim countries. A wall was a wrist, an ankle, a filament of flesh, an object of longing and craving, something with which one might have a brush but never possess.

⚜

The rain felt well timed, bracing. Maybe he'd been dozing through the relationship of late. Dots were there for the connecting. All along, he should have foreseen her betrayal. Clues peppered everything down to their jokes, obvious jokes, obvious clues. He, she claimed, was the stereotype of a projectionist: aloof, holding himself at a distance, never *taking action*, never revealing anything significant about himself and projecting—of course—onto others: accusations, quibbles, warts—able to see himself only via others. And he played into it, too—"Or maybe I'm just projecting here," he would say, rolling his eyes at the lameness even while conceding its likelihood.

No kid dreamed of becoming a projectionist. It was akin to dreaming of becoming the person who cleans the space suits. Nah, the kid wants to be the astronaut, free-floating from a tether, waving to the marble world, next in peril, oxygen dwindling, some critical part burned to a crisp and the world holding its breath. The kid wants to be *aboard* the *Apollo 13*, second wants to be the actor, third to direct it, fourth do the makeup, fifth to hold the lights, tied with fifth to screen the film, tied with fetching water for the actors.

Always, she'd assumed she'd wake up next to a filmmaker someday, thought this whole projecting gig was one long temp job. And for a while he'd talked about going back to school. But it hadn't happened. Over time, he'd come to embody projectionism, fused with his projectors in a sort of Buddhist oneness. Some might have been ashamed of the job, but not Wes. He embraced it, went as far with it as you could go. Not just anyone could land a job at 1.2.1, right smack downtown against the smooth side of an old granary with the antiquated equipment, antiquated except that it was the only stuff that could really do the job, which he'd tell you about if you had an hour and nowhere to be. Did you know there were anywhere between three and nine (nine!) reels that had to be loaded on to get through the film? Did you know those things weighed ten pounds, that he had to carry six at once sometimes; who needed a gym? Or that Wes had two blocks and had worked five once when some exotic flu was going around? Anyone could operate the digital stuff, be a robot like the automated system they tried to replace them with every few years, but it took a special breed to do what Wes did. He mixed films into one another like a DJ, blending them together, running closing credits into opening ones, dissolving like his hands were acid. One night he took a nature documentary and draped it, like sheer fabric, over a thriller about investment bankers. The sharks, gray apparitions too long deprived of sun, wended their way through cubicles as if the office had just that day filled with water. Was that *plankton* in the vending machines? Marvelous.

Word got around—Wesley was *one to watch*. He fancied himself a grand master with chessboards lined up and down, snot-nosed prodigies from all nations put in their places as he slid his retinue of warriors and church officials around the board. Or a Vassilonian chef who juggled several complex dishes at once, undaunted by the dozens of burners. His mom boasted about him to her bridge club, that he had a girlfriend and a lease, and assured him that his father would've been "busting his buttons." The only ones he couldn't seem to dazzle were the only two he wanted to, Inez and Gunther. Dissolve into—

Gunther. They are kids, still, on the tracks. They are, what, nine? Ten? In his memory it is a single long take, the day endless, tracks extending through industrial complexes and abandoned fields and farmland, the ties never letting you settle into an exact rhythm, the boys hatching schemes for derailings, robberies, and kidnappings of secretly willing ladies.

Gunther grabs his shoulder. "Stop."

Between ties, they pause, listening. Wes hears nothing. In the distance, the blocky yellow lights of warehouses and streets, not the single white one growing closer.

They walk on, Gunther chanting some hip-hop tune of his own devising.

Wes knows even then that Gunther wants the actual train, the giant projectile of steel bearing down on them. He knows Gunther will bail from the rails but wants the blowback of air, his clothes billowing outward, his hair splaying, intimations of death and danger. Wes wants these things but does not. He wants Gunther to like and respect him and hang out with him. He wants to go to movies with Gunther, but Gunther does not like to go to movies. Gunther likes girls, real ones.

Flash forward to full-grown Gunther, an avowed, unabashed anticinemite. "Just wait," Wes's mother had insisted, "he'll come around," which he'd always believed, but lately he'd begun to concede it might never happen. Gunther was staunch.

It was something of a cliché: You'd go anticinemitic in college and then become some industry clone a year after graduation. There were, too, the older ones who predated the Dimming and still spoke nostalgically of before, right up to the citywide debates that trialed their tongues and brought forth arguments of such verve and eloquence, they were sure they'd triumph. But the darkness had gone forward. Some had had the wherewithal to leave, but for others where would they go; how would they relearn the topos of sidewalk and curb, find an edible knish, decent shoes, and so they stayed on, their grumbling a steady soundtrack even as film lashed at their laundry lines, and it was fortunate that many were hard of hearing and kept to their apartments.

Gunther was old at heart, Wes's mom said, but Inez begged to differ, saying, rather, that he'd never grown up. Like Wes, he'd been steeped in film from the womb, his mother one of the balloon-bellied who spent hours of her pregnancy under the endlessly looping sonogram in 2.5.6. Just being there, the scientists told them, brought the unborn bliss, for they would sense always a womb that limned the world.

Gunther and Wes had played on streets that were studios and sets and theaters. How, then, to account for his demurral, his stoic resistance? Some wanted the zoning laws to be stricter, wanted to preserve some streets as oases of contemplation (as if there weren't contemplative films. See *Fog Line*, see Tarkovsky passim). But Gunther wanted it gone, all of it.

Of course he and Inez butted heads. He'd stare into his plate when Wes tried to bring them together; "Dinner with the Dim," Gunther had dubbed it. He'd held his tongue, at least, refraining from accusing her of "nocturnocidal tendencies," part of his larger rant about how the whole *city* was an anthill of cinaddicts, not just those with the wrist chains.

"It was like I wasn't even there for your asshole friend," Inez told him that night. "Your nut case, paranoid recluse of a friend. I don't get it. I don't understand the basis of your friendship. You're going in opposite directions in life. I hope."

"It's largely racquetball-based these days," Wes told her, which bore some truth. Play they did, though ball whacks were interspersed with confidences and discussion of Deleuze.

She shook her head. "This boy loyalty, I don't get it. If you were brothers, it would be one thing. Tell him to grow the fuck up."

⋗⋘⋗⋘⋗

He had the sudden urge to see Gunther, wanted his ear, wanted to talk to someone who'd known him since they were measured in inches. Maybe Gunther could offer something, make it go away. He changed course, ducked into another alleyway, little more than a crevice. Gunther's neighborhood was riddled with these narrow old-city vestiges, too close-quartered to squeeze films into. They were sanctuary for the Gunthers and, if you believed certain newspapers, terrorist breeding grounds. It was the most ethnically mixed part of Palamoa, neighborhoods that huddled close and went dark early. He hadn't memorized the way but remembered a temple and a botanica, and if he could find one of these, he knew he could find Gunther's.

Oh but the darkness was a balm. At that moment he would've stepped straight into another one of Gunther's meetings. The pitchest black he'd ever been in. Literally, they'd led him underground, blindfolded, far enough down that street noise receded entirely. Somewhere in the city's guts. It was cold, and even when his eyes adjusted, there was nothing upon which to anchor his vision. That was the idea: light purge. They sat in silence for a while. He heard his own breath, no other, and felt attuned to the slightest twitchings of his brain. An ululation arose, followed by something hornlike, and then, one by one, like surfacing orcas, the voices broke:

". . . out of a hundred . . . maybe twelve to pursue further, two of whom said they might come not sure if they're among us right now."

"One is."

". . . helped a seventy-two-year-old move to New York."

". . . alongside scientists on studies of lungs and particulate matter."

". . . book, *Palamoaization and the Posthuman* due out next year from . . . University Press . . . academic respectability . . . infiltrate the higher institutions of learning . . . the classrooms."

Drawn originally by curiosity, Wes knew Gunther wanted to win him over to the whole shebang, including the orgy at the end, nakedness and exploration of touch that shrugged off gender or orientation or background or number involved. Thankfully Gunther had warned him; Wes pictured Gunther himself reaching for him, or returning to daylight not knowing, and so he had opted out of this part of the night, which was fine. Plus he'd just started dating Inez at this point and had no intention of cheating on her.

"It's not even sexual, really," Gunther had insisted. "It's a bracketing out of everything that Palamoa stands for and embracing all that it rejects."

"Sure, not sexual." Wes wondered whether Gunther had really deluded himself so thoroughly in the name of disillusionment.

⸺◈⸺

Maybe he and Inez just needed to get away more. Inez had accompanied the higher-ups to a couple of festivals as part of her job, but the only trips they'd taken together were to Colorado, where Inez's parents had retired after the farm sold. They'd flown into Denver a year into their relationship, made a vacation of it. Altitude or psychosomatic reaction, the first couple of days for Wes were a continuous migraine, everything too sharp, vertiginous. The third evening, he strode into a moment as incontrovertible as déjà vu. They were on some street in Lodo closed to traffic, and after dinner and drinks they strode by a Cuban place where a live band out front blared a sweet old mambo, trumpets darting around a sultry crooner. A few feet ahead of Wes, a woman sashayed in a tight black dress, the correspondence between her movement and the sound track so exact, he was spellbound, and he wanted to point it out to Inez, who, to his delight when he turned, herself looked like a screen star. She'd been watching with him and declared, "You want her," and he'd tried to convey what he'd experienced, but she wouldn't hear of it. "You're human," she said. "It's okay." Then, suggestively: "Make it up to me later."

As they'd gone on arm in arm by the light of the closed shops, headed back toward their hotel, the windows arranged and decorated to snare attention, lit to magic, he had the sense that he was watching a film slowed down, frame by frame, and a further epiphany came on, something that couldn't be confused with sexual desire as easily as a woman's swaying. It was something like: Every city desired to be Palamoa, to be at once frame and light and motion. Palamoa itself, possessing all of these, was yet unsatisfied, for it, in turn, desired to be a single film that encompassed all, an ideal one that ran through all projectors at once, infinite, one that you would clip at intervals only so that you could splice more, newer footage into the old. He felt that if he could've only expressed this he would've endeared himself to Inez forever.

⧉

Maybe he should've called first, was his thought as he rapped Gunther's knocker. Gunther opened the door enrobed, like someone just awakened. For a bachelor, he lived well. His unshaven face and the extra pounds, Wes supposed, would not be liabilities in the dark. Gunther always had some blue-haired chick on his arm, some girl who'd quiver, electrified by his "opiate of the masses" talk. Usually the relationship lasted till the girl wanted him to move away from Palamoa, and Gunther steadfastly refused, citing Socrates-like noblesse oblige.

"Shouldn't you be at work?" Gunther asked. Wes caught alcohol on his breath mingled with something from the kitchen that had once been in the sea.

He explained it to Gunther—what he'd seen, how he'd killed the film.

"You're sure it was her?"

"Positive. I doubted it at first. I made sure."

"A telltale birthmark? A chipped tooth?"

"It was her."

"Come in."

Within, sure enough, was the girl du jour, her hair not blue but with the ripped T-shirt and spiderweb stockings and the Che button and one with a red slash through a film icon.

"My oldest pal," Gunther introduced him, and then, shaking his head as if he couldn't believe it, "a pro*jectioneer.*"

"Hey, man, I don't judge," said the girl, whose name turned out to be Aurora. "You're just the hands of the system anyway, not even like the kidneys, much less the brains."

"No offense."

"Sorry," she said. "You've had a rough night. Let me kick you when you're down."

Gunther spooned him some grilled scallops over salad and poured him wine, then launched into his spiel. Of *course* Inez had cheated on him. She was cheating on herself, living in a world of simulacra piled atop simulacra, nothing underneath, no foundation but for her makeup, sleeping her way to the top, but, as in an Escher, the top was the bottom; she was just a product of her society, her episteme, etc., etc., etc. Wes knew he should feel grateful, but the rhetoric felt canned—he wanted something about Inez and only Inez, something that would make him hate her and leave the rest of the world unaffected.

"Frankly, no woman's worth losing your job over." It was Aurora.

Gunther nodded in agreement. This took him aback. He'd been sure Gunther was going to seize the opportunity to recruit him for the cause. And he was on the brink of signing on for the anticinematic resistance himself, ready to plaster a wall, to disrupt a screening, to grope and be groped in the dark.

Aurora went on. "How long ago did you leave? How quickly can you get back?"

"I don't know. . . ." He, always vigilant about time, having lost it. Had it been an hour?

"This 'backup reel' is still . . . backing you up?"

"Maybe," said Wes, on his feet now.

Gunther sounded righteously aggrieved now. "Are you going to allow her to ruin your life, take away your means of production?"

At once he felt lucid, poised, coiled. To have allowed her betrayal to steer him astray, how foolish.

"I should go back, shouldn't I?"

"Can you?"

"It may be too late. They may have shut me down."

"Okay," said Gunther, pursing his lips. "Look. Here's what we do. *You* cut the film, right? No, the film was already cut. A small-scale civil disruption. Our ensemble, we'll own up to it. I'll make the call. We do that, you know. Monkey wrenches in the works. Switched reels, power outages . . . hasn't happened to you yet, has it?"

In Gunther's eyes, he could see that all this time he'd protected, spared. "No, it hasn't," he said as Gunther and Aurora stood there and waved him, parentally, off into the downpour.

⊰⊱

He had braced himself for almost any eventuality, but not the one he found: both films still going—*as if he'd never left*. Methodically, he switched the other film on the next block, then headed for the booth where he'd done the deed. He threw his full weight against the door to jar it open. Within was bedlam, since the first projector, never shut down, had been unspooling film all the while, hemorrhaging it onto the floor and the counters and every available inch—tentacles and tendrils of film curling and extending from floor to ceiling, a morass he could wade through, feeling it shudder beneath him. Like a drunk who stumbles across a highway unharmed, the film seemed to have avoided passing in front of the second projector's lens. Thus it hadn't eclipsed the other, had in some mysterious fashion altered nothing, and the crowd—the seats were still mostly full—watched on, blissfully ignorant. He tugged at random strands, knots, pulling on them and holding them up to the light. None yielded Inez. He could make out a house, some establishing shot, a strange beauty in its sheer repetition.

Releasing it, he flicked the switches, and both projectors fell silent. Soon enough this would become a crime scene. Maybe Gunther had already called, the authorities on their way. His time was waning. He flipped on the streetlights and could see their faces—*Again?*—and, film trailing behind him, he hoisted the giant reel and carried it down the stairs into the canyon.

"Ladies and gentlemen," he announced, "we're all the victims of a minor disaster tonight." He urged them not to panic. The anticinemites, it would appear, had struck. He searched their eyes for fear, rage, but found none, so, emboldened, he went on. Maybe they could help him find the spot where the film had been torn asunder. Together, they could salvage it, reconstruct it. Maybe—he heard a new intensity infuse his voice—they could stand up to whoever had done this, show the film, damn it, through to its end. Wordlessly, then, they began to rise to their feet, some quicker than others, and reach out, tentatively at first, then with growing resolve, for the film, each of them taking a small strand, positioning their fingers carefully, pinching at the edges. To disentangle it, they had to spread out, and the line that began to form went in both directions, up the stairs, down the block. He could envision a whole new way of watching a film, walking beside it, even zooming along at twenty-four frames per second— what a ride that would be! Their arms were outstretched: matronly women, businessmen with sleeves rolled up, a woman in a wheelchair, familiar faces and new ones, arms with wrist chains and bare ones. Even Gunther, it struck him, could get behind this. In the lamplight, they resembled nothing more than mourners bearing aloft a long, winding casket. All films, he thought—everyone—should be held like this once. Eventually they'd locate the end, the fatal wound, and remembering as much, he made himself slow in his movements, as if he might prolong this forever, might never find Inez, might instead slip inside one of the intervening frames and dwell there indefinitely, unknowing.

The Conversations

The first of the Conversations had taken place at once in Rome, in Vegas, and in Hoboken. No one knew then what they were, of course; they just seemed the talk of talkers, mundane as could be, the little dramas that unfold in the lives of all in front of the private audience of the participants and whoever else happens to be within earshot.

In Rome: a couple argued over whether or not it was safe to rent a motorbike and go zipping around the city. She cited the blind curves and the age of the cobblestones and the profusion of stray cats who might straggle their ways across his path, and reminded him that he himself admitted he shut his eyes sometimes when he sneezed on their own wide, clearly demarcated American highways, seconds when he might as well have been in an alternate universe, might as well have been tripping out again like he did in his frenzied youth, which she was glad she'd only come onstage for at the curtain call—and as an afterthought, she almost added, What about the possibility of a flashback? She didn't approve, left the room when he so much as broke out the pink Colman's mustard tin in which he stored his joint-making sundries. Now they were going around and around like the ceiling fan in the café, and the waiter, a squat, dark-skinned older man with a Father Guido Sarducci mustache and enviable teeth, was ready to spike their cappuccinos with a local liqueur in order to placate them just a touch, take the edge off their bickering. He, the waiter, didn't follow the news all that closely, being mostly consumed, when he wasn't working, with his collection of vintage early-twentieth-century opera 78s, his Gigli and Tamagno, but he knew enough to note that the griping of Americans had led them to the brink of global economic collapse and that this wasn't good for him, or anybody, and here again this American couple was demonstrating that most characteristic trait that marred their nation: noncompromise *en extremis adolescenti*. She should let him go off and ride his bike and pump up his virility, since that is what it was all about (though the motorbikes, in his opinion, were unbecoming and puggish), and meanwhile she should go off and flirt with some of the local men (ahem) to make herself feel better, preferably as her guy rode by on his motorbike at the nexus of a moment when he'd catch her in the act and—if he were to crash, then, at least it would be noble and meaningful. He was about to offer them a free dessert, which would surely catch them off guard—a tiramisu that the chef had recently perfected, its admixture of custard and mascarpone so sublime that he himself had eaten some left behind by a couple earlier that day, she who was dieting and he who was diabetic, and he'd laughed, the waiter, unapologetically downing the residue in the kitchen in the presence of the chef, honoring him rather than scraping his art into the trash. The tiramisu he was bringing them he had taken from the refrigerator and had sensibly lopped off half, still sizable enough to serve as a full portion in many places, Merulana, where he used to work, among them, that pen of miserly oafs and fifth-rate thugs, and now he proudly bore the dish toward the bickerers, anticipating their broadening smiles of surprise and then, shortly after, when the spoons met their mouths, the murmurs of pleasure that would inevitably follow, and he was making his approach when the Conversation ruptured and blew apart the room, glass counters raining down shards, chairs left spinning from warped overhead fans, bodies reduced to semiskinned skeletons that would still be smoldering when the sirens came.

In Vegas, a father and a son argued about how the son had played his poker hand. The father was a lifelong cardplayer who'd taught his son to play at a formative age, maybe four, five, getting him a leg up on his generational brethren, since the strategies of poker were among the eternal verities, as worthwhile to instill as alphanumeric characters and the hitting and pitching fortunes of the Yankees. The son was inclined toward long bouts of staring into inclement weather, mesmerized by window-splatter and downflowing rivulet, and for a while the father thought there was maybe something wrong with him, that his swimmers hadn't traveled in first-class, but later on in life it turned out that this same son had been even then composing rudimentaries (his word for the early symphonies), been absorbing rhythms and, as he would later describe it in an interview on public television, synesthetically allowing the notes to fall upon the staves of the mind. When the father listened to the son's compositions—and he did, he really tried, spent hours, reset his ringtone so it played none other, pushed himself on the treadmill to his kiddo's homage to Lugosi or Ligeti—he heard randomness, chaos, a defiance that his son had never exhibited behaviorally (his dad had all but told him how to sneak out, all but lowered him onto the limb that extended by his window, all but signed a contract to the effect that he'd look the other way if the boy wanted to meet up with one of their cute neighbors, the blond—what was her name—Nichole or the other one and run down by the creek and smoke a bowl and do some undershirt groping and some grinding). No, he'd been unswervingly a good boy, and the father listened intently to the music in hopes of gleaning traces of lust—for power, for nubile flesh, for market share, for bragging rights in the AL East—none of which was in evidence. So here they were out in Vegas, the trip arranged by dad, turned the big six-oh. All he wanted was to spend some alone time with his boy without his mom's platitudes, her admonitions and her sayings and most especially her voice, its cloying the sound equivalent of that godawful soap she insisted on torturing them all with in the bathroom, that floral ambush. And so he'd flown him out here, where the kid kept ordering some kind of lemon slushie business, and he must've reviewed the rules a dozen times, no exaggeration, made him a cheat sheet with the terms—*flop*, *turn*, *river*—not even anything technical, played out a slew of open hands with him in the comfort of their suite, slipped him a crisp pile of bills to play with (though whom, exactly, was he trying to impress with those tips?) and brought him to the 50/100 no-limit table, and the kid stood by and watched at first while his dad showed him the ropes, and when the seat emptied next to him and his son put down his lemon ice and got dealt in, it reminded him of when he'd taught the boy how to drive, a wavelet of nostalgia until he remembered that then, like now, his son proceeded to do everything wrong, got the wheel locked, drifted over the median, and now he's playing it too thin-icy when he's toting three jacks, then playing his next hand like he's got the nuts and the next thing you know, he mucked the hand, as if he zoned out comp*lete*ly mid-play, still that kid at the window, at the wheel, only now he's ruining not only his own fortunes but his dad's and, frankly, this whole trip. His dad pulled him aside, and while he would've settled for an explanation of the thrown hand, what he meant was, *What's going on in there?* and wanted to know *What will be enough?* and *Will we ever be any way other than this?* Whatever words he was going to drive at these were swallowed in the shattering, flesh rending, everyone diving for the closest table or bolting for the exits, a panic of smeared colors, till all that could be heard was the music of the slot machines and a roulette ball, its hops growing farther and farther apart until it came to rest.

◁◈▷

Part of what made it so difficult to detect the Conversations was their pristine logic, their lavishness with detail, the intricacy with which it felt like someone had put them together. They were camouflaged in the way a flounder picks up six or seven shades of stones from the bottom and presents itself, an unfinished mosaic, one whose tiles haven't yet been glued into place, and might just keep shifting.

The other thing that made it difficult to pick up the Conversations is that no one had the faintest fucking clue as to what they could possibly be.

—<◇◇>—

They were, it ought to be emphasized, about everything and nothing. They were about the best place to get bubble tea in all of Tokyo. They were about whether anime was a fundamentally self-aware genre. They were about ghost sightings and the existence of paranormal beings. They were about ridiculous roommates who left their shit *everywhere*. They were about whether that dress made her look fat. They were about whether it was ever okay to scroll through someone else's text messages. They were about whether the affiliation of Walt Disney with the L.A. Philharmonic was ultimately a good thing. They were about whether or not to stay in/leave/go deeper into Park Slope/New York/an affair. Loosely, they could be grouped under the heading of "disagreements." What they weren't were online chats, phone conversations, small talk, screaming matches, Skype exchanges, the letters pages of *The New York Review of Books*, the catacombs of blog commentary threads. They were face-to-face, live theater in the round, and called for mouths and throats and sweat glands and gestures intended and incidental and facial tics. No one knew exactly how long the Conversations had been going on before it was recognized what they were. It took a damned spot of time to figure these things out. To realize that some of the slaughtered had not only been at the epicenter of the blast but that they had been the fuses.

It was only with the design of the pocket black boxes that it became possible to trace them, to record them as they transpired and then play them back. Even given their survival rate in blasts, it was surprising that the black boxes made it through the Court's strenuous weeks of deliberation. They did, with the proviso that the only time their contents would be open to screening would be after a Conversation or if a Conversation was strongly suspected to be imminent. Over time, the free market took the boxes and compressed them, made them compact and funky, allowed you to personalize yours so that you felt some ownership over it, the sides aglow with yellow-green, imprinted with your floating genome map or a rotating skull. It was, like, your life. It would outlast your body.

When Conversations erupted, the recordings were scrutinized, weighed against the chatter of suspected terrorists. Translators for every conceivable language came to be in high demand. Voiceprints danced, nightly, across monitors. Crack cryptologists each took their swings. They manhandled the messages, parsing them every which way for code, from syntax to semantics, the shapes of glottal stops, the lacunae. They were checked against the Koran, Shakespeare, the Ramayana, the whole damned library. One by one, the usual suspects were ruled out. No shortage of terrorist organizations vied to take credit for the blasts, but their claims, to a one, were exposed as hollow. The sole thing that the Conversations appeared to have in common was this Rome-like quality—all roads led to the blast.

Once the authorities had ruled out earthly sources, naturally the zealots and the rabbis and the televangelists and the imams all weighed in on what was happening, since it was clearly the handiwork of some god or other, such that if we could peer into the souls of the dead, we'd know the very contours of their weaknesses and their sins, could see the *waswasas* that had afflicted them and driven them into these back alleys, from which they could escape only through expulsion from their bodies. A prominent televangelist, his church the size of a small stadium, giant television screens blaring his message hither and yon, decreed that this was God's *way of reminding us that He is in every single conversation, not merely those that praise and glorify Him and His Works, not only those that pertain to the way that his Word is to be manifest and its seeds sowed across the face of the earth, not only those that would chastise and rebuke those who have strayed from the path that He has clearly delineated, but in the most humble, ordinary of matters, the talk between a man and his wife, between a father and his son, He is unabashedly present in all of these things.* The rabbis convened to discuss the implications, as well. What could God mean by causing these events to happen? What sense could be made of it all? Was this simply more evidence of His inscrutability, His mysteries? Was not the history of Judaism itself one of conversations constructed in the margins of previous conversations, Talmudic and Midrashic debates that went on over the course of centuries? These conversations they began to carry on, themselves, in writing, kneeling upon vast pieces of paper like children doing some activity, their handwriting spreading till entire floors were covered. Until more was understood of God's intentions and the purport of His message, it would not do to speak aloud about it.

—◇◇◇◇◇—

If Tad McGill and June Miet hadn't survived separate explosions roughly contemporaneously, and if the youthful, slightly cocky journalist named Jason Tubbs hadn't been granted access to the survivors and put *dos y dos* together, who knows how much time would have passed before the Conversations were discovered? As it was, Tad lay in a coma for several weeks before his eyelids began to flicker and nostrils twitched. Slowly, he began to hoist himself out of that vegetative state, and after that it would be months before he could speak, and weeks more before his memory of the moments leading up to the explosion began to undissolve back into focus for him. Finally, there was the last leg, wherein he needed to be able to trust that recollection and accounting of events in the face of the obvious trauma, even with the parade of would-be biographers, Hollywood producers, politicians, gold diggers, corporate executives, et cetera, coming through his room. Tubbs clung to his bedside like some long-lost brother, tirelessly zapping his heat compress in the microwave, slipping him nicotine patches, you name it; Tubbs got close to Tad and made sure that—if and when there was something to confide—he'd be the one privy to it.

At first, he didn't even pick up the parallels between Tad's situation and that of this woman June thousands of miles away in Massachusetts. No one did. That both Tad and June had been engaged in conversations with loved ones (both of whom had, sadly, been killed in those same blasts)—well, these things happened. And then there was the interior experience of the event. When Tad came around, he described it to Tubbs, that sense he'd had that he was reading someone else's lines, lines that made an astounding, uncanny sense in the context of his relationship with his wife. There was a slowing of time, and it felt as though his tongue was operating completely independently of his brain and mouth, had broken away.

Plus, there was the mint.

"Mint?" Tubbs asked.

"Mint. I'm remembering it now. Like the strongest breath mint you've ever had . . . only, like, ten thousand times more potent. I can't possibly describe it to you."

The whole thing, he said, bore more than a passing resemblance to déjà vu—that sense of removal, of observing the world around one and even oneself through a haze, at a distance. And he'd assumed, naturally, that what he was experiencing *was* some variant of déjà vu or, shit, an aneurysm or a seizure or something, one that in the most literal sense tied the tongue, twisted and tugged at it. It was actually kind of pleasurable, in an odd way, a relief—like you didn't have to figure out what to say next, didn't have to censor yourself; all that felt as though it had been taken care of for you. And, as would become increasingly plain, the Conversations tended to occur after an impasse of some sort had been reached or at a point of extreme frustration, where those involved had been "going in circles," or had "already talked about this, in one form or another, a thousand times." Tad had been discussing with his wife whether or not it made sense to get their daughter, Samantha, tested for a learning disability the way two of her friends had recently been. Tad himself had struggled in school and only as an adult had figured out that maybe someone had slipped up. The Conversation had started faintly, like gum with its flavor already mostly chewed out of it, and then gone into a rather sudden crescendo.

ALEXANDRA: I just don't know if it makes sense to label her. She's *seven.* . . .

TAD: It's not a question of labeling. We all get labeled eventually. I'm an assistant accounts manager. That's a label. [flash of mint]

ALEXANDRA: That's an empowering label, rather than a stigmatizing one.

TAD: Right. Do you not appreciate labels at the grocery store? [mint rising] Organic versus conventional . . . aren't they all . . . how did you put it?

ALEXANDRA: I don't remember my exact words.

TAD: Something about power.

ALEXANDRA: Power . . . I don't know. It's besides the point.

TAD: Yes. So you're shopping, let's say, in the produce aisle.
[mint surging]

ALEXANDRA: Tad, our *daugh*ter is not a tan*gel*o. . . .

And then, as smoke and vapor at Cape Canaveral come gushing over the booster engines, subsuming the launchpad at the moment the rocket takes leave of it, the mint came on, a storm, a mint tsunami. When, over time, he came to recuperate the memories, he recalled that Alexandra herself had looked like she didn't quite buy into what she was saying, was a little too emphatic, surprised him just a touch with her gesticulations, her word choices. "Stigmatizing"? Really? How often *did* she address him by name? A "tangelo"? I mean, it wasn't as if her vocabulary was simplistic or anything, but those details stood out, like the way if your spouse was dressing a touch more provocatively than usual, or suddenly devoting a lot of extra time to grooming, it might raise some red flags about how s/he was spending evenings. But so much else was going on at the same time, such derangement of the senses, such weird weather. And maybe he was wrong. Maybe she loved tangelos; maybe the tangelo was her favorite fruit, her favorite *thing* on earth. Maybe she'd torn one open in her most unguarded moment, peel falling away, juice spritzing against her cheeks but sparing her eyes, a subsequent gush revealing the ecstatic itself. He'd been wrong before.

―◈―

Unlike Tad, June recovered right away. She'd been talking with Brendan, the boyfriend (she used the definite article), about this habit he had at gatherings, where in the company of attractive young women whose cleavage likely exceeded hers by more than one cup size, he would tell these humorous stories about things that had happened to the two of them together but would fail to include her at key points in the story, as though he was Photoshopping her out—he was adept with such programs, like when he made that card for her that depicted her as a fifties housewife, gasping at her own prowess with a blender. He was saying, "Okay, but they're just stories, and we both know that exaggerating some things and downplaying others is an intrinsic quality of storytelling. . . ." Brendan was a grad student in literature, his thesis an unwieldy sandwich of postcolonialism and media studies, and they were in the stairwell, having halted a few steps up from the landing. They were both treating this conversation as though it needed to be held then and there, before they entered Apt. 2BF, as though they might be able to resolve it outside in some public way, before some tribunal (for they could often hear, from her bedroom, conversations that took place in this very same stairwell), and to be honest, June was thinking about getting on with things and doing mad, slalomy things involving Brendan's cock, not rehashing the particulars of some forgettable exchange with Gillian Sando*val*. She caught a whiff of something that she thought might be carbon monoxide, was about to call a time-out so that they could either crack open her apartment door to check it out or evacuate. I mean, people die from that shit all the time—you see them on the news. But then she thought wasn't CO odorless, and this was sort of *minty* in a vague way. This made her want to laugh, but was her desire to laugh the sort of thing caused by the invisible gas, or was it caused by how Brendan could be such an astute reader of sub-Saharan African literature but miss the very glaring subtext of his own words and nomadic eyeballs? But before she could answer, the purple paisley in the wallpaper had started to slither its way into her brain instead of staying out there where it belonged.

When June told him this over the phone, Jason Tubbs had this strange recollection of the York Peppermint Pattie commercials of his childhood. The mention transported him back to Ottawa, to his grandparents' place, where either he'd seen those commercials or which he just associated with them because of the cold and because his grandparents gave him lots of treats. All of those old commercials could now be easily watched online. They were cheesier than he recalled, but he couldn't get around the resemblance between what went on with them and the accounts of these explosions. Tubbs broke the story, and Homeland Security brought in teams of chemists at the next explosion, which occurred at a DMV in upstate New York, to try to suss out any trace of mintiness, the residue of any sort of chemical, like some gas that might've mimicked mint seconds before combusting. There was no chemical known to do this, though certainly terrorists were always trying things, and so it was not outside the realm of possibility that they would've stumbled onto some new concoction. But there was nil of mint in the math of after, only the char of fabric and flesh and paper.

❖

Tad became an apostle of the Privacy Movement. Poster child, wheeled up to microphones by his younger, blonder second wife and his daughter, who had ultimately not been classified as learning-disabled and done just fine, thank you very much. His trademark shirt read on the front THE ORIGINAL BLACK BOX, a play on the notion that he had "recorded" his Conversation—that is, could recall it—without the government shoving its wires into his personal space, and on the back, REMEMBER TO REMEMBER WHY WE REMEMBER, which, if repetitive, made a sort of sense and had an alluringly chantable and stampable rhythm and echo rhyme. The message was obvious: if there was anyone who had every right to argue that the government should do whatever it took to get to the bottom of these attacks, it was double-amputee, three-time blood-transfusion-recipient Tad, but he was not calling for these things. He'd never been antigovernment before, but the blast changed him. He teamed up with those who were all-out conspiracy theorists, who deemed the whole thing an inside job. He refused to carry a box or don a roomsuit, and he kissed a lot of babies.

—◈◈◈—

The Mint Industry, for its part, tried to turn things to their advantage at first. The "Mint: Part of the Solution?" campaign flopped, though. Suddenly, it seemed that nobody wanted anything to do with mint toothpastes and chewing gums and teas, breath mints and mouthwash—all yoked by association with the most chilling and senseless deaths. Folks wanted it out of their houses, their lives. Kids drove around stockpiling boxes left out back behind pharmacies and convenience stores, wanting to re-create those mintgasms on their lips and tongues as vividly as possible, barely able at times to carry on a conversation, much less a Conversation, with all the hard candy bobbing in their gargle. They were stoned on top, half the time.

The effects on conversation itself were more slippery, tougher to measure than that on industry. Some would say that verbal interactions became less rancorous as people minded their words more carefully, noting that conflict was close to a universal in the documented Conversations. Others said that was a myth, mere wishful thinking. There were countless false positives, people who panicked in mid-sentence, slamming on their tongues' brakes, sure that they were about to be reduced to smithereens. It can't be said that anyone escaped fully from the shadow of the Conversations' impact. Everyone had to feel some added self-consciousness, some doubt that their words, at times, were their own, though of course it was pointed out by wiser thinkers that they had always felt this way to some extent, that these events had merely delivered to awareness a suspicion that had long lurked for most everyone. Still, who could help but feel a bit of envy for the mute, volitional and otherwise, the hermit, the idiot, the monk, even the taciturn and the plain agreeable?

‹◇›

They gathered in the Sonora, as suitable as anywhere for trying to gain a new foothold on the universe, conjure new prepositions, put an end to the bloodshed. All of them, the thinkers and tinkerers, the particle-accelerator designer and linguists, anthropologists and cosmologists, and one playwright. Anyone, looking up upon arrival, would've thought that the mathematicians had arrived early and been granted the ability to play with the sky. Linda Mesner was there from Cal Tech, as was Abe Dodson, who'd come out of retirement for the occasion. As they registered and passed through the labyrinthine security system, they were all fitted for customized suits, for the conversations, it was obvious, would get heated, ran the risk of turning on a dime into Conversations. They fitted themselves into helmets whose glass was as thick as walls, voices amplified and played through a centralized sound hub so that groups could talk freely. Picture them, then, standing amid the cacti—the suits protected against the spines, so that you could bounce around out there with impunity, barbs landing on you harmless as raindrops till you became, yourself, "part saguaro," as one participant put it on his blog, until it was taken down the next day for security reasons. They worked feverishly for eighteen-hour stretches and then climbed out of the suits, so that they wouldn't feel entirely claustrophobic and could go back to their bodies, which, it was felt, would be salubrious for their minds. According to the waivers that they'd signed, they all had to remain silent for the rest of the night, the only exception being their sleep talking, which, it was decided, couldn't be controlled and, moreover, wasn't likely to be very dangerous. Many crumpled in exhaustion, retreating either to their tents or to the cabins that had been put together for the occasion. Others, however, were so charged up at the end of the workday that they couldn't possibly have slept, couldn't sit still. They unzipped their tents, still feeling the weight and girth of the roomsuits, which had come to feel like skins. Their senses revived as the stars began to multiply in the sky, more and more, it seemed, with every minute that passed, and some were led to dance, others to kiss, and still others to wander like bedouins or pariahs. The only sound was that of the wind throwing itself against the ironwood and the palo verde and the ravines and a single looming butte where its whipping was already etched firm. It is hard to fault them for believing that what they were hearing was the sound of the universe in full accordance with itself. In the distance, a coyote loosed an occasional howl, as if unable or unwilling to share in their compact with silence.

⸺◈⸺

One who came with them to the desert was a philosopher of mind named Gavin Walters. An ex-philosopher, maybe. He came down from Oregon, where he was legendary even then, even before, against all odds, he made his contribution to unraveling the mystery of the Conversations. At forty-nine, he'd spent the past few years shunned and disgraced, living in a shack and spending whole days where he'd talk to no one but the postman, who became his best friend. His former students and colleagues had no shortage of theories about his mental decline—it was widely accepted that he was ill, ironic, given that his early papers, on which he'd built his reputation, had been on the question of whether there was a class of delusions that could be said to be extensional entities.

You could say that he invented the field; uncontroversially, he took it further than anyone else had to that point. The idea was to ingest as many and as various substances as he could track down, legal and illegal alike, and describe them. Just describe, bracketing out any expectations, any hangups about what society felt about them and about your using them, or what you were supposed to feel or taste. He scraped mold from rotting pineapples, ingested the hottest chilis he could land, plus the classics, weed, ibogaine, the full gamut of prescriptions. For him, coke that was cut with different things was more compelling than the purer stuff. He went on to document them like a wine critic, venturing far beyond the traditional descriptive armature of taste, trying, rather, to map the path the substance took within his body and beyond, how it altered what he defined as his body. He smoked bean curd and mashed pomegranate seeds and munched on talus.

He chose a set of baseline activities that he could use to measure the effects against some standard. These activities were playing chess, manipulating a cat's cradle, writing poetry, and having sex, broadly defined. He scavenged the hindquarters of stores when mint was being dumped and then wildcrafted it in the fields behind his cabin. His outpost drew protégés—young and disaffected, bored with food, as well as the more readily available drugs. Like some latter-day Aquinas, he had them all contributing to his *Encylopedia of Substantive Phenomenology*, scribbling his dictated words and their own. By the time he got to the Sonora Summit, he was long past burnt, the envisioned book a chimera of ambition and appetite, part gourmand's ramblings, part Husserlian explorations, part Proustian contemplation, and many parts schizoid rant.

How he'd even found out about the Summit was a mystery. Uninvited, he'd hopped the rails down and talked his way into a car with an algorithm expert and a quantum physicist. When he got there, they let him stay, even though his name wasn't on any list, the physicist he'd ridden over being willing to vouch for him based only on their conversation on the long, unremittingly straight road. Walters had this theory that there was some alien sentience, akin to body snatchers, but rather than bodies, they were stealing conversations, and that maybe their sense of time was different enough from ours that they were outgrowing them, exploding them as they outgrew them, or maybe they were exploding them to open up new dimensions that they could then colonize. Over the weekend, he went from being seen as a colorful outlier to an integral player. So that people actually listened when he described the opposite of the Conversations, what he called "kismet," meaning moments when people found common ground in an almost transcendent way. For Walters, kismet was no less tangible than kumquats, the balm that healed those ruptures in the cosmic fabric that had been opened up by the Conversations. But of course it was impossible to test this theory, because such moments had to arise spontaneously, couldn't be staged, prefabricated. Was he a crackpot or a visionary or both? Was it possible that perhaps the most plausible explanation was being offered by someone who anyone with an ounce of sanity would have long ago consigned to the realm of the insane?

That night, linguists slept with cosmologists, engineers with translators, and a woman allowed Walters to do things with her and a *Bufo alvarius*. Her moans, an inarticulate report in the air, alternated with those of the coyote, who may or may not have been responding. Rolling off her, he reached for his notebook, taking down a description, followed by a poem whose greatest lines, in his estimation, were "the haptics of venom" and "the gravid gash that spitfires intratime, outgabbing itself." He drifted off, more content than he'd felt in many years, she next to him, and at some point during the night he came awake and muttered something about the poem, wanting to share it with her, the her in it. She bolted upright, startled but quickly regaining her composure, reminding herself that there oughtn't be any talking whatsoever, not even to prevent talking, so she shook her head emphatically and made noises to smother his words. He gave up, lay back again. At daybreak, he had occasion to glance at the poem, and not only was that line not there but the whole thing was written in a language he couldn't understand, maybe no language at all. They made it to morning showers without ever talking about what had happened. At breakfast, the playwright recounted a dream of coming eyeball-to-eyeball with a scorpion that had taken up lodging inside his roomsuit. He remembered it that morning only on slipping back into his suit.

⊰⊱

It would be years before the Conversations petered out into nonexistence, and by that time people had grown inured to all the changes wrought by them. What changed, what led to their end? Either we'd become Conversation-proof or the protective measures that had been set into motion finally kicked in, or maybe Gavin Walters's theory was spot-on and there were enough instances of kismet, the cultivation of which had become a sort of an art form in and of itself, and the alien beings had sealed themselves off or gotten lost in endless warrens of cosmic dimensionality. We started back, started to come back. We started to talk again. We started to meet one another again—in cafés, in barrooms, at swimming pools, in esplanades. We poked our heads out from the rooms we'd borne with tortoise resignation. We began to fight again, to argue, to quibble, to provoke, to annoy, to tell off, to haggle, to opine, to agree to disagree, to politely suggest, to reprimand, to stammer, to plead, to refuse to plead, most pleading of all in our refusals. When there were no more Conversations and only, again, conversations, we stood gratefully in one another's fires. Eventually, mint, too, made its comeback, and this was a blessing, because we could smell one another's breath, and that had not always been pleasant. We licked mintsicles and took mint baths. And for a short time, at least, we went back to having conversations, all the conversations we'd never had that we should have had, all the conversations that someone hadn't wanted, orphaned, banished for years to who knew where, now made their triumphant returns to where they belonged— all we'd wanted to say to lovers and would-be lovers, what we should've said to aging parents, to pastors and teachers and coaches and nemeses and spouses and friends and those we'd told ourselves were friends, those who'd loaned us their shoulders for any purpose whatever, those who'd hurt us and those we'd hurt—all leapt giddily from our tongues and pounded on the drums of our ears and tremored our chests and left us blissfully intact and craving only more.

Tilkez

Confession time: I've been keeping a journal post our-conversations, not, I hope, the creepy kind, but of course that's what everyone thinks, right? Give me a chance, though, and what you'll find, I think, is that when it seemed like I was off dwelling on my own agenda, covering my own beat, glued to another channel, I've been tuned in, no "going through the motions" over here. I really *was* taking in everything you were saying, the small talk and the large talk and the medium-size, too. Like a whale, sifting it through my, if you will, baleen. And all the stuff about your dissertation—let me say I have found that to be some fairly meaty plankton. Plankton you could serve as a roast, or kabob, or slap on a bun. Medium-sized talk—not *Can the Yankees polish off the Indians in Cleveland*, not *is it supposed to rain on Labor Day it is crap, 'cause we're supposed to have Ted and Ellis over, but I guess we'll just have to wait and see what it* does. No, not trivia like that. But also not on the grand scale of your tiff with God that all started with—let me be meticulous on this, because we've talked about things of such significance and at times intricacy, and while I could make it my business to keep track of every shiny button of a detail that rolls off you, I also have, you may recall, a little something called a job that occupies a fair amount of my attention, and, moreover, there are some other little things like paying bills and keeping some of my married friends from one another's throats, keeping them from adulterating themselves into the *Guinness Book: Relationship Edition*—I think you'll know the friends to whom I'm referring—so that lest what you tell me blur on one side into the quagmire of quotidia or tumble on the other into the Sea of Melodrama, I write things down, okay? In order to be able to go back and reread them and say, Hey, look, she took an art class in her early twenties that she loved even though her teacher made multiple passes at her and then scathingly dismissed her final project in a supremely public manner—I believe the phrase "Doritian, as in the aesthetic kin to Doritos" may still have some resonance for you. Or your irrational phobia about tollbooths—I use *irrational* only because I haven't heard you trace your fear back to some decisive ur–brush with booth that would have had long-term ramifications for your psyche. I must point out that nowadays, though you'll go through them, you tense and throw up a wall, clenching your shoulders like so, and you fail to appreciate well-intentioned humor: "PTSD—post tollbooth smacking disorder?" and stay grumpy for miles, till you finally forget, usually when *Weekend Edition* morphs into *All Things Considered*, et cetera. And if there *was* a pivotal tollbooth encounter, I didn't write it down, which reinforces my point about the value of writing things down. If it ain't jotted, I'm not going to go so far as to argue that it didn't happen, not some "*p*onderous *p*ostmodernist" as you'd spit it, but there's a far slimmer chance that I'm going to be able to recollect it.

I'm admitting to you, therefore, that I not only write things down that you tell me on a regular basis but that sometimes I'll reread them seconds before we go out, which is to say you could have just called to notify me that you were marching up the block, making your final approach—you could even be at the buzzer and I might be just behind the door, notebook flipped open, the spiral coil slightly cold, a nervous student once again, brushing up on *you*, cramming for *you*, trying to soak up as much last-minute information as possible—a couple of eleventh-hour monarchs and conquests, a few more onerous taxes to irk the colonists closer to revolt, whatever, it probably won't even be on the exam. Still, it's this booster shot of confidence, this sense of knowing you, and on several occasions, let's face it, I've surprised and delighted you with items recalled, like about your soft spot for the napoleons at Lulu, where you yourself didn't even remember having said anything and so it fell unto me to convince you, such that I even doubted myself, forcing me back to my notebook after the fact to verify that, indeed, you'd effused on their "imperial" qualities. All of which is to say that instead of relying on chance and memory, I've an archival sense of our relationship, have the data backed up, if you will, though ironically not on any computer, because, for whatever reason, I have to handwrite it, get to know your inner monk, you know? So when I'm cribbing at the door, it feels like I'm unzipping, even though there's no actual compression and decompression going on, so in that sense starkly different from my day job, what they pay me the big Krugerrands for, what lands me the triple-wide cubicle, though sometimes it feels as though reading my notes on you is a kind of zipping, seeing as how I am embedding them in this concentrated form deep down in my brain, where they will then crouch, waiting like guests at a surprise party to surface at the optimal moment, and sometimes bringing them forth feels like an unzipping, like I'm taking thoughts that I've encoded in a few words and breathing life into them in the very act of reading, and it is this ambiguity, about whether, in fact, reading my journal is more like a zipping or an unzipping (could say "data transfer" but, come on, now, can you get any flaccider than that), that makes . . . well, in the end I'm not sure it matters; what matters for my purposes now is that all this talk about zipping and unzipping brings me to my true subject: the boudoir.

To continue somewhat bluntly and in an inescapably data-driven way, I have also been compelled to record the instances

in which we've been intimate: initiating event, salient circumstances, degree of success as evidenced by noises evoked,
nipple ascendancy, the glow factor, the last of which especially
I can admit is somewhat subjective. And if the recording of
your anecdotes has been an act of refusal to consign to the
waste bin of memory, you might ask is the same true of this
record of physical intimacy, and the answer, I think, would
be no, that all the jottage on *real* unzipping bears a rather
different purpose from the scribbling about, say, the time you
peed your Skivvies at a wax museum, nor is this just some
compendium of exploits that might become fodder, a refresh
button for my alpha-male status. No, this chronicling of sexual acts is more akin to what you've talked about in terms of
your graduate work, which, looking back, I can pretty much
see that I was sort of aholeish about at first, probably as a
result of my never having heard so much as a whisper, before
meeting you, about endangered languages. Obviously, you
brought me up to speed quickly enough, and I became, if not
a connoisseur, at least an appreciator of the delightful factoids
you'd bring home, like the one about the tribe that had like
a built-in GPS system in their brains. But there was that one
you always seem to circle back to, Tilkez, not a dialect but a
full-blown language, as you explained to me—very lucidly, I
might add—one of the thousands around the world that are
not being passed down to the younger generations, who instead are fixated on American sports apparel and "the Snooki
situation" and the differences between the PSP2 and 3 rather
than mastering the nuances of some creaky old language, and
what, I ask, in my extremely pragmatic fashion, which we can
both admit is something you find quite alluring, what is the
purpose, exactly, of preserving a language if it is in its death
throes, prolonging its frail, post-double-hip-replacement existence? It would seem that natural selection has made its choice
and, for whatever reasons, fair or un-, this "Tilkez" has not

made the cut, been pink-slipped—we need the bed. I mean, it's not as though these people have suddenly been rendered mute, not like this language is uniquely essential to them, like their glottal muscles and lips are simply incapable of forming the shapes necessary to speak otherwise, not like they can no longer say hi, communicate what to plant and how many rows, convey that leopards have been sighted in the foothills. No, they can do this as matter-of-factly as ever before, maybe *better* is what I'm thinking; maybe it wouldn't hurt them to learn the new ways. It's like old programming languages—the only ones piddling around trying to keep them alive are the guys from whom technophiles derive their reputations for insufferable geekiness, I mean, anyone who's sitting around and *compiling* Pascal and Basic A and Ada and Forth, well, we've talked about this, of course, how compiling means something totally different in our respective fields, in yours it would actually be collecting, whereas in mine it relates to translation to machine blah blah blahnguage, but my God.

Yet, at the moment when I took a staunchly, some would say classically masculine pragmatic stance, a look came across your brow, an expression like a bank of clouds covering— nay, smothering—the moon, and you told me about how beautiful Tilkez was, that once you got to know a language, not "know" in the sense that you could speak it, because you couldn't, then or now, so it's not that, but know . . . well, the way you described it to me triggered, as I was writing it all down afterward, what I can only call a pang of jealousy toward the damned language. Yes, I know, I sound like a little bit retarded just confessing such a thing, but the way you talked about it it was like you were describing a person, and to me Tilkez is undoubtedly guy, buff/chiseled/loaded, maybe because you told me all about the very masculine Tong-th-song ritual accompanying adolescence in the same conversation, not that the language has anything particularly to do with that grueling hunt and the chewing of raw flesh and the ritual garb and the ornamenting of bone and the thigh scarification, and not that the women don't speak it just as much and, if our own women are any measure, probably a lot more than the men, but something about the way you knew the tiny quirks of the language, the exceptions and inflections—how the *a* rises musically through the ribs in words related to good fortune, how *th* and *thht* distinguish the two clans split by the river, how their eight words for types of fog use all thirty-seven consonants—and the passion with which you told me about these, demonstrating with your hands and mouth and throat, and the way, as we played Scrabble, you lamented the "tragedy" of not being able to put down words in the language, and even though you were joking, partly, you still imagined moves you might have made, tallied points accordingly, rearranging your tiles, for all I know, so that they spelled out little things in Tilkez, all this even while you lacked the ability to speak it fluently, only enhanced the sense of your being in a *relationship* with him/it.

If you'd merely spoken it, that would've been one thing, but it was precisely your distance, your fascination coupled with an intimacy, an ever-growing knowledge of it, plus throw in a nurturing tendency that I think we can both agree that you possess in more than average amounts—all of that conspired to make me, I can admit, feel somewhat vengeful toward this language, even, however insane this sounds, murderous, though the fact of the matter is that I could never, as I'm sure you know, bring any harm to any living being, but a *language*, a language is another story, especially one dying on its own, maybe due to its own inherent weaknesses or its not quite measuring up against its peers, or maybe its time has just come. And on seeing those clouds flutter over your face, I said, "Why not just leave it to die? It ain't gonna be the English of ever," and you seemed personally wounded by this, which might have been the reaction I wanted (I can't quite recall, and strangely, I neglected to write about this, so I am operating on sheer memory now, climbing harnessless). But suddenly I could see that perhaps this language that you wanted to preserve and revive and celebrate was, in fact, maybe not like a lover with whom I'd be in competition, but more like a child, a sickly and needy child who needed, above all, you, and given the complexity of all of these feelings, I was able to step back a bit, inhale, take a larger view: maybe it was okay if this child-language was suckling at one breast and I was sucking *on* the other, maybe we wouldn't be in competition ultimately because the language, sated and milk-drunk, would toddle off to sleep, given that it had been feeding and I was doing something altogether other, which is to say that I was in truth then encircling your nipple and bringing it to life, feeding *it*, in a manner of speaking, breathing little bumps into it, patterns and ideas for further patterns, and after the child-language drifted into blissful sleep, I'd have both of your breasts to myself. And moments later, like magic, they'd become tits, just like that, in an instant, and when was the transition, exactly, was there one bump, one lick with which this transformation had taken place, this transformation in its way as profound as the emergence of tits themselves from the most ordinary prepubescent chest, never a problem for you, I know? Regardless, these tits would stay tits until the baby cried out again, the infant who, remember, is just a language, not even a flesh and blood infant, so let it sleep, and let the tits stay tits for a while now that they've gotten themselves to that point. This very moment when I'm swiveling around the tits, sweeping over them like a master zamboni driver, or, better, a calligrapher, yes, of tongue, is when it occurs to me—and this next will constitute a larger confession—that I do some of my best thinking when I'm making the circular and semicircular and the changeably elliptical orbits of the tits. It's then that I had the stupid thought about the Tilkez language being like a child, and on top of it then the thought, stupider by a magnitude of two or three, that if the Tilkez language *was* a child, then, since children require that "window of learning" for language development (conversations of 4/16, 5/30, 6/1, 6/10), Tilkez would *itself* be learning a language, was itself picking up on average something like four to ten words per day in the heyday of its "explosion" (your figures, your word); in other words, lying there slumbering while I was expending my energies and, if all continued in this way, would soon exhaust them in orgasmic explosion of my own, all while the child was lying next to us insensate, nursed and coddled, accruing words, getting fatter and stronger on hearty nouns and zesty verbs, growing new incisors that could sink into chewy adjectives, pull adverbs from the bone, swallow whole the indigestible fiber of prepositions, all while I was doing all the work, the very type of work that brings children, each and every one, into being— I had to catch myself at this point and remind myself that this was only metaphor.

Staying with this, I swept around your nipples, the right one slightly lower and rotunder, and you seemed in no rush for me to move on, and that's when I got the Sapir-Whorf hypothesis stuck in my head like a syrupy pop song. That class you'd taken in Social Dimensions of Language and Something-or-other, hijacked, as you put it, by the insistence of certain blowhard classmates of yours to debate endlessly about these dudes, Sapir and Whorf, and remember how for the longest time I got mixed up and thought they were on opposite sides and not, like, an illustrious dynamic duo? It's a bit revisionist, the way I'm telling this, because as I was circumnavigating your areolas I wouldn't have remembered their names, which certainly make their appearance in my spiral bound (3/12, 3/24–31 passim, 4/12, etc.), but at the time I was fully focused on when to exit this rotary and head north, eventually south, but north first.

Soon enough, I knew, we would be going at it, but that was the very matter that brought me up short and made me realize that we needed to have this conversation. The words that occurred to me in that instant were *going at it*, and while I didn't remember Edward Sapir or Benjamin Whorf, I did remember your having wavered back and forth about how you felt about their argument, and how in the end you sided with them over Chomsky, who, of course, I've heard of (*syntax* another word we sort of share, same same but different). Eeny meeny miney moe, you wound up believing, against McKay, even though he had to sign off on your diss, you dissed him; you thought that it made a difference, the words you used, or, as you put it, those available in any given language were the tools you could think with and thus the words that shaped what existed for you, that if you didn't have the words for, say, *cornflower blue*, you wouldn't see it as different from, oh, *Persian blue*, and if you didn't have a word for *blue* at all you simply wouldn't see the color or it would appear the closest color whose name you did, in fact, know, maybe *black*, and I had thought about this a little bit, though admittedly not too much until I was figure skating—the cold of the rink because I was reliving the whole Eskimo snow thang in my mind (no longer on that cumbersome zamboni, though)—round the nipples.

And at some point in my looping, I realized that if those guys were right, if how the words you used actually *determined* what you were thinking and thus what you could do, that "getting it on" was precisely the problem, that we talked about "getting it on" and thus were fated to "get it on" or "mess around" or "make love" instead of doing certain other things, like that "fucking" would be a far cry from "getting it on," an utterly different act, though maybe not the one wanted, but what if it was, and maybe your aversion to that word, to *fucking*, was as woeful as the case of the boy you told me about who refused to learn the various words for reindeer—the rideable,

the skittish, the recently castrated—and whose herding ability would thus pale when stacked up against his dad's and *his*
dad's before that, and what if on occasion fucking was exactly
what both of us wanted and needed, and what, then, about
screwing, which would mean that one of us, probably you, was
getting screwed, but maybe that's okay, maybe not such a bad
thing—but inside a cunt? A mons? A vagina? A pussy? A *kitty*?
And are we talking a standard slotted? A Phillips head? A Torx?
A hex socket? Maybe we could start out getting it on, then
cross over, sublimely but profoundly as breasts turn into tits,
to fucking, or to something else entirely, schtupping or boink-
ing, dogging or banging or humping or shagging or hitting the
skins or making love or doing it, though what is this "doing
it," a great big fuzzball over our genitalia like a blur lens on
network TV? I didn't stop the action at that moment but knew
that we'd have to have this conversation. Or, since you and
your fellow linguists seem to love nothing more than a good
conference, here, let's call this the First Annual Colloquium on
Our Future Sexual Nomenclature, zipping and unzipping allowed and even encouraged, and okay maybe I'm not saying all
this, maybe this is just what I've written down to be able to say
a small portion of, maybe this is the last conversation on the
topic we'll have, ever, or the last period, you and Tilkez going
your way and I mine, no child support owed to a language, not
my kid anyway, plus, a language that, quite frankly, is going to
die, may as well bear a fatal illness deep in its chromosomes,
no matter how motherly you are and no matter how much love
you pour onto it, how tenderly you nurse.

Even so, I can't help but want us to come up with some
other ways to express what we want/need from each other,
maybe splinking or frooling or enchpeshing, or maybe the
–ing is all wrong, maybe reen or gruph or oozanoo, maybe
we'll rotate through 'em, try them out one by one, me calling through gritted teeth, "Sapir me!", you with your throat

thrown back, "Whorf me just so," and maybe one word will
shoot straight to the part of my brain that controls my cock
(paltry name), which, in turn, too often I can admit, controls
me, or by some fluke of random chance we'll wind up with
something like the Tilkez term for it, or perhaps they'll have
more terms than you'll ever know, secret, magic-charged ones
they'd die sooner than confide to some fancy-braided linguist
living and teaching in the US of A and occasionally swooping
down to interview them, but maybe somehow you can trick
them into teaching you one, seducing one of their paragons
of virility, making yourself irresistible, dabbing yourself with
that perfume that makes you seem like you're wearing leather
that someone spilled absinthe on, slipping into that black neg-
ligee that shimmers over you like liquid mica, starting each
of your words with a consonant our language simply doesn't
possess, formed by lips against skin, pursing and releasing, and
you'd know just enough Tilkez to get you into the room, but
it would be your fluency in gasp and touch that would bring
him in the dead of night to such a point of agonizing arousal
that in his own home, or hut, he'd betray, to his horror, at the
cost of his honor, that most longed-for word, a word that,
once he'd fallen asleep, you'd steal away with into the darkness, risking your own limbs to bring it back, clutching it like
a fragile object on the plane, sweating while bearing it through
customs, a word that climbs its way through the ribs three
and four at a time, obliterating the names of body parts and
feelings and whole rooms and all those things for which we
formerly thought we had names.

Urban Planning:
Case Study Number Eight

T he life of an urban planner is at once both more and less
exotic than it might appear.

⋖⊗⊳

Raedmeon is a city built by committee, riding in on slow, lumbering beasts of burden, Weston a committee man if ever there
was one. Among his secret joys is the way the dry cleaner folds
and boxes his shirts, the new-map sensation of the creases cascading over his shoulders and chest each morning. He likes
that he knows what the competing interests in the room are at
any given moment: Camilla Barber's predictable cooing about
"sustainability," Martinez's operatic enthusiasm for x, y, or z,
swelling with his Adam's apple in the hour before lunch, then
retreating into an afternoon of spent indifference.

⋖⊗⊳

Each night, the ancient elevator hoists Weston up to the sparse
apartment where he finds himself amidst light and shadows,
a furnace that talks him through the night in Hephaestian
tongues. A cot does for him; he is not impervious to the image
of himself sunken in four-poster opulence in a spread of red
paisley satin, maybe backed in goosefeather, but recognizes the
chances of this are remote. Sleep may be luxury and indulgence
for some out there, those in the elegant apartments his eye falls
on beyond his sill, with its gouges and blackened wicks. For
him, sleep is as crude and functional as fuel. It catalyzes him

250

for eight hours of sifting through statistics, rendering diagrams and schematics, the endlessly rigorous and recursive tasks of engineering a veritable universe packed into 14.82496 (he can go on) square miles.

⫻

A pragmatist! Very well, then, let them think it, though in reality it is no exaggeration to say that his "plans"—if one is to call them that—derive wholly from the dream life that runs riot across the proscenium of his skull. If he were to reveal this, it would be dismissed at first, then, if he insisted, treated with suspicion, and finally *he* would be dismissed. It's not as if he proposes Raedmeon as surreal playground—dripping, oozing plazas, grids with walkways and staircases spiraling up to their own nadirs, reservoirs that digest locals and belch the remains of the sun by dusk. Who, though, could possibly understand the way the orderliness he harnesses and maintains has its origins in his *dream life*? Least of all his colleagues, drab bureaucrats to a man (and Camilla Barber).

⫻

When and how did he come to be "the Bread Machine"? At the holiday party one year, someone arrived with a fresh-made loaf, and they were all talking about it. Next thing you know he's spittle-lip drunk and someone's magic-markered some manufacturer's name in the ample region between his hairline and the eyebrows that he raises, by habit, in lieu of his voice. The moniker's no accident, though, never was—it's too perfect an analogy for how he operates, and he dons it with pride. So into the Machine go the problems that beleaguer any self-respecting city: overcrowding, crumbling infrastructure, de facto segregation, inadequate power grids on nights of anomalous heat or cold, the bombardment of pollutions ocular and aural, the endless teeter between the chorus of the old and the sirenry of the new. Out come Proposals. Solutions (or leastways Disasters Narrowly Averted).

◄◦◊◦►

Into the Machine, too, go daydreams, the yearnings and desires of the forty-six-year-old eccentric loner whose lunch hours are spent browsing in the most unlikely locations—pawnshops, restaurant-supply stores, sequin-manufacturing concerns. He will not join them in the company cafeteria midway up the black cylinder they relocated to a couple of years ago, despite its panoramic views of the city. He needs to move in Raedmeon's streets, to sniff out the sources of its pumpernickel, needs to see if its homeless veterans have updated their cardboard pleas or of late changed their bandages. In taking all of this in, he's no saint, no deliverer of alms or answers; he is merely feeding the dreams that provide him with, for lack of a better word, his Ideas. After work, he'll walk home through microcosmic cities of sheet vinyl and salvage just across from the abandoned tanneries, all the while chewing on the pumpernickel loaf he bought earlier. The Bread Machine indeed.

◄◦◊◦►

What none of them knows about is the pinch of yeast that goes into the Machine: 450 milligrams of Evanescet, sleeping medication not yet available to the general public, still in Experimental Trial Phase 3.3. No rat fatalities or illness beyond the usual side effects—involuntary twitching of the whiskers, diminished proprioception. At staggering doses only, catastrophic kidney malfunction. In order to swallow such doses proportionate to his own body size, Weston's guy in the pharmaceutical industry assures him, he would have to slug pills all day long, quite literally alternating with coffee sips for hours on end. It would be virtually impossible to consume enough, his friend insists, to induce kidney problems even if, let's say for some reason, he wanted kidney problems. *Let's just say you wanted kidney problems*—he likes the way the guy says it, smirky but winning, traits he doesn't see enough of at Urban Planning.

(He tried imitating this friend for a day, but it fell flat, and it was pointed out that something he said verged on harassment, so he dropped that tack at once).

—⟨◇◇⟩—

Weston, stooped over, sloped with patience, a gift for waiting over the vast, cosmic sprawl of time his job demands, a knack for knowing and abiding by every procedure, doing everything fairly, hearing out all contractors and bidders, checking off all the boxes, refraining from jumping in until he's heard all parties speak, Weston *will* not, damnit, *sit around and wait* for the government to approve Evanescet for common, everyday use. He needs the stuff *now*, needs the way it makes him swim through nights like a glowing set of eyes, springs him sated from the cot at daybreak. He loves the galvanic vigor that lingers in him on the bus as it wends its way downtown through the Raedmeon he's helped make block by block. He's tried other means of inducing sleep—drugs of the government-sanctioned variety, herbal blends, witches' incantations. Nothing comes close, and as far as he can tell, his kidneys are stalwart as bighorn sheep.

—⟨◇◇⟩—

On the bus this morning, he notes the tree-lined medians and open-air market, the vistas opened up by demolition and then the reassuring density of new construction encased in the fragile, spiny promise of scaffolding. Weston wants to cry out "O Evanescet!" like it's some lover whose hips are enmeshed with his own, wants to sing the praise of this muse with a bard-like fervor. But he wills himself silent, yoking deep-diaphragm breaths to images of retirement, a mere eight years away. They'll send him off with a gold-plated bread machine; of that he has no doubt. By then, Evanescet will be procurable in patch or chewing gum, either that or banned utterly but available at the right price, scored in a dark alley in needle form. *Note to self: Preserve a handful of dark alleys.* His upper lip twitches while he worries the pill crumbs in the inner lining of his coat pocket with his fingers, relishing the thought of devoting himself fully at last to the Raedmeon he's been quietly constructing all along, one that would never appoint a committee, where the streets are lined with luminous balustrades, and planning means nothing other than dancing in the pineapple rotundas of an untranslatable night.

Acknowledgments

Givens: that there are too many to thank, that thanks are never quite adequate, that their ink allotment here can only hint at the true scope and scale of my gratitude.

Thanks to Steve Mounkhall for being the ideal reader, the extra lobe of my brain, a presence even when we have not spoken for stretches.

Thanks to Michele Filgate for reminding me that reading is, indeed, a variety of breathing, and for sharing so many inhalations and exhalations with me.

Thanks to the Seacoast Writers Circle, and most especially its core members—Donna Kirk, Josiah Eikelboom, W.B. Berman, Jim Kozubek, Tamara Collins, and Tammi Truax, who kept my nose within a spark's breadth from the grindstone for years. And for sharing your brains, your words, and your laughter, and your Sunday evenings.

Thanks to David Fisher and Ross Kaplan for your unwavering support and continuous advice over the years.

Thanks to my stellar colleagues at Chester College of New England, Monica Bilson, Mark Sleiter, Eric Pinder, Chris Anderson, and Jenn Monroe—what fortune to be part of this amazing, sui generis department.

Thanks to writer and artist friends: Rebecca Makkai, Greg Gerke, Gabriel Blackwell, Matt Bell, Alison Lobron, Joshua Cohen, Kate Christensen, Brian Boyd, Steve Himmer, John Madera, Anna Wexler, Steve Almond, Lance Olsen, Krista Knight, Jacki Lyden, Beth Ann Miller, Chris Sumner, Judd Ehrlich, Alice Andrews, Becca Derry, and Mildred Crow; you have offered crucial support, conversation, and solace, and led by the example of your own pens and brushes.

Thanks to mentors Alex Parsons, Bud Pollak, Morrow Jones, Charlotte Bacon, and David Huddle, who shaped my literary sensibility, but something far larger—a way of being in the world, a way of becoming, still ongoing. I strive daily to emulate your passion, humor, wisdom and work ethics.

To my UNH brethren, Jason Ronstadt, Joel Rice, Mohan Ravichandran, Dylan Walsh, Kate Megear, Nate Graziano, and Debbie Upton Harrison, there at the dawn of what has become a new life for me.

Thanks to Tom Lee for letting me gallivant in the woods in Forest Communities of New Hampshire, the first and most primordial of the understories.

Thanks to Bob Simmons, projectionist, for letting me climb up into the booth.

Thanks to marvelous editors: Melvin Sterne, Scott Garson, Bill Henderson, Mark Mirsky, Paulette Licitra, Ander Monson and Sarah Blackman, Kevin McIlvoy and Nick Voges, Carol Novak, Rachel Kendall, Phuong Pham, Derek White, Steven Church and crew at *The Normal School*.

Thanks to David McNamara, for bringing *Circulation* into the world and providing it with maps so it could roam.

Thanks to Bradford Morrow, who, through *Conjunctions*, did so much before we ever met to shape the writer I would later become, and whose friendship I count invaluable.

Thanks to the Corporation of Yaddo for the sanctuary of time and the enduring friendships that you afforded me.

To all the wonderful people at Bellevue Literary Press, and most of all for Erika Goldman, my editor, a special declaration of gratitude, for finding me and for perceiving in these stories a unified sensibility and shape.

Thanks to my brother Greg for sharing your love of language, literature, and ideas with me over the years, and for being such an astute early reader of so many of these stories.

To my mom and dad—to thank you feels like thanking myself, so thoroughly do your visions and personalities suffuse these stories. I am grateful, too, that you surrounded me with books and an ever-replenishing thirst for getting to know the world.

Finally, most of all to Mary Ann and Ella. Words are least sufficient here, given how many joyous roles you play in my life, how much and indelible a part of me you are. Not only do I love you, I relish being able to share with you the adventure of our lives.